HAVELI

BY

Suzanne

Fisher

Staples

ALFRED A. KNOPF ✦ NEW YORK

THIS IS A BORZOI BOOK
PUBLISHED BY ALFRED A. KNOPF, INC.

Text copyright © 1993 by Suzanne Fisher Staples
Jacket illustration © 1993 by Steven Rydberg
Map copyright © 1993 by Anita Karl and James Kemp

Library of Congress Cataloging-in-Publication Data
Staples, Suzanne Fisher
Haveli / by Suzanne Fisher Staples
p. cm.
Summary: Having relented to the ways of her people in Pakistan and married
the rich older man to whom she was pledged against her will, Shabanu is now the
victim of his family's blood feud and the malice of his other wives.
Sequel to "Shabanu, Daughter of the Wind."
ISBN 0-679-84157-1 (trade)
[1. Pakistan—Fiction. 2. Sex role—Fiction.] I. Title
PZ7.S79346Hav 1993   92-29054 [Fic]—dc20

Manufactured in the United States of America

To Jeanne Drewsen, my agent, whose faith has been constant;
Frances Foster, my editor, whose wisdom is an inspiration;
and the many people in Pakistan who gave of their time, energy,
and hospitality to make it possible for me to travel
and learn about their wonderful country

Names of Characters

italicized syllable is accented

Aab-pa (*Aahb*-puh)—A healer and herbal doctor
Abdul Muhammad Khan (Uhb-*dool* Muh-*hah*-muhd
  Khahn)—Pathan murdered by his brother
Adil (Uh-*dihl*)—Shabanu's male cousin
Ahmed (*Ah*-mehd)—Rahim's only son, betrothed to Zabo
Ali (Uh-*lee*)—An old servant in Selma's household
Allah (Ah-*luh*)—Arabic word meaning "God"
Amina (Ah-*mee*-nuh)—Rahim's first wife, mother of Leyla and
  Ahmed
Auntie (*Ann*-tee)—Dadi's sister-in-law

Bibi Lal (*Bee*-bee Lahl)—Phulan's mother-in-law
Bundr (*Buhn*-duhr)—Mumtaz's stuffed monkey (Urdu word for
  "monkey")

Choti (*Choh*-tee)—Mumtaz's pet deer (Urdu word for "small")

Dadi (*Dah*-dee)—Shabanu's father
Dalil Abassi (Dah-*lihl* Uh-*bah*-see)—Dadi's proper name
Daoud (*Dah*-ood)—Selma's late husband

Fatima (Fah-*tee*-muh)—Shabanu's cousin, Sharma's daughter

Guluband (*Goo*-loo-buhnd)—Shabanu's dancing camel, her
  childhood favorite

Hamir (*Hah*-meer)—Shabanu's cousin, murdered by Nazir

Ibne (*Ihb*-nee)—Rahim's faithful manservant

Khansama (Khahn-*sah*-muh)—Rahim's cook
Kharim (Khuh-*reem*)—Murad's cousin

Lal Khan (Lahl *Khahn*)—Phulan's brother-in-law, murdered by Nazir

Leyla (*Leh*-luh)—Rahim's eldest daughter, betrothed to Omar

Mahmood (Muh-*mood*)—Cloth merchant

Mahsood (Mah-*sood*)—Rahim's younger brother

Mali (*Mah*-lee)—Rahim's gardener

Mama (*Mah*-muh)—Shabanu's mother

Muhammad (Muh-*hah*-muhd)—Holy Prophet of Islam

Mumtaz (Muhm-*tahz*)—Shabanu's daughter

Murad (Moo-*rahd*)—Shabanu's brother-in-law, Phulan's husband

Nazir Muhammad (Nuh-*zeer* Muh-*hah*-muhd)—Rahim's youngest brother

Omar (*Oh*-muhr)—Rahim's nephew, betrothed to Leyla

Phulan (*Poo*-lahn)—Shabanu's sister

Rahim (Ruh-*heem*)—Shabanu's husband, a major landowner

Raoul (Ruh-*ool*)—Nazir's farm manager

Rashid (Ruh-*sheed*)—Son of Zabo's servant

Saleema (Suh-*leem*-uh)—Rahim's second wife

Samiya (Sah-*mee*-yuh)—Shabanu and Mumtaz's teacher

Selma (*Sehl*-muh)—Sister of Rahim, Mahsood, and Nazir

Shabanu (Shah-*bah*-noo)—Daughter of nomadic camel herders, fourth wife of the wealthy landowner Rahim

Shaheen (Shuh-*heen*)—Selma's lifelong servant

Shahzada (Shah-*zah*-duh)—Keeper of Derawar Fort

Sharma (*Shahr*-muh)—Shabanu's aunt, cousin of both of her parents

Tahira (Tuh-*heer*-uh)—Rahim's third wife

Uma (*Oo*-muh)—Mumtaz's name for her mother

Xhush Dil (*Hoosh* Dihl)—Camel owned by Shabanu's family

Yazmin (Yahz-*meen*)—Servant girl in Selma's household

Zabo (*Zeh*-boh)—Rahim's niece, daughter of Nazir, betrothed to Ahmed

Zenat (*Zee*-naht)—Mumtaz's *ayah*

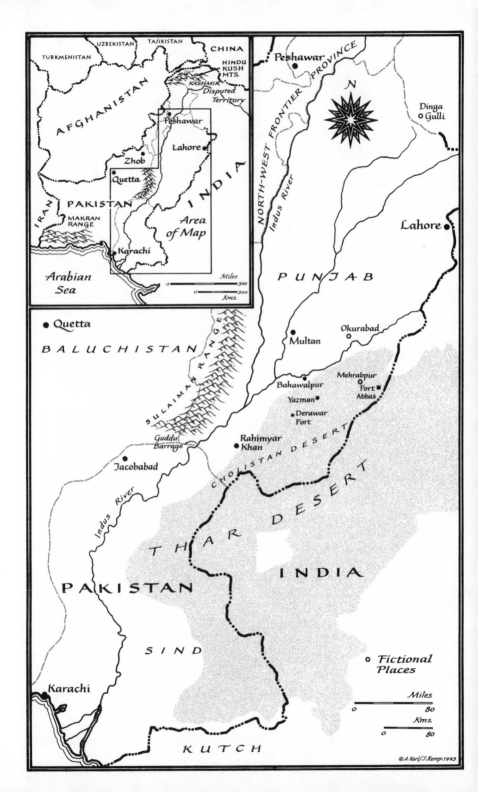

chapter 1

Shabanu awoke at dawn on a cool spring morning, with the scent of early Punjabi roses rich and splendid on the air, warm as the sun rising through the mist. The *charpoi* squeaked lightly, string against wood, as she rolled over to gaze at her sleeping child.

But Mumtaz had slipped out, perhaps before first light. Shabanu closed her eyes again and waited for the sun to creep through the open doorway of their room behind the stable.

She lay on her back and stretched her arms over her head. Mumtaz was nearly five, and there was little time for her to be free in this life. She would be safe enough within the ocher mud walls of the family compound near the village of Okurabad on the road to Multan.

Shabanu did not force her daughter to stand to have her hair untangled every morning. She allowed her to wear her favorite old *shalwar kameez* with the legs halfway to her knees, the tunic faded to a grayish wash. Soon enough Mumtaz would have to stay indoors and wear the *chadr*. For now Shabanu wanted her to have whatever freedom was possible.

Shabanu remembered how she'd rebelled when her mother had forced her to wear the veil that reached to the ground and tangled around her feet when she ran. It had been the end of her climbing thorn trees and running among the sand dunes.

Outside, the sun dappled through the neem tree, and Shabanu imagined her daughter hiding behind the old giant, her matted head against its leathery bark, the dirt powdery between her toes.

The spirit stove popped as old Zenat started a fire for tea in the kitchen beside the room. Already flies darted in and out of the doorway. Shabanu rose from the *charpoi* and stretched.

Dust rose around her bare feet as she moved about, folding bedding, then gathering things for the child's bath— tallowy soap and a rough, sun-dried towel.

Shabanu went to the doorway. A flash of sunlight caught in the diamond pin in her nose, sending a glint straight to where Mumtaz hid behind the tree. The glass bangles on Shabanu's arm clinked as she whipped her long black hair into a thick knot at the base of her neck. She turned back inside to reach for her shawl and saw from the corner of her eye a small movement as Mumtaz flitted away, silent as a moth.

Wrapping her shawl around her, Shabanu followed her daughter toward the old wooden gate that led to the canal, where Mumtaz loved to play in the water. The small dark head bobbed beyond the bushes that framed the inner courtyard of the big house where Shabanu's husband lived. Shabanu was the youngest, by eight years, of Rahim's four wives, and Mumtaz was his youngest child. The other wives lived separately, in apartments in the big house.

Shabanu and Mumtaz had lived with Rahim until early in the winter, when Shabanu had persuaded him that life would be easier for her and the child if she could take up residence in the room near the stables while he was in Lahore, capital of the Punjab 150 miles away, for the winter session of the provincial assembly.

There had been incidents, a few of which she'd told him about—the scorpion in her bed, the rabid bat in her cupboard. Rahim had raged and demanded to know who had done these things. A small, thin boy was offered as the culprit.

Then Rahim said there was no need for her to move out of the house. Why would she rather be off, away from the rest of the family? Why would she give up the convenience of running water, electricity, servants? But Shabanu knew that the danger lay precisely in her staying, and she had remained firm in her insistence. At the last moment before leaving for Lahore, Rahim had acquiesced.

The others said the stable was where Shabanu and Mumtaz belonged, and laughed wickedly behind their veils. She didn't mind. It gave her privacy from the insolent servant women who walked into her room without knocking, and reported everything back to the other wives.

Shabanu followed the child to the stand of trees past the pump, where Mumtaz stopped. On the broad veranda, beyond the wide silver pipe with water dripping in sparkles from its mouth, stood bamboo cages in which desert birds blinked their fiery eyes.

The birds came from the dunes of Cholistan, where Pakistan meets India, a land of magic and camels where Shabanu had spent her childhood. Mumtaz never tired of her mother's stories of the desert's wizards and warriors.

She was fascinated by her father's birds. She loved to come in the first morning light to help the old *mali* remove the linen covers from the tall domed cages. Shabanu stopped to watch her daughter approach, her hands stretched out toward the feathers that shone brightly from between the thin bars. The *mali* returned with pans of maize, clucking and mewling to the birds, and asked Mumtaz to lift the cage doors.

When the birds were fed, Mumtaz turned again toward the gray weathered gate leading to the canal. Shabanu was about to call to her when a tall, dark figure sped from the veranda. In two strides the figure was behind Mumtaz, and a long, pale hand with crimson nails flashed out from under a dark green *chadr*. The hand grabbed the child by the hair and yanked her from her feet.

"You filthy urchin!" It was Leyla, Mumtaz's eldest half sister. "How dare you spy on my father's house!"

"He's my father too," said the child, her voice piping. Leyla flicked the wrist of her hand that grasped the child's hair. Mumtaz bit her lips and squeezed her eyes shut against the pain in her scalp. Leyla turned back toward the house, pushing the child before her like a prisoner of war. Mumtaz was small but strong, like her mother, and when she struck out at Leyla with her wiry arms, Leyla tightened her grip on the child's hair to keep her moving along.

"Thank you," said Shabanu, appearing at Leyla's side as if from thin air. She took Mumtaz by the hand and stepped between them. Leyla's mouth, the same deep, shiny red as her nails, went slack with surprise for a moment. She shook her fingers loose from Mumtaz's tangled hair and withdrew her hand gracefully under the folds of her *chadr*.

"How can you let her run loose like a street rat?" Leyla asked. "She's wild. She scares the chickens."

"That's enough, Leyla." Shabanu's voice was calm.

Mumtaz's eyes remained tightly shut against tears as Shabanu knelt before her and held her by the shoulders.

"I'm here, pigeon," she said, turning toward Mumtaz again. "That will be all, Leyla," she said without looking up. Mumtaz slumped into her arms and buried her face against her mother's neck. Shabanu held her for a moment, then removed her to arm's length and brushed the hair from her eyes. Her gaze held the child's.

"Come, we'll feed the ducks, and then you can bathe in the canal," Shabanu said, as if Leyla had ceased to exist.

It was Shabanu's refusal to defend herself, as if she had nothing to defend herself against, that drove the other women of Rahim's household—Leyla, her mother Amina, the other wives, Leyla's sisters and half sisters—to hate her. If only she would *say* that Mumtaz had as much right as the others to run about the courtyard, and ask what harm the child caused. But Shabanu refused even to acknowledge their resentment.

Shabanu was the favorite of Rahim—"the Merciful"— their powerful father and husband, the landowner and patriarch of the clan. The other wives hated her pretensions to dignity.

Each wife had her own private grudge. Leyla's mother Amina, the first and most important of Rahim's wives, was the eldest, the best educated among them all, and the only one who was his social equal. Amina also was the mother of Rahim's only surviving son, a poor quivering thing called Ahmed.

Amina had borne two other sons, also sickly and defective in one way or another. Like all of Rahim's sons, with the exception of Ahmed, both had died in infancy.

Amina had long since stopped sharing Rahim's bed. While her position gave her an unquestioned advantage over the other wives, she guarded her jealousy with a keen eye.

Ten years after Rahim had married Amina his attentions began to wander, and that is when he took a second wife. She was Saleema, who had captured his fancy one hot July when he visited his family at their summer retreat in Dinga Galli in the Himalayan foothills.

Saleema had come to see Amina, a second cousin, with her elder sister. She was a shy, slender girl with large dark eyes and a serious mouth. Saleema was far from beautiful. She inspired no jealousy in Amina, who had grown weary of her husband's physical demands. They culminated in pregnancy after pregnancy, each of which ended, to everyone's great disappointment, with a defective son or a daughter—three girls in all.

Then there was Ahmed. And by then Amina had had enough. It was such a relief not to have Rahim come to her bed at night when she was tired and wanted only to sleep! She had borne a healthy son. It was not until much later that Ahmed's weaknesses became apparent.

Saleema bore three daughters and two sons, both of whom died within a matter of months. Rahim's disappointment seemed to diminish Saleema with each birth. Amina watched with satisfaction as Saleema grew thinner and paler, until there seemed to be nothing left of her but her large black eyes and a straight line for a mouth.

Eight years later, under similar circumstances, came Tahira, who at the age of fifteen became Rahim's third wife. Tahira still was beautiful. After five years she too had borne three daughters and two feeble sons, both of whom died within a year. In that time she had been the chief co-occupant of Rahim's bed.

While Saleema had lapsed into bitter resignation that she had been replaced in her husband's affections, Tahira still harbored hope that Rahim would tire of Shabanu, return to her bed, and give her a healthy son who would inherit his father's land. For it was not at all certain that Ahmed would survive. And although Tahira was eight years Shabanu's senior, still her skin was smooth and her waist was slender, and the need for a viable heir should have been of paramount importance to the aging leader.

But from the time six years ago when Rahim first met Shabanu, a girl of twelve with budding breasts, wisdom beyond her years, and a dazzling smile, he had eyes for no other woman. In truth it had been too long since he'd had any appetite for his third wife, whose dainty approach to love made her seem insipid to him.

When Shabanu produced only one female child, those close to Rahim advised him to divorce her and take another wife who would produce a healthy heir. But Rahim demurred. His total indifference to all women but his fourth wife could only be explained as witchcraft.

Amina could not conceive of anyone else's happiness being achieved without expense to her own, and she viewed anyone who made her husband smile and whistle as he walked about the farm—as did Shabanu—with the deepest suspicion and contempt.

The women of Okurabad couldn't understand what attracted Rahim so powerfully to Shabanu—the way she went about barefoot, wearing the heavy silver ankle bracelet of the nomads, and no makeup. She, a lowborn gypsy, dared to regard them with contempt! They were all daughters of landowners like Rahim, holy men, tribal leaders whose ancestors had descended directly from the Holy Prophet Muhammad Himself, peace be upon Him!

Shabanu's father was a camel herder. She was a daughter of the wind.

They all knew how to dress and behave in the best houses of Lahore. Shabanu walked about the courtyard singing gypsy songs in her wood-smoke voice in Seraiki, the language of the desert. She'd never even been to Lahore!

They said among themselves that she practiced evil magic.

They were frightened of Shabanu, of the levelness in her eyes which they mistook for a conceit, a certain knowledge that Rahim would side with her against his elder wives.

For many weeks now the entire household had been preoccupied with preparations for Leyla's approaching marriage. Although the ceremony was not to be for several months, Leyla was busier than she ever had been before, and for some time had not followed Mumtaz about the garden as once was her custom. Shabanu cursed herself silently for letting down her guard.

Leyla growled low as a cat and turned swiftly away, her *chadr* swirling out around her like a green flame. When she was gone, Shabanu shook the child gently by the shoulders.

"You mustn't go to Papa's house until I'm awake and can go with you," she said.

Mumtaz said nothing, and Shabanu pressed her fiercely against her breast for a moment. Then they walked holding hands to the canal, which ran like an opal ribbon through the morning haze.

chapter 2

Rahim returned from Lahore during the day, and that evening Shabanu sat at her dressing table and watched in an ivory-framed mirror as Zenat took a heated rod from the fire. The old *ayah* arranged curls around Shabanu's face to soften the strong line of her chin.

Shabanu removed the silver cuff from her ankle and replaced it with a fine gold chain.

Mumtaz sat quietly watching the ritual of her mother adorning herself for her father. Shabanu lifted strands of pearls and rubies from red velvet cushions and twisted them together, then held them up for Zenat to fasten at the back of her neck.

"How do I look?" she asked, glancing from the mirror to Mumtaz's face. Mumtaz stuck a finger into her mouth and ran to her mother.

"Like Papa's birds," she whispered, and clasped her arms about her mother's waist. She buried her face in the silken folds of Shabanu's deep red sari, which hung from her knees heavily, weighted by embroidery of golden thread at the hem.

"Come away, Mumtaz. You'll mess your mother," said Zenat, circling the child's wrist with her clawlike fingers.

"Oh, let her be," said Shabanu. "God knows there's little enough time for her to sit in my lap like a baby." She hugged Mumtaz, who breathed in deeply, as if she wanted to keep her mother's rich, dark perfume all to herself.

Shabanu put the child to bed, telling her a story of the desert wind. The wind, she said, was a poet whom God had sent to live in the desert. His love dwelt among the stars. He could never reach her, and was doomed to spend eternity singing among the dunes.

When Rahim's servant rapped on the wooden door, Shabanu blew out the candle, kissed the smooth curve of her daughter's cheek, and left her in the careful guardianship of Zenat.

Rahim's servant held a lantern aloft, and its light glittered in the mirrors of his black velvet waistcoat and gleamed from the starched fan at the front of his turban. Zenat lifted the wedding *chadr* on which Shabanu's mother had embroidered desert flowers so perfect the individual stitches were invisible, and Shabanu bent her head like a bride as the *ayah* arranged it over her hair.

Rahim was standing before the heavy wooden mantel of the fireplace in the grand front room of the old house when Shabanu entered. The electricity was off in the house, diverted to the pumps that carried water from the tube wells in the farthest fields, where the cotton was newly planted. Candles glowed from silver holders on the mantel, and crystal oil lamps beside the draped windows threw golden glints from the mirrored ceilings. The ancient mud walls were painted with fat melons and trellises bent with the weight of heavy-headed flowers.

Rahim's square shoulders belied his sixty years. Shabanu lifted her head and removed the *chadr,* letting it slip down over her shoulders, and Rahim watched her silently. The turbaned servant reappeared at the door with a silver tray and offered Shabanu a glass of apple juice.

"Are you well?" Rahim asked, his voice rich and warm. Shabanu nodded. The incident with Leyla was not important enough to bother him with, especially not on his first night home. She saved the most serious of Amina's and Leyla's acts of malice for her argument that she must find a place away from Okurabad where she might live with Mumtaz one day, when Rahim was no longer there to care for them. He was forty-two years older than Shabanu, and she was truly afraid to be at the farm without him.

"See!" she'd said to him two weeks before, when she'd presented him with the body of Mumtaz's favorite puppy. She had found it with its neck wrung at the edge of the stableyard. "What will become of Mumtaz and me when you are no longer able to protect us?"

As always when these things happened, an acceptable explanation was found for the puppy's death. It was said that Mumtaz played with the pup in the stable, which was forbidden. Rahim and his brother Mahsood kept their stallions there. The least disturbance could cause a hormonal storm that might rage within the high-strung beasts for days.

"You must keep the child under control," Rahim had said to her. He dismissed her fears, and she'd had to let the matter drop.

Rahim put his hands on her shoulders and kissed her forehead gently.

"My old soul is always better when I've laid eyes upon you, my love," he said.

The deep lines in his face softened as he smiled in the flickering light. His hair was as gray as his silk *shalwar kameez*. A woolen Kashmiri vest fit flat over his middle, and his trousers billowed out from under the tunic before narrowing again above his soft polished shoes. He was straight and slim, but Shabanu thought he looked weary, and wondered what weighed so heavily on him.

"Would you like to visit Zabo?" he asked, and Shabanu's heart lifted.

"When?"

"I'm going to Mehrabpur tomorrow. I thought you and Mumtaz would like to come along."

"Yes, of course," she said quickly, and lowered her eyes. Shabanu was afraid to show pleasure at the thought of seeing her one friend, for fear something would happen to prevent her going. It had been so long since Shabanu had been with anyone her own age with whom she could talk freely.

Rahim lifted her chin and looked into her eyes.

"I wish I could do more to make you happy," he said. She did smile then, and his eyes lost their dark worried look for a moment.

"It will make me very happy to see Zabo."

Rahim tapped her chin with his knuckle.

"But I need your help," he said. "I am going to ask Nazir for Zabo to marry Ahmed. Will you persuade her?"

Shabanu thought at first that Rahim was mistaken; he couldn't mean Ahmed!

"But Ahmed is . . . not right!" said Shabanu.

"He's been to doctors in Lahore, and he can give her children," Rahim said quietly, not looking at her.

"But what if they're like him?" Poor Zabo! She was lovely and fair as a spring day in Cholistan. Shabanu's stomach tightened and her mouth felt dry.

"I know what you're thinking," Rahim said softly. "But she'll be safe here with Ahmed. You and she can spend all your time together. You need someone to talk to and laugh with. You will persuade her?"

"If Zabo marries Ahmed, she'll never have anything to laugh about—ever again!" she said. "Must you?" She looked into Rahim's face, but his eyes would not meet hers and finally she looked away.

"I must find ways of forcing Nazir to cooperate after Leyla's marriage to Omar," he said, his voice taking on the formality he used as a shield against her. Nazir, Rahim's youngest brother, was greedy and difficult. He was known for his huge appetites for food, drink, and women, and for cruel treatment of his wife and servants. And he was known for taking anything that caught his fancy.

Nazir was jealous of Rahim and Mahsood, their middle brother. The marriage of Leyla to Mahsood's son, Omar, would reunite the clan's land for the first time in two centuries. And this no doubt had increased Nazir's jealousy.

"Nazir has tried to find a suitable match for Zabo since she was ten," Shabanu said. "But no decent family wants a son, even a lowborn son, to marry Nazir's daughter. And he'd never accept a son-in-law unless he had a large land-holding."

Rahim remained silent. Among Pakistan's landowning classes it was the custom for cousins to marry in order to keep land within the family. Marriages were never made without thought of expediency.

"You can't ask me to persuade my only friend to marry an idiot boy who would give her idiot children!" said Shabanu.

"Zabo will marry anyone her father wants her to marry," said Rahim.

"You'll have to deed thousands of acres to Ahmed to get

Nazir's agreement," she said. "Do you trust your brother not to grab such a large piece of your land?"

"Ahmed will listen to me," Rahim replied. "He may be slow, but he knows enough not to trust Nazir. He's a good boy, Shabanu. Zabo would—"

"Zabo would be miserable!" Shabanu's eyes snapped.

"His mother and I have decided," Rahim said, and she knew there would be no more discussion.

Shabanu suddenly saw clearly Amina's hand in the arrangement. It was better to obscure such a cruel union as that of Ahmed and Zabo in the shadow of a major event like the wedding of Leyla and Omar.

One day Omar would inherit the family's largest landholding. His marriage to Leyla would be the marriage of the century. It would rejoin thousands of acres of ancestral land that had been divided and divided again by feuds that spanned every generation since the clan had settled in the Punjab. The future leadership of half a million clansmen depended on the sons Omar and Leyla would produce.

No expense would be spared in the preparation. Nothing would be left undone. Talk of clothing, jewelry, the house where they would live, the ceremony, the food, the dowry—details heaped like grains of sand on a dune—occupied the entire household. Already there were wagers on the timing of the birth of the couple's first son.

Leyla also was Amina's child, but the mother's ambition for Ahmed, her only son, was fierce. Ahmed had little sense. He had a limited ability to learn some things—such as riding and caring for horses and hunting deer and birds in the desert—all things he loved to do. At other things, such as his formal lessons, he proved hopelessly inept. Ahmed was a good-natured boy, but there were times when his brain seemed to depart his body, and he would sit rocking by the day on a straight-backed chair, his eyes glazed, a thread of spittle attached to his chin, wetting his shirt.

"I shall come with you and console her," Shabanu announced, reaching for the bell to signal the servants to bring dinner.

chapter 3

The next morning they arose early. Shabanu had returned at midnight from Rahim's bed in the big house to her room beside the stable. While the sun still lurked below the line of trees beyond the garden wall, she sat with Mumtaz between her knees, brushing the tangles from her daughter's newly washed hair and thinking of the day she'd first met Zabo.

Rahim had sent Zabo to help prepare Shabanu for her wedding. Both girls were barely thirteen. Shabanu had made her farewells to the desert; to the sapphire night sky that dazzled with more stars than anywhere on earth; to the shimmer of sunlight on the water in the *toba* where she'd spent her childhood; to the red dog-faced blossoms of the *kharin* that crunched peppery and sweet between her teeth; and finally to the camels, whose grace and courage had been the center of her happiness.

Her father had let her ride Xhush Dil, their finest camel, out of the desert the day she'd left. Usually when Shabanu rode Xhush Dil she'd sing, and he'd lift his great leathery feet in rhythm to her husky voice. But there had been no singing that day. And Xhush Dil had walked quietly, as if to acknowledge the solemnity of the occasion.

They'd seen Zabo coming along the track through the shimmery white edge of the desert in a pony-drawn cart more than a mile off. Rahim's servant Ibne accompanied her, riding his white stallion ahead of the cart.

"Uncle Rahim wants us to be friends," Zabo had said after making her *salaams* to Shabanu's mother and father. Shabanu hadn't looked at her directly at first. She kept her eyes on the ground, as befitted a bride and suited her mood.

But later, when they stopped for tea beneath a stand of trees in the green area near the irrigated land, Zabo spoke with great sympathy, and Shabanu began to listen.

"It's very difficult, I know," Zabo said quietly. "I've known my aunts all my life, and I still feel uncomfortable with them. But you'll get used to them and learn to go your own way."

Zabo sat staring at her fingers as she twisted the edge of her gray *chadr* around them.

"I don't mean to sound disloyal," she said quickly, and her soft brown eyes searched Shabanu's for understanding. "Uncle Rahim is very kind and fair."

Shabanu could see from Zabo's eyes that she too was unhappy. She soon learned why. Zabo lived a prisoner's life. Despite her beauty no one wanted a son to marry Nazir's daughter, and Zabo was considered unmarriageable. Nazir was the least prosperous of the three brothers, and he guarded Zabo's virtue as his greatest prospect for gaining more land.

As the other women of Rahim's household came to despise Shabanu, they also hated Zabo for being Nazir's daughter. While both the girls were young and beautiful, they also were very different: Zabo was tall and slender, while Shabanu was small and compact; Zabo spoke Punjabi, the upper-class language of the area, and Shabanu spoke Seraiki, the poetic tongue of the desert. Perhaps what the others despised most of all was the unpretentious and open affection between the two girls—so rare a quality within the hothouse of intrigues that shaped the other relationships at Okurabad.

Together Zabo, Shabanu, and her family reached the farm at the edge of the desert where her sister, Phulan, lived with her husband and his family. Phulan's belly was swollen with her first son. Her beautiful sloping eyes radiated contentment.

Zabo began by teaching Shabanu the Punjabi language and what she needed to know about the strange customs of the wedding—so formal and stiff in comparison to the joyous cacophony of family weddings in Cholistan.

She made Shabanu wear shoes with heels on them. They laughed together as Shabanu tottered and finally fell headlong into the dust.

"U-ma! You're pulling too hard!" Shabanu jumped at Mumtaz's cry and finished off the end of the plait with a piece of thread. Tears glistened in the corners of the child's eyes.

"I'm sorry, pigeon," Shabanu said, smiling at her daughter. "Go tell Zenat to get your pretty blue *shalwar kameez* ready. We want to show Auntie Zabo how grown-up and pretty you are!"

Mumtaz skipped off, trailing her tattered blanket behind her and happy to be finished with the ivory-handled hairbrush. Shabanu sat silent in the lantern light, turning the brush over between her brown fingers.

The day she left Cholistan, Shabanu felt as if she'd entered an alien land inhabited by people like her sister, whose happiness was difficult to comprehend.

"The secret is keeping your innermost beauty, the secrets of your soul, locked in your heart." Shabanu could hear the words of Sharma, her wise aunt who lived with her daughter, Fatima, in the desert. "Trust yourself. Keep your inner reserves hidden."

At the time, Shabanu had thought she hadn't any inner reserves to hide. But Sharma's advice had guided Shabanu's life. She tucked away each small happiness so that it glowed within her. And Sharma was right: Rahim was mesmerized by her mystery. He reached out to her in every way he knew, but he never quite touched her.

"Uma! It's time to go!" Mumtaz came clattering in her patent leather pumps, her toes turned slightly inward. She looked like a calf, her elbows and knees grown too large as the baby fat fell away.

Shabanu handed Mumtaz her sewing basket, and Zenat carried a canvas bag sagging with Thermoses of tea and water, hot fried bread, and roast chicken wrapped in a towel. They waited in the curtained backseat of the huge sedan. Mumtaz sat daintily on the white linen covers that crunched over leather seats, and ran her hands gently across the tan velvet curtains that shielded the windows.

A crowd of Rahim's constituents, humble people from the desert wearing turbans on their heads and *lungis* around their thin hips, stood in their bare feet inside the gate, although the sun was still below the horizon.

The driver stood at attention beside the door of the European sedan, a gun strapped across his chest. He had been up for hours, checking and polishing the car. The secretary came after Rahim as he adjusted a shawl around his shoulders in the doorway and gave instructions to the farm manager, who stood inside. The secretary wrote down everything Rahim said. The crowd fell silent, then pressed forward, waving petitions and shouting to ask Rahim to hear their cases.

"I've been here all week!" shouted one.

"My son is dying!" said another.

"Please, *Sahib*! Sign this!"

"My cousin has taken my cow, and now my *toba*!"

The driver and another guard rushed forward and pushed the crowd aside with bamboo sticks held horizontally like fence rails.

Ibne held the car door open for Rahim, who stepped in beside the driver. A cloud of French scent entered the automobile with Rahim, and Mumtaz bounced up and down on the seat.

Another car left the long, palm-lined drive ahead of Rahim's, sending up sheets of dust that the sedan parted with its shiny snout. The great lion carved over the gate in the ancient garden wall bade them farewell. The crowd of petitioners would be there when they returned.

As they gathered speed, two men leaned from the windows of the car ahead, shouting to clear the road of goats, sheep, and cattle being driven to market. The two cars hurtled through a green tunnel of acacia trees planted by the British colonists eighty years before. They sped past camel carts loaded with timber, oxcarts with wooden wheels, overcrowded Bedford buses that looked like huge, luminescent beetles with *charpoi*s and crates of chickens tied on top. Men stood beneath the trees staring at the official car with green provincial assembly emblems above the license plates and important people inside.

Everyone in the district recognized the sound of Rahim's horn more than a mile before they saw the car. But each time it passed they stood by their cycles or sat in their carts and stared, not in awe or fear or envy—simply stared, slack-faced and dull with the inevitabilities of poverty.

Rahim and Shabanu spoke little, he not knowing what to say to her in her anger, and she having nothing to say to him. She would never change his mind about Ahmed and Zabo.

The trip lasted an hour on the main road along the canal. If the road had not been cleared of carts, pedestrians, bicycles, and animals, it might have taken three hours to reach Mehrabpur, a dusty village where flies rose in clouds from carts piled with fried dumplings.

On the other side of the town stood Nazir's house, invisible from the road except for the thick mud walls of the fortress within which he lived. Nazir was ten years younger than Rahim. He was a less important politician and landowner, but he had more enemies.

Four men with thick black mustaches stood staring straight ahead beside the heavy wooden gate. They wore khaki uniforms and poppy red turbans and held ugly automatic rifles across their chests. Their eyes looked as if they had seen much violence, and Shabanu sensed they would easily be provoked to fire their guns.

Rahim didn't come frequently to Mehrabpur, but Shabanu knew the guards recognized him. Still, they insisted they must have the guns of the driver and bodyguard. The two men refused, but Rahim ordered them to hand over their weapons. They closed the windows and drove through the gates.

"God knows what trouble Nazir is brewing now!" said Rahim.

Mumtaz's eyes were wide, and she hugged her stuffed monkey tight against her chest.

The car stopped under a canopy that covered the driveway, and Shabanu and Mumtaz stepped out without waiting for the door to be opened for them. A servant opened the trunk, and an old *ayah* took the picnic hamper. Shabanu turned to say good-bye to her husband but his back was turned, and he walked toward the main front door where Nazir stood bareheaded, his billowy trousers and tunic stretched over his enormous belly, his mustache thin and sinister-looking.

"Shabanu!"

Zabo came bounding out of the house and threw her arms around her friend. "I couldn't sleep last night. I couldn't wait to see you." Shabanu hugged her back, and Zabo bent her long, graceful frame to pick up Mumtaz, who clung to her neck. They all stood looking at one another the way thirsty people in the desert look at water before they drink.

The main hallway in the sleeping quarters area of the house was dark and narrow and smelled of dust. But in Zabo's sitting room the windows were flung wide open to the garden, with lace curtains billowing in the breeze. Bolsters embroidered with animals and flowers were scattered around the room. The furniture was simple—wood and string *charpois* and footstools—but Shabanu recognized the style of the embroidery. Zabo had spent years before fires and in the corners of parlors, bent over her needlework to make her own world in the simple room where she'd slept since childhood.

"Let me look at you!" Zabo said, taking the old stuffed monkey from Mumtaz's arms. The toy had been a gift from Zabo. "You look so pretty, and you've grown so tall!" The child stretched her neck to look even taller. Zabo slid a large package wrapped in bright green paper across the floor.

"This is for Bundr and you. I'll hold Bundr while you open it."

The child tore at the paper and squealed when she saw the wicker pram. Inside were a quilt and a new wardrobe for the monkey.

"Let's take Bundr out to show Rashid," Shabanu said, and the two women walked out into the back garden with Mumtaz, who snatched the toy monkey back and pushed it in its pram to find the young son of the servant who would look after her for the afternoon.

Zabo and Shabanu sat on a willow bench under a banyan tree at the edge of the garden.

"I've got new boots from England for hiking at Dinga!" said Zabo, clasping one knee with her long, supple fingers. She and Shabanu joined the other women of Rahim's and Nazir's households each summer at the family's summer house at Dinga Galli, in the Himalayan foothills. They hiked and gathered wild flowers along the mountain footpaths while the men hunted panthers among the granite peaks above.

"Zabo, I have something to tell you," said Shabanu. She couldn't bear a second of dishonesty with her friend. Her voice sounded formal and unfeeling, and she stopped speaking for a moment. She looked into Zabo's eyes, and her heart crumpled.

"Oh, Zabo!" Shabanu reached for her friend's hands and fought the tears that built pressure behind her eyes.

"What?"

"Rahim has come to propose that you marry Ahmed."

"Ahmed?" she asked with a small laugh, as if Shabanu had misspoken. Then her eyes widened with disbelief. "He wants Ahmed to marry? Me?"

"He's offering a fortune. Rahim hates this quarrel with your father. He's proposing several hundred acres!"

Zabo covered her face with her hands for a moment. Shabanu could hear her friend's heart—or was it her own?—thumping wildly. Slowly Zabo straightened her spine and dropped her hands to her lap. Shabanu put her arms around Zabo's shoulders and drew her close.

"Forgive me," said Zabo. "At least you and I would be together."

Shabanu sat immobile for a second, then she pushed Zabo's hair from her high forehead.

"I am so angry with Rahim," she said quietly, and Zabo looked up when she heard the cold edge in Shabanu's voice. "All he thinks of is the family name, the family land, the family, the family! He doesn't care a parrot's whistle for me, except as his possession. Or for you, except now as a peace offering."

"Finally I shall escape this prison," said Zabo, looking over her shoulder at the cracked gray walls of the house. "Since Mother died I have always been afraid I'd never leave here, just as she never left."

"You won't even try to persuade your father that it's wrong for you to marry Ahmed?" asked Shabanu. But she knew Zabo was unlikely to disobey her father. She'd never run away as Shabanu had done when she'd learned her father had promised her to Rahim.

"Don't waste yourself on the things you cannot change." Shabanu heard Auntie Sharma's voice, speaking to her as if it had its own will to come on inside her head like a radio. Sometimes Shabanu felt she'd never learn patience.

"Duty is not so difficult when there's no alternative, Shabanu."

"Oh, Zabo, I still want to run away sometimes! We could disappear into the desert."

"My father would hunt us down and kill us," said Zabo. "It can only be as he wishes."

Shabanu thought of the armed guards always within a few feet of Nazir. They never smiled or spoke. Nazir had reason to fear so many people that he regarded everyone as an enemy.

Shabanu knew Nazir's cruelty too well. She thought of a late afternoon six years earlier, when the sun left a sheen on the canal like sun-ripened melon. She and her sister were gathering water to take back to their camp at the edge of the desert, where their family had come to plan Phulan's wedding to their cousin Hamir.

When their pots were full, the girls walked down the canal path, talking. Phulan was saying how handsome Hamir was, and how if she ate plenty of lentils and butter she would have fat and healthy sons that would look just like their father. Shabanu was daydreaming about her own approaching marriage to Hamir's brother Murad, and thinking this might not be such a bad place to live after all.

"Who is this?" asked a deep voice from the bottom of the bank. Shabanu looked down to see a fat man in a silk tunic and drawstring trousers leaning on a hand-carved shotgun. This was her first glimpse of Nazir. Laughter boomed out from the bushes.

A second man, younger and slimmer than Nazir, stepped out from behind a tree. He also had a gun. Both men wore elaborately embroidered caps, finely woven vests, and gold watches. A third man appeared, and a fourth—a young man, still part boy.

"How about this one?" Nazir asked the youngest man.

Phulan stood defiantly before them, shaking the glass bangles back on her brown arm, a water jar and a basket of wet laundry atop her head. Her face was uncovered and lovely, her nose disk glinting in reflected sunlight, her graceful pale fingers molded around the curve of the water jar on her hip.

"Yes," said Nazir. "The one who bags the most quails gets that one."

"What about me?" asked one of the others. "I shot the only blue bull. I should have her. Give the boy the other one."

"I'll pay you handsomely," said Nazir, turning back to the two girls. "Land, jewelry, money—anything you like."

Shabanu's heart had raced. Some families would be grateful for the payment and would willingly forget the indignity. But Shabanu had been certain her father and Hamir would not. The thought of Nazir sweating over her sister made her ill, and she snapped her head forward, tossing the water jugs down the embankment. The men scattered as the jars broke, splashing mud onto Nazir's silken trousers.

Shabanu swung up onto the neck of their camel and pulled Phulan up behind her. Nazir spluttered with rage, and the other men bent double with laughter, slapping their knees and choking on tears as Shabanu and Phulan escaped to the camp at the edge of the desert.

After dark, Nazir and his men came in a jeep to the house where Hamir and Murad lived. Hamir was overcome by anger. Blood was the only redemption he could see for the insult to his honor. He took his father's old country-made shotgun outside, where darkness had settled around the farmyard.

The landowner and his friends sat in the jeep, laughing

and talking. They had been drinking. Their voices were loud, their words slurred.

"Where are they?" Nazir demanded when he saw Hamir.

"They've gone into the desert," replied Hamir. He brought the gun up in front of him and held it under his arm, the muzzle pointing casually toward the jeep.

Nazir was silent for a moment, and the other men sobered.

"Then bring us your sister," said Nazir.

Without moving a muscle, Hamir squeezed the trigger and a shot exploded into the side of the jeep. Nazir's friends scrambled out, falling over each other into the dirt in drunken disarray.

Hamir's mother and brother came running around the corner of the house just in time to see the flash from a large foreign-made shotgun—much louder than Hamir's. Hamir flew from his feet like a puppet being yanked from a stage. When the dust cleared, Hamir lay in a bloody, tattered heap, his body nearly halved at the waist. His family buried him in the floor of the house before they too fled into the desert.

It was true, Shabanu thought. Nazir would kill his only daughter if she did not obey him.

She and Zabo sat without moving from the garden bench through the warmth of the afternoon. The *ayah* brought them lunch, and Zabo sat quietly, picking invisible crumbs from her lap.

Shabanu talked about the things they'd do together in Okurabad after Zabo's marriage to Ahmed. The leaves sparkled and danced in the spring sun, then the shade thickened around them.

Shabanu talked until her throat was scratchy, and she felt drained dry as the Cholistan sand at the height of summer.

"I wanted to say something wise—something to comfort you," she said at last. "I want you to believe we will be all right if we are living in the same household. The truth is, I don't know what to say."

"There is nothing to say," Zabo said quietly. "Truly, I do just love to hear you talk. I love to hear what we will do together. The other things can't be helped. We may as well speak of the blessings."

"Perhaps Rahim will allow me to go with you to Lahore to shop for your dowry," said Shabanu. And they talked of that for a while.

chapter 4

T he wick on the candle sputtered, and Shabanu looked at Rahim. His face was quiet on the pillow. The silk whispered as she drew the coverlet down, and his eyes opened as she reached for her shawl. He raised himself up on one elbow and caught her hand as she stood to draw the shawl around her shoulders.

"Come back," he said softly.

"I can't," she said, trying to tug her hand away. But he held her fast.

"You must," he said, and pulled her back toward him.

"You're hurting me!" He said nothing, but neither did he release her wrist. He pulled her down to lie beside him again.

"Mumtaz will be frightened when she wakes."

"I've already told Zenat she's to spend the night with Mumtaz."

"You have no right!" she said. "*I* make the decisions about Mumtaz."

"No right?"

She propped herself on her elbow and turned to face him.

"She's too small to be shoved off with servants. . . ."

"I won't have you spending all your time with her!" A diversion of Shabanu's attention from him when he wanted her was the only thing that made Rahim unreasonable. She knew better than to argue with him now.

"You'll see her in the morning," he said, taking her into his arms again.

Shabanu barely acknowledged her resentment. She stuffed it back into her heart, just as she and her sister had once stuffed feathered quilts into camel bags before they traveled to a new water hole in the desert.

Rahim's hot face scraped against hers, and she reacted lazily at first until her body responded to the rhythm of his passion. But her eyes stared into the dark, at the ceiling, and, as they turned in the bed, at the wall, at the pillow. All the while she murmured sweetly against his ear, and her plans took shape in her mind.

She thought about the incident with Leyla. If Amina had not yet brought complaints to Rahim about how Mumtaz dressed and ran freely about the farm, no doubt she would soon. Shabanu decided to make a change in her daughter's daily schedule.

She thought about how to make dressing Mumtaz and combing her hair every morning into a game. It wasn't as if Mumtaz's half sisters were so well turned out every day. In fact, Mumtaz looked no worse. It was her spirit of adventure—her fearlessness around the animals and her interest in climbing trees and playing in the sand, heedless of snakes and scorpions—that set her apart from the others and intimidated them.

But Shabanu decided to see to it that her daughter looked

better than the older children without limiting Mumtaz's freedom to play. That might defuse Amina's complaints.

Shabanu felt pleased with her decision and turned her thoughts to her first trip to Lahore to shop for Zabo's dowry.

Her mind buzzed with excitement long after Rahim had fallen asleep again.

She had already decided that she and Zabo should stay at the *haveli,* the family's ancestral house in the old walled city of Lahore. Rahim had lived there with his brothers when they were boys in school. His sister Selma, a widow, lived there alone now.

Rahim's elder wives hated the drafty old wood building. They all stayed in modern stone and glass bungalows in the more fashionable Cantonment area of Lahore. Selma looked after the *haveli,* and Rahim often stayed there when the provincial assembly was in session.

Shabanu had never seen the *haveli,* in the heart of the Mogul city. But now she imagined herself sitting in a window high atop the dilapidated old house, with trees and ferns growing out of drainpipes outside the third-story windows. She would look out through the carved wooden screen onto the street, watching the horse-drawn carts as they clattered over the cobbles below.

Long after the candle had flickered out in the tiny silver stand on the table beside her, she breathed softly and stroked her arms under the crumpled linen of the sheet. But she never closed her eyes. The thought of Lahore and the *haveli* electrified her.

Before first light, she slipped out of bed and wrapped her shawl tightly about her. Rahim lay snoring, turned on his side, his shoulders lifting with each breath. She spread her jewels on the table beside his pillow, then folded her sari and left it on the floor under his shoes. She scrubbed her face in the basin and whipped her hair into a knot behind her head. She put on an old *shalwar kameez* she'd left in his cupboard, and slipped out.

Mumtaz had not been afraid in the least the first night Shabanu had spent away from her. In the morning when Shabanu came back from the big house to bathe and breakfast with her, she had found the child asleep with her arms around Bundr's neck.

Usually Shabanu rose early—earlier than the sun, earlier even than the serving women—and went to bathe in the women servants' bath across the courtyard.

This morning, after checking on her daughter, she took the brass bucket from her room to the pump, and her heart rejoiced at the splash and gurgle as only the heart of a desert woman can rejoice at the sound of water. She loved the way the darkness chilled her, as if she were the only soul alive.

"Why do you want to spend your days in that dusty room behind the stable?" Rahim had asked her again and again. "There's no water, no heat. You could be here with servants."

"I'm still a peasant girl," she'd said, making her smile dazzle.

It excited him to have her come to him in the evenings and leave again in the mornings. It was like an illicit love affair, though he continued to insist she move back into the house. But she held on to the room, and the arrangement continued in the same way, week by week.

Living in the room behind the stable was as close as Shabanu had come to freedom since she'd left Cholistan, and the morning hours before the household awoke were her freest time of all.

Streaks of green appeared on the horizon, outlining the inky black trees around the courtyard wall as she brought the bucket back and lit the fire in the stableyard pit. The darkness diffused slightly, and stripes of orange appeared beneath the green, and the stars dimmed, and the animals began to stir, and it seemed the day had begun to happen all in one instant.

Shabanu loved being close to the animal sounds in the morning, as if the horses moving about, the cocks crowing, the cows lowing with their udders full were all intent on letting her know the world was safe for another day.

By the time the water was heated, the light glinted watery and pale from the rim of the bucket, and steam rose as she carried back her bathwater. The rising sun shone purely, for the air was still free of the dust that would gather as activity increased about the farm.

Precious as her time grew as each day wore on, with mending and looking after Mumtaz and cleaning and storing the wheat and rice from the market and a thousand other household chores assigned her by Amina, Shabanu spent a long time in her bath.

Though water was plentiful here at Okurabad, Shabanu still prided herself on being able to bathe in very little. When she and her sister were small, her mother would pour a thin stream of water over each of their heads, soaping their hair, then rubbing the soapy water into their shoulders, backs, and bellies. By the time each girl was rinsed, only a single cup of water had been used.

The air felt cold and astringent as Shabanu pulled her

kameez over her head and, loosening the string of her *shalwar*, stepped free of her clothing.

She loved the bare austerity of the servant women's bath, with its swept-smooth dirt floor, whitewashed walls, thick, tallowy soap, and rough, wind-dried towels. The baths in Rahim's house puzzled her—their pale pink tiles, perfumed soaps, and soft towels that refused to absorb water seemed frivolous and useless.

She stood on a small platform of thin wood slats beside the drain and scooped the hot water from her pail with a plastic cup. She shivered with pleasure as it ran over her scalp, through her hair, and then splashed cooler over her shoulders and down her spine.

The soap smelled clean and honest, and produced a slippery lather as she rubbed it over her shoulders and chest. She ran her hands over her full round breasts.

As she stood there in the bath, Shabanu thought of her many blessings, the things that brought her pleasure and made her life worthwhile: First, of course, was Mumtaz, who grew stronger and cleverer and more beautiful by the day; then there was Rahim, who treated her well and wanted enough for her to be happy that he allowed her these small freedoms, and who gave her beautiful gifts of jewelry and clothes; and there were the gifts themselves—she loved to wear them, but, more important, they gave her a sense of material well-being, as they might always be sold if she needed money; and the women she loved—Zabo, Sharma and Fatima, her mother and Phulan—for, though she saw them seldom, their strength, wisdom, and beauty were folded in and around the chambers of her heart, as if they had become an organic part of her.

That same morning she asked Mumtaz to stand before

her to have her hair brushed. In the afternoon Shabanu took her to the bazaar at Multan and let her pick her favorite colors in cotton lawn so fragile and light the *darzi* clucked his tongue over it when he sat down to cut it into pieces for small *shalwar kameez*.

As the days began to lengthen, Rahim noticed the change in how the child looked. He stopped now and then to speak to Mumtaz in the courtyard, and she curtsied to him.

Still Mumtaz played by the canal and climbed thorn trees in her new *shalwar kameez*. Every afternoon when she came back for her nap, Shabanu undressed and bathed her and sat down to mend the rips in the knees and sleeves of the soft cotton garments as Mumtaz slept.

One afternoon Rahim returned from a hunt in the desert, the jeeps dripping blood from their floorboards. Mumtaz stood watching as the men unloaded the dead deer, their delicate hooves crossed and pointed toward the sky.

Her father saw her and went to the back curtain of his big four-by-four, returning with something in his arms. Mumtaz stood her ground, unaware that the small, angular bundle was for her. He stooped before her, and the first thing she saw was a timid face with large, brave eyes shining brightly from it.

Rahim held out the fawn, and Mumtaz lifted her hand gently to touch the velvety place between those beautiful eyes. The fawn struggled, kicking out its legs, and Mumtaz withdrew her hand quickly. Rahim set it on its feet. Its legs were so slender that Mumtaz was afraid they'd break as the fawn bucked to get away from them. Its soft pink tongue licked out at its shiny black nose, and Rahim let it go.

"She'll be back," he said. "She's looking for her mother, but she won't find her. Go ask Zenat to warm some buffalo milk with sugar, and get out one of your old nursing bottles so you can feed her."

From that day on, Mumtaz and the fawn were inseparable. The tiny hooves followed her, *tak-tak-tak,* across the courtyard and down to the canal. The child tied colored ribbons around the fawn's neck, and the animal's coat became thick and shiny from the rich buffalo milk. The *mali* fed her grain in the mornings when he tended the birds. Mumtaz was totally absorbed in her pet, and it lifted Shabanu's spirits so that Rahim noticed a new warmth in her.

In the dead still afternoons the heat began to accumulate, and Shabanu and Mumtaz napped. The air shimmered up from the dirt in the white light outside their door. The mosquito netting hung heavy and limp around them as they lay side by side, sleeping behind leaden eyelids. The air felt too hot to breathe, and the *charpoi* strings prickled their shoulder blades through the rough cotton sheet.

They had been napping for more than an hour on such an afternoon when a shrill scream pierced their heat-drugged sleep. Shabanu pushed aside the mosquito netting. At the doorway she paused to grab her *chadr,* and as she emerged into the shade of the tarpaulin that Zenat had stretched over the doorway, she saw two men scuffling, their feet raising clouds of dust from the parched earth. One of the men wore a smartly starched turban.

The screaming went on, and Shabanu saw a veiled figure slip away to the edge of the stableyard as other menservants came in their undershirts from doorways behind which they'd been asleep. Some wrapped limp turbans around their heads as they ran.

"I saw him in her room!" the voice shrieked, over and over. The voice was strange but familiar. Shabanu knew it was the voice of Leyla, though the veil and dust muffled the sound. The voice quavered, and its pitch seemed oddly higher, as if Leyla was trying to disguise herself.

"The mosquito nets were heaving! I was afraid he was trying to strangle her!" The voice trailed off, thin and ghostly.

Through the dust Shabanu saw the twinkle of mirrors on Ibne's vest. His proud white turban fell from his head in the scuffle and was trampled in the dirt.

He struggled silently with the other men, who grunted and wheezed as they fumbled to pin his arms to his sides and pull him to the ground. Ibne's eyes slid wildly from side to side until they found Shabanu's in the shaded doorway.

She thought of the times Ibne had brought Rahim's gifts to her in the desert, he riding his shining white horse, and she sitting with her father astride a camel.

In all the years Shabanu had known Ibne, this was the first time their eyes had met. His held an urgent plea as the servants wrestled him to his knees. He didn't make a sound as they dragged him away. When the dust cleared, the dark veiled figure had disappeared.

Zenat came to take Mumtaz in the early evening so Shabanu could dress for dinner, and Shabanu asked what she knew about the commotion in the stableyard. The old woman worried her long, widely spaced teeth with her tongue and kept her eyes lowered. She pulled at her stained white *chadr*.

"They said he was caught in your room, *Begum*," she said.

"They!" Shabanu said. "Who are *they*?" The old woman kept her eyes on the floor.

"The women, *Begum*," she said.

"Was it Leyla?"

"I don't know, *Begum*," Zenat muttered. She was rescued by Mumtaz, who came in with her dolls and Bundr tucked into the wicker pram. The fawn trotted behind her, raising and lowering her velvet head.

When they were gone, Shabanu sat in the corner of her room, where she could keep an unseen eye on the dusty haze in the stableyard. It turned golden as the sun sank over the walls. Flies darted in and out of the doorway, and someone walked Rahim's stallion past on its way to the stable. Birds twittered in the trees.

Amina and Leyla had trapped Ibne. Shabanu saw it as clearly as if she were watching the plot of a movie unfold. Amina had arranged the incident to cast suspicion on Shabanu.

Amina set the tone for the other women's attitude toward Shabanu. She enlisted the servants, her daughters, and the other wives to wage war against this unwanted member of the household. If Amina was the general, Leyla was her field commander.

Amina and Leyla said she manipulated Rahim. They believed he protected her while she seduced him into misappropriating property and possessions that rightfully would be theirs when he died. They would be shocked to know what Shabanu really wanted was to be gone from them, away from this place, rid of everything that would remind her of it, and alone, when Rahim was gone.

Shabanu stood and crossed to the rough wooden cupboard, where she moved stacks of bright-colored tunics and saris until she found a silver shot-silk *kameez* and a tight-fitting *churidar* pajama in the same silver, striped with black. She flicked the tiny silver bells embroidered into the pattern on the bodice, and her heart lifted with their delicate rings.

She wouldn't let them cast their shadow over her life. She would show Rahim exactly what had happened. She would shine a light so bright over herself and Mumtaz that there would be no darkness in their world.

chapter 5

R ahim questioned Shabanu about Ibne that night almost as if he didn't want to know, so anxious was he that she not be hurt by the accusations he'd heard. She told him the simple truth, and he nodded while he listened.

"He never entered your room?" he asked when she had finished. "Could you have been too sound asleep to know?"

"Ibne would never come into my room alone, even if he knocked first. Not even if I asked him to! It was a lie planned to make you distrust me."

"Ibne said the cook sent him with a message. And the cook said he sent no message. The cook has been with me for twenty-five years."

"And so has Ibne," said Shabanu. "And his father before him."

Rahim rubbed his chin with his forefinger and tightened his lips over his teeth.

"You don't think he'd risk everything—his job, his dignity, your respect—by trying to hurt me? It doesn't make sense." She spoke calmly, keeping all urgency from her voice.

"You're a beautiful woman, Shabanu. Never underestimate a man with desire in his heart."

She threw up her hands and let out her breath in an exasperated puff. Forgive me, Ibne, she thought. I can't let him think I'm trying to convince him. He must decide on the truth in his own heart.

"Will you let your most trusted servant go because of a foolish screaming woman?"

"Leyla is not—"

"Ha!" Shabanu said, and folded her arms. "So it was Leyla!" He stiffened at the coldness in her voice. "And you believe her?"

"I know you think Leyla and her mother have tried to hurt you, but they're good women, Shabanu. You're too sensitive about your background. . . ."

"I'm proud of my background! I wouldn't trade my family or growing up in the desert for a *crore* of rupees!" she said. But she allowed him to soothe her and tell her how honorable her father was.

Shabanu spent the night with Rahim, and although she was very tired, she took special care to please him, giving him jasmine tea and rubbing scented oil into his skin until he fell asleep.

The next morning she was up early. In the low-lying haze she and Mumtaz walked beside the canal, the fawn following behind, ducking her head and throwing out her feet in delicate kicks. A bell jangled from the red braided collar around the animal's neck, and Mumtaz stopped for a moment and watched her speculatively.

"Uma, why is she so small?" she asked. "Her ears get bigger, and she eats a lot. I want her to grow as big as Guluband so I can ride her!"

"Guluband was a camel," said Shabanu. She thought of herself at Mumtaz's age riding the majestic Guluband among the dunes, his feet lifting in rhythm to her songs. Shabanu turned to look at the fawn, and both she and Mumtaz watched as the animal gazed back at them with her long, graceful ears pitched forward.

Mumtaz is right, Shabanu thought. The fawn had not grown at all in the month since she'd come to Okurabad. Perhaps losing her mother at such a young age had shocked her, or her confinement within the courtyard had stunted her growth.

"This little one will never be big enough for you to ride," said Shabanu. "Shall we name her Choti, and she'll always be your little one?"

Mumtaz nodded solemnly and took her mother's hand. They walked on without speaking.

A little farther on they met Tahira, Rahim's third wife, a slim woman with fair skin and a deprecating air. Tahira had deep-set eyes and a gentle manner but little sense of humor. When Shabanu had first come to Okurabad, the women would summon her to tea each afternoon. They would assemble formally in the parlor and catch up on the household gossip. They'd watched her carefully, and after she'd left them they'd talk about her, inventing things they claimed she'd said to them.

In those days Shabanu had wanted to befriend Tahira. But Tahira would have no part of her. If Shabanu spoke to her, she would look at the floor and pretend not to hear. Never in her life had Shabanu felt so alone.

Tahira adjusted her shawl studiously, not looking at Mumtaz and Shabanu as they passed on the canal path. Her daughter, a few years older than Mumtaz, turned and ran back to pet the fawn. Tahira came after her quickly and grabbed her by the wrist, shaking and scolding her as she dragged the girl away.

It didn't matter whether Rahim decided Ibne was innocent or guilty, Shabanu thought. It was *her* guilt that Leyla and Amina hoped to prove, as surely as crows are drawn to a corpse.

Ibne and Zenat were the only exceptions within the household at Okurabad, where the attitudes toward Shabanu ranged from indifference to viciousness. The longer Shabanu lived in Rahim's house, the more clearly she saw how cancerous the relations between the family and the servants had grown.

At first they had seemed rather normal to her, if intricate and fragile, shaped by traditional codes of behavior of which she was thoroughly ignorant. She decided not to even try to understand. She would never fit in with the family women, and even the servants regarded her as beneath their station. Instead, she approached each person on his or her own terms.

These were some of the things Shabanu observed:

While the family rooms were kept in good repair, the mud interior walls plastered and repainted in their original Mogul designs, the walls of the rooms where the servants worked were cracked and bulging. The furniture in the front rooms had been repaired, the springs retied, the horsehair fluffed, and new covers sewn. In the house's interior, derelict chairs and tables slumped in corners.

During rest periods, the male servants dragged their *charpois* from their rooms into a circle in the courtyard, where they sat gossiping and drawing on their tall brass *hookah* pipes. The servant women spread basketfuls of neem leaves over the grime on the dirt floor so they could sit and talk behind the kitchen. If anyone not included in the conversation approached, the group fell silent until the intruder had passed.

In the family's quarters the windows were opened during the day to air out the rooms. They smelled of sunshine, jasmine, lime trees and roses from the gardens, and sometimes of burning sticks of incense. The interior stank of years of rancid *ghee,* animal blood, the droppings of rodents, and more than two centuries of dust. To Shabanu it smelled of evil.

In the family quarters, relations between the wives seemed placid on the surface, with the women cooperating, socializing, and even commiserating among themselves. They shopped and gossiped together, laughed over their triumphs, and wept over small injustices. Their communion seemed innocent to Rahim, who surveyed his family with the satisfaction of a shepherd.

But in the world of the servants, alliances were drawn and plots were hatched openly. Relationships were what they were, without pretense or hypocrisy, and at times the servants' quarters had the atmosphere of a battlefield.

But the women's gentle camaraderie and the laughter that rang out from the family *zenana* in truth covered something else. Behind their veils the women also plotted and schemed, usually one against another, often several against one or two, occasionally all united against one, and that one most frequently was Shabanu.

In the servants' quarters much of the scheming was done on behalf of members of Rahim's family. Some servants plotted also for their own gain.

But all of the servants, regardless of how well or ill they were treated, derived their own power from the master or mistress they served.

Zenat was the oldest and weakest among the servants. She had nowhere else to go. When there was trouble she ducked her head, took blows as she had to, then dove for cover. Because she was nearing the end of her days of usefulness, she was assigned to work for Shabanu and Mumtaz.

Zenat would come scuttling into the room by the stable, looking over her shoulder like a ground squirrel being chased by a fox.

"What is it?" Shabanu would ask.

"Nothing, *Begum,*" the old *ayah* would reply. "I'm too old for trouble."

And that was how Zenat got along.

Sometimes the servants favored by Amina tormented Zenat beyond reason, simply because she was Shabanu's servant.

One day when Mumtaz was an infant, Khansama, the cook—who was Amina's creature, body and soul—asked Zenat to fetch some *ghee* from a cupboard in the courtyard. The entire kitchen staff watched from the doorway. Zenat was afraid, but she dared not disobey, for Khansama stood, arms folded over his chest, to see that she did as she was told. An angry buzzing vibrated the cupboard, and Zenat raised a trembling hand to the rusted latch.

Through the crack, swarms of angry bees darted out into the sunlight and stung her dozens of times on her face and neck. She flailed her gnarled hands, and the little furry creatures flew up the loose arms of her tunic and stung her there, got inside her bodice and stung her chest.

Khansama and the kitchen servants laughed until tears of mirth streamed from their eyes; they bent at their waists and slapped their knees until they were weak. Then one by one they grew bored and drifted back to gossip on the *charpois* on the veranda by the kitchen door.

Zenat sank to her knees, the bees still swarming about her. Shabanu heard her cries and ran to the old woman, swatting the bees as she helped Zenat to her feet. She tore open Zenat's tunic and freed the bees trapped inside. Then she half carried, half dragged the servant to her room, where she stayed three days, with Mumtaz on a cot beside Zenat's bed.

Shabanu bathed Zenat's swollen face and chest with spirits of ammonia and eucalyptus oil and held her head, forcing spoonfuls of ginger tea between her lips. Slowly Zenat began to mend. While her body improved, her spirit seemed to have retreated to a dark place within her, and the old *ayah* was never the same again. But she remained loyal to Shabanu and Mumtaz forever after.

Later in the morning, after their walk along the canal, and after Zenat had brushed Mumtaz's hair and taken her out to play, Shabanu covered herself with an old *chadr* and crossed the courtyard to the main house. A guard stood at the corner of the veranda, and when he turned his back Shabanu slipped through a side door. Once inside she turned immediately down a narrow passage and climbed the iron stairway to the dark balcony just under the painted and mirror-encrusted ceiling of the great *baithak,* the men's sitting room. The balcony, which was part of the *zenana,* was enclosed with walls, and carved screens covered the narrow, curtained windows that looked out over the room below.

In the old days, the ladies watched from behind these screens as the men below celebrated harvests, hunts, and battles. The women laughed and gossiped, their perfumed breath trapped within silken veils, falling silent only when the dancing girls entered the *baithak* to entertain the men to the rhythm of tiny brass bells strapped in rows around their slender ankles.

Shabanu went to the farthest corner of the musty balcony and pulled aside a curtain, brushing a cobweb from the cracked shutter.

In the crowded hall below, men stood facing the doorway through which Rahim would enter. The room had been built more than two hundred years before, and its grand proportions reflected the significance of the life-and-death decisions made there over the generations.

But it was a public place and, like most public places these days, bore evidence of profound neglect. Moss grew in the cracks of the damp tiled floor, visible between the ancient threadbare rugs. A grand chandelier hung from a gilt medallion in the center of the ceiling forty feet overhead, but the crystal was draped with cobwebs and dust, and fluorescent tubes blinked at intervals around the mostly dim room.

Rahim's secretary had collected a dozen petitions from people whose cases would be heard that morning. He stood waiting with them in his hand—crumpled pieces of paper carried with care from every corner of the tribal land by men who could not read but trusted in the saving grace of the signatures the slips of paper bore.

Two dozen other men waited quietly, hopefully, clutching their own tattered papers. Some sat with legs crossed on cushions or on the worn ruby carpets; others stood with their backs against the ancient cracked walls inscribed with words of the Holy Prophet and painted with trellises and vines along the casements, arches, and rails. Still others milled about, muttering to the relatives who had come with them.

One man had brought his wife, a thin young girl in a

tattered *chadr,* wearing a large pair of men's shoes. The girl stood stiffly, as if trying to ignore the pain caused by her husband's pride that she should not have come barefoot. She was the only woman in the room.

A servant brought Rahim's embroidered bolster and placed it with other cushions on a canopied dais. The murmuring hushed, and Shabanu watched as the men's reverent eyes focused on the doorway.

Rahim arrived fresh from his prayers, a blood-red velvet cap embroidered and set with diamonds on the back of his head. And to Shabanu's surprise, behind him came Ahmed, wearing a cap like his father's—a cap that identified him among his clansmen as the next *syed,* a religious leader descended from the Holy Prophet Muhammad Himself.

Ahmed appeared proud to accompany his father as he held court, and Shabanu was certain Amina had schooled him on the importance of the occasion and how he should behave. He watched Rahim from the corners of his eyes and imitated everything his father did. When Rahim scratched his nose, Ahmed did the same. So total was his concentration that a thin thread of drool escaped his lower lip and fell to his lap.

Shabanu leaned her head against the shutter. She still had trouble comprehending that Rahim had arranged Ahmed's marriage to Zabo. It was too cruel to them both. It wasn't just the humiliation Zabo would endure; Shabanu was sure Zabo would suffer on Ahmed's behalf as well.

The first petitioner presented to Rahim was the man with the thin young wife. He complained that he had bought her from her father at the price of four goats and a *kanal* of land, and she had not yet conceived. He wanted his property returned. The girl stood with her head bowed. She clutched a bundle of clothing against her chest, expecting to be returned to her family.

Had he other wives and other children? Rahim asked. No, the man replied. He'd had the misfortune of having two barren wives before this one. He was nearing his fortieth year, and Allah still had not blessed him with a son. Would Rahim grant his request so that he could afford to take another wife?

Rahim asked how old the girl was. The man looked back at him blankly.

"When were you born, child?" Rahim asked the girl. Unaccustomed to being addressed directly, her shoulders swiveled back and forth out of nervousness.

"She wouldn't know, *Sahib*," said the man.

"What do you remember about your childhood?" Rahim asked. Her shoulders were still for a moment while she thought.

"In the year of the drought our animals died, and we fled our village."

"Were you old enough to walk?"

"Nay," she said. "My father carried me."

Rahim looked at the man.

"This child is too young to conceive," he said. "Take another wife if you must. Leave her here, and we will take care of her. She'll work in my house. I will pay you. When it's time, she can return to you." Rahim tossed the petition aside. "And perhaps you should pray," he said, turning back toward the man. "If you've had two other wives and no issue, the problem may be with you."

The man's face went dark with shame, but he handed the girl over to the bodyguard, who led her into the back part of the house toward the servants' quarters. She shuffled forward a few steps, then stopped and bent to remove the shoes. She handed them to her husband and turned again to follow the servant without another word, still clutching her bundle of clothing to her chest.

Rahim listened next to a long technical discourse on a dispute over water. Ahmed began to look around the room. His eyes came to rest on something beneath the balcony where Shabanu stood behind the screen, and she was unable to see what had caught his wandering attention. His expression changed from the slackness of boredom to a sly grin. He tried to keep himself under control, but his lips quivered and he giggled several times, trying to cover his mouth with his sleeve. Several people in the front rows looked over their shoulders to see what Ahmed was laughing about, then, apparently seeing nothing, turned forward again. There was an embarrassed shifting upon cushions in the front ranks of the room.

Rahim, without interrupting the talk about water, reached over and laid his hand on his son's arm. But rather than quiet Ahmed, the gesture seemed to break his thin margin of self-control, and he fell over on his side, laughing hysterically. Rahim gestured to a servant, who came and helped Ahmed to his feet and led him from the room.

Shabanu pitied Ahmed. His mother had told him he was important and desirable from the day he was born. While he was spoiled, he was neither cruel nor arrogant. It was the only plus for Zabo that she could think of. At that moment Amina's evil seemed horrifyingly powerful and palpable throughout all the rooms at Okurabad, even the balcony where Shabanu stood—almost as if Amina had the ability to snatch the house away from its long history and use it to her own purposes.

Rahim heard five more cases before clearing the room. He conferred with the secretary for a while, then Ibne and the cook were brought before him. Both men wore white *shalwar kameez*. Their heads were bare. It was the first time Shabanu had seen Ibne without his mirrored velvet vest and starched turban arranged in a knife-sharp pleated fan. He stood straight and looked directly at Rahim. His black hair was oiled and neatly combed. The cook, who was rumpled and splattered with sauces from the kitchen, hung back and kept his eyes on the corner of the dais where Rahim sat.

"Hassan Ibne, on the afternoon of April second, you were apprehended outside the room of *Begum* Shabanu," Rahim said. "Is that correct?"

"*Ji, Sahib,*" Ibne answered.

"Tell me why you went there."

"Khansama asked me to deliver a message to *Begum*—"

"He's lying, *Sahib*!" said the cook. "I gave no message."

"Be quiet!" Rahim said. "Go on, Ibne."

"Khansama gave me an envelope that bore your seal. He said it was a message from you and that I should take it directly to *Begum*'s room. When I got to the edge of the courtyard, a woman was standing there watching, and when I was near the door she began to scream. Then the cook's helper came running and shouting and woke about five house servants, who also came running. There was much confusion. The woman was screaming, and the cook's helper was shouting that they should grab me. I was too shocked to struggle, and they dragged me to the ground. The envelope disappeared in the scuffle."

Rahim listened carefully and turned to the cook.

"Where did the envelope come from? Who put my seal on it?"

"He's lying, *Sahib,*" said the cook, who looked up at Rahim's face then. "He went to *Begum*'s quarters because she summoned him. It wasn't the first time. . . ."

"Enough!" said Rahim, and his voice was cold with rage. He asked to see the cook's helper, a tall boy who kept his frightened eyes fastened to the floor. In a barely audible voice he corroborated the cook's story. His ears, red as blood, stood out at right angles to his shaven head. There was no one except Shabanu to give a second testimony on Ibne's behalf, and she knew she would never be called.

Rahim's face grew darker, but Shabanu wasn't sure whose story he believed. In the end he dismissed all three servants, saying they must leave Okurabad immediately.

The cook wailed loudly and put his fingers to his lips, imploring like a starving beggar. Ibne heard his sentence quietly, with his head high.

Oh, Ibne, Shabanu thought, if I could have saved you, I would have tried. But it would have been worse for all of us. Forgive me for saving myself and my daughter, and not you. Damn Amina! Damn her and Leyla to hell!

Rahim got up from the dais, and Shabanu left quickly, the way she had come—down the iron staircase, through the side door, and out onto the veranda. She hesitated behind the trellis, for in the wooden garden swing just a few feet away sat Amina, her sleek silver head leaning against the swing's painted headrest, a faint smile on her heavily rouged mouth, her kohl-rimmed eyes closed. The rounded toe of one shiny black slipper touched the grass, and the swing glided back and forth with a faint groan, as if of its own accord.

chapter 6

One morning Shabanu rose early to mend Mumtaz's ever-growing pile of *shalwar kameez* that had torn as she played among the thornbushes near the canal and climbed trees in the garden.

The mornings were still cool, and a heavy mist hung about the topmost branches, descending into the open spaces above the lawn and rose beds.

It was very quiet; even the horses in the stable were still sleeping. The pearly air slowly grew lighter as the sun rose above the fog. Across the courtyard the back of the house seemed to stare at her through its dark doors and windows. Shabanu wrapped her shawl tight about her shoulders, then sat on the front step outside the door to her room. She listened for the soft breathing of Mumtaz, who lay sleeping on the baby *charpoi* just inside. Choti lay curled at the foot of the cot, her chin tucked among the angles of her folded legs.

A gentle breeze blew in from Cholistan, across the canal, the air wafting alternately warm with the peppery-sweet scent of *kharin* and cool with the damp smell of irrigated land.

Shabanu hoped it would soon clear the fog and let in sunlight to warm the garden.

She placed a candle on the small table that stood just outside the door. Lifting the lid to her sewing basket, she put her hand inside. Nestled among the skeins of embroidery silk, spools of thread, and scraps of cloth, she felt something at once hard and soft. She was puzzled for a moment, but then horror rose in her as her fingers found the sticky end of the thing.

A sick feeling settled into her stomach as she withdrew the severed foot of a baby camel from the basket. She thought of her own baby camel, Mithoo, who had followed her into the desert when she'd tried to escape from her family before her marriage to Rahim. Mithoo had fallen into a foxhole and broken his leg. Rather than leave him to the vultures and jackals, she lay down beside him and waited for her father to find them. Thus she had committed herself to the future her family had planned for her.

Out of the corner of her eye, Shabanu saw a curtain move slightly, and anger replaced the sick feeling as retreating feet slapped on the bare floor of the hallway that led from the back of the kitchen.

Would she never be able to relax her vigilance? Even in the earliest part of the day, before the household awakened, must she be wary of everyone and everything? She was never quite able to put behind her the last intimidation or incrimination when the next was upon her. She sat still for a moment, listening to the birds in the neem trees. Then she wrapped the foot in her handkerchief, buried it back under the contents of her sewing basket, and stood purposefully to wake Mumtaz.

For the next few days she was filled with rage at Amina's persistence and small-mindedness. But the rage was good, she thought; it kept her watchful. She must be careful that her reactions should not embolden the others to progress from their evil mischief to more serious things that might endanger Mumtaz or herself. She worried most about Mumtaz. Without a mother to protect her, who knew what would happen to her daughter?

Then came the day of the two invitations.

Everyone at Okurabad had been talking for weeks about *Basant,* the spring festival of the kites. For days the household was alive with talk of the *Basants* of other years, when the men and boys of Lahore had flown kites from the rooftop of every *haveli* in the old walled city. The women watched from the roof of the cinema, which stood taller than the *havelis*, with only the minarets of the neighborhood mosques to obstruct their view. They talked about it until Shabanu could see in her mind's eye the bright-colored pieces of paper against the afternoon sky, and boys leaning over parapets with brooms of twigs tied to the ends of long poles to capture kites cut free by the glass- and resin-coated strings of more skillfully flown kites.

Mumtaz had pestered her.

"Uma, please, can we go?" she asked, standing high on her toes and yanking at the sleeve of Shabanu's tunic. "Please, Uma!"

Finally Shabanu shooed her away, and the child took to telling Choti how she would make her own kites that looked like her father's desert birds. She imagined that if they could fly, kites must have wings.

The invitation came in an envelope marked only with her name, a plain white card inviting Shabanu to a picnic on the roof of the cinema. Part of her longed to go. It was the first time she'd been invited to *Basant.* And her dearest wish was to see Lahore.

But the memory of the baby camel's foot against her fingertips made her shiver. She was afraid to take Mumtaz to the cinema rooftop, four stories above the old city. She began to worry that it would be rude of her to decline unless she had good reason. The sun grew warmer, but she shivered every time she thought of the kites and the crowded rooftop. With everyone looking up at the sky, it would be easy for someone to push them over the edge. Their fall to the street below would be a convenient accident.

And then the message came from the desert near Mehrabpur, where Shabanu's sister, Phulan, lived with her husband, Murad, and their sons on their farm at the edge of the desert. A thin, solemn man wearing a faded blue turban was admitted unceremoniously to stand just inside the back gate of the house. Shabanu was summoned for the recitation of an invitation from her family.

They had traveled to the edge of the desert, where they hoped she would join them to be with Phulan following the birth of her fourth son, the messenger said. The infant had come early, but both mother and child were well.

Just the sight of the soft-spoken desert man lifted her spirits. And a visit with Mama and Dadi, Phulan and Murad and their sons, Sharma and Fatima, and Auntie and her two sons couldn't come at a better time!

The summons from her family was good enough reason to send her regrets for *Basant*. She wouldn't miss seeing them for anything in the world!

Rahim wouldn't return from Lahore for several days. When he wasn't at Okurabad it didn't matter much to him what she did, as long as he knew where she was and that she'd be there when he returned.

Without even placing a trunk call to Lahore to tell Rahim, Shabanu told the messenger to ask her father to come for her as soon as possible. She would be ready. She gave the messenger a ten-rupee note, which he refused. But she pressed it into his hand, and he folded the note into a package of country-made *bidi* cigarettes that smelled of cloves and tucked it into his breast pocket.

Early the next morning, a *tonga* cart carrying Shabanu's father emerged from the cool mist of late spring. The servants made him wait outside the gate, but Zenat had been watching for him since before daylight. She ran to the stableyard to tell Shabanu and Mumtaz, who were ready and waiting.

Shabanu saw him through the gate. He stood in his embroidered slippers with turned-up toes beside the hired horse cart, his *lungi* and *kurta* clean and fresh, the breeze playing with the end of his turban. He looked awkward, his calloused square hands hanging loosely at his sides, squinting at the wall as if puzzled by why it should stand between him and his daughter.

"Dadi!" she shouted, and he ran to the gate as she flung it wide. His beard was flecked with gray. But Mumtaz leaped into his arms, and he swung her high over his head. He was still strong and straight as a young man, and Mumtaz squealed with delight when he caught her, just as it seemed she would fall to the ground. Even Zenat gave a rare grin that showed the entire length of her wide-spaced loose teeth.

Shabanu and Zenat carried baskets of food and gifts of sugar and jasmine tea and cardamom and a large brass water pot for Phulan.

The morning held the promise of warmth in the fog that swirled around the pony cart as it made its way through the outer edge of the irrigated area. The acacia trees were pale and fragile with new growth. Even the meanest desert shrubs were misted in pale green veils of leaf buds.

Shabanu's heart turned over and over again as they neared the dunes of the desert. Seeing the blue ribbon of smoke from her mother's cooking fire curl lazily toward the sky, she could almost taste the sweet milky tea, and already she heard the camels' growls and mutters, transporting her back in time to her Cholistan childhood.

Her family stood to greet her in a small clump, their bright cotton tunics like flowers against the pale gray sand.

Shabanu flew into her mother's arms.

"Sh-, Sh-, Sh-, Shabanu," her mother crooned softly, and cradled her youngest daughter's head against her shoulder as she'd done when Shabanu was a child.

Her cousins, aged eight and ten, had grown tall and thin. Their hands were coarse and broad, but their faces were still soft and childlike.

Dadi held Mumtaz as if she were a treasure, and Choti pranced at his feet as if she too wanted to have a fuss made over her.

Mama's face was lined deeply, though her shoulders were still straight and square. Phulan's eyes were pinched at the corners, and pockets of flesh were forming beneath them. Creases had developed around her lovely mouth, although she had not long ago reached only her twentieth birthday.

The desert ages people too fast, Shabanu thought sadly. She'd never noticed before.

Mama wore the same turquoise tunic she'd worn when Shabanu was married. It was worn and faded, but it still showed the strong lines of her mother's tall, slim body.

At Shabanu's wedding the women of Rahim's household had stared at the desert women's rough handmade slippers and tunics sewn in graceful lines that fitted their full breasts and slender waists. The women of Okurabad wore more stylish cuts of splendid fabrics that hid their plumper fig-

ures. Shabanu still loved the simple embroideries and mirrored designs of Cholistan far more than the beaded chiffons
the women of Okurabad wore.

Her relatives wore their hair plain and pulled back in long
thick braids, while the women of Okurabad wore theirs
carefully coiffed in fluffy bobs. The hands of the Cholistan
women were rough with calluses from hauling water, their
nails cracked and split from patching the walls of their houses
with dung and earth and water. The idle hands of the women
of Okurabad were manicured, with long lacquered nails and
soft white palms.

Shabanu's family had stood silent with a natural grace,
while the women of Okurabad laughed at them behind their
silken *dupattas*.

Shabanu was glad to see every one of them—even Auntie,
whose lips had grown thin and crooked from years of purs-
ing them with disapproval. Shabanu embraced them, one by
one, inhaling the desert-clean smell of their hair and clothing, as if to dispel the outer layers of the Okurabad woman
she'd become to reveal the Cholistan girl who remained inside her.

Auntie took Mumtaz by the hand, and they all sat beside
the fire. Auntie had felt sorry for Mama and Dadi when
they'd had no sons to provide for them in their old age. But
now because of Dadi's fine camel herd and Rahim's generosity, they were far more prosperous than Auntie and
her husband, who still worked as a government clerk in
Rahimyar Khan and visited his family only occasionally.

Auntie hugged Mumtaz and kept her close, perhaps
mourning the daughter she would never bear.

Mama handed Shabanu a cup of tea. She cradled it in her
hands, and the warmth of her family enfolded her.

Phulan held her newest infant son against her breast. Her

second son, who was three, ran about, barefoot and bare-bottomed, herding chickens with a stick, while the third toddled after him. The eldest, who was five, sat nearby with the men.

While Phulan seemed content and thoroughly absorbed in her four sons, the changes in her saddened Shabanu. Just seven years earlier, when she was married, Phulan's skin glowed from weeks of massages with oil of jasmine and golden powders—turmeric, cumin, and saffron. Her hair shone from rubbing it with a paste of sandalwood and mustard oil during the wedding preparations. Her arms and cheeks had been round and sleek from a diet of yogurt and honey, carrot pudding, nuts, butter, raisins, and sugar. She had been like a ripe peach, round and golden and fragrant.

Now Phulan's skin was checkered and lined. Her hair was dull, with limp strands that flopped over her forehead. Her body was spindly and slightly stooped from hard physical labor on her husband's farm. Although Phulan was still young, Shabanu could imagine clearly how her once-beautiful sister would look as an old woman.

Men came and went throughout the morning, squatting with their backs against makeshift shelters, smoking and talking about prices for hauling produce. Dadi and his cousins contracted out their camels to haul sugarcane to market during the busy harvest season. They calculated how many more camels they'd need for the overlap of the cotton, mango, and orange crops as the season wore on.

Late in the morning Shabanu's mother brought out the old wooden bowl, and Shabanu took it from her to mix dough for chapatis. Her aunt brought out cloths folded and tied around sweets from the bazaar at Rahimyar Khan.

As they were about to eat, the sound of gongs and plunks from the bells of animals reached them from where the dunes

undulated into the desert. Within moments the unmistaka-
ble husky voice of Shabanu's Auntie Sharma shouted out
above the melody of the bells, and Shabanu thought she'd
never heard a sweeter sound.

They saw the goats and sheep first, then the ancient female camel carrying Sharma and her daughter, Fatima, slipped
into view like an apparition from behind the edge of a dune.

"Ho! Can you have such a gathering of women without
me?" Sharma demanded.

Shabanu hiked her skirt to her knees and ran headlong
toward her aunt and cousin. The three clasped one another's
waists and danced in circles, their bare feet sending up clouds
of dust so thick it muffled their laughter.

Sharma was Mama and Dadi's favorite cousin. There were
many who disapproved of Sharma because they said she had
been a disobedient wife. Many believed she was a witch.
Shabanu believed she was the wisest woman on earth.

Sharma's husband had beaten her after Fatima's birth. He
was disappointed when she'd failed to produce a son. Sharma
had accepted her punishment and said nothing. Slowly she
began to build the herds of goats and sheep she tended at
the edge of the desert near Fort Abbas, where her husband
owned a small farm. Every week she would bring a twig
whisk or a bowl or a blanket from her house and bury it in
the sand. There, unbeknownst to her husband, she'd built
holding pens of thorn branches for her rapidly growing herds.
In the last week she also brought red clay pots filled with
ghee, a sack of flour, and goatskin water bags.

One day during the cotton harvest, which coincided that
year with a series of sandstorms in the desert, Sharma strapped
Fatima to her back and announced to her husband that she
was going to pick cotton in the fields of the local *zamindar.*

Her husband was a proud man, and he objected to Sharma's working in the fields. But Sharma's will was powerful, and her husband, ever greedy for money, had acquiesced. Sharma gathered the muslin sacks she intended to fill with cotton and walked down the road toward the *zamindar*'s fields.

There she made a sling of her *chadr* and tied it between the branches of thorn shrubs that were strong enough to hold Fatima but supple enough to bend with the breeze. She left the infant to be tended by the older children of the women who worked in the field beside her. She spent the day picking cotton, bent from the waist until she felt her back would break.

A storm rose in the afternoon, and Sharma thought surely it indicated that Allah had blessed her plan.

Instead of taking the cotton she'd picked to the weighing station, Sharma headed toward home with Fatima strapped to her back and the bulging sacks of cotton piled high atop her head. She leaned into the wind, and clouds of blowing sand stung her face and arms. Halfway home, she left the road and circled around to where her husband's camels were tethered.

She took the oldest female, because it was the quietest and most dependable animal in the herd. Also, the old camel never strayed, so her husband never hobbled and tethered her. In a sandstorm he would think she had wandered away, and he would miss her least of all his camels when she failed to return.

Then, in the midst of the howling wind, which tossed baskets and branches and small trees about as if they were as light as the sand itself, Sharma and Fatima struck out to gather their penned herds and entered the desert several miles away.

It never occurred to her husband that Sharma, a mere woman, would have the strength to ride a camel four days and four nights through a storm without stopping, until she was so deep in the desert that he'd never find her. It never occurred to him that she could find her way among the dunes under such conditions with the skill of a tracker. It never even occurred to him that she'd have the courage to leave him, despite his regular beatings and verbal abuse.

So, not wishing to acknowledge any dishonor to himself, her husband chose to believe that Sharma and the child had died in the sandstorm. When they didn't return, he never went to look for them.

It didn't displease him, really. Sharma was the second wife who'd borne him only daughters, and he couldn't afford a third and still feed them. But without Sharma and Fatima he now could ask his cousin for the hand of his eldest daughter, who was just reaching a marriageable age. She would bring no dowry, but he'd watched her breasts bud and her backside grow round. Perhaps finally he'd have a wife who would give him sons!

Fatima had grown fat and healthy in the desert with her mother. They sold the cotton to buy cloth and food. When they needed more sugar or tea, they sold their fine strong animals. Sometimes they harvested wheat in the fields near Rahimyar Khan, far away from Sharma's husband.

When she came of age, Fatima decided she would not marry at all. Her mother was delighted that her daughter had chosen to stay with her.

Sharma and Fatima were self-sufficient. Any man who had ever tried to harm or cheat them had fallen on hard times.

Once a goatherd had stolen their spring lambs. The foolish man bragged of this deed to his cousin. The very next day the lambs and his entire herd of goats disappeared from the edge of the desert where they grazed. He looked for them for days, but they'd disappeared without a trace, and he never saw them again. The man was ashamed—not of his thievery, but that he'd been outsmarted by a woman—and never mentioned his misfortune to anyone.

Before long Sharma and Fatima were known widely to be witches, and their reputation shielded them well. They seldom had need to protect themselves.

"You're just in time to eat," said Mama, smiling at Fatima and Sharma through the steam of the roasting bread.

"You could time your *chapatis* to their arrival," Auntie said sourly. Phulan rolled her eyes, and Shabanu had to turn her head away so her laughter didn't show.

The women talked and talked until the sun was high in the sky. When it grew too warm, they stretched a *chadr* between the lean-to and two poles and moved under its shade, never once interrupting their talk.

Shabanu luxuriated in a sense of belonging. She'd forgotten how it felt to be accepted, not to have to watch for danger over each shoulder, not to examine the motives behind everything that was said to her. Not being afraid to let Mumtaz out of her sight was entirely new to her.

"Jamil's wife still has only daughters—four!" Phulan said with some satisfaction. "Poor Jamil. Perhaps he should take another wife."

"But Adil," said Mama, "now has three sons! Perhaps he'd give one to Jamil." How like her mother always to hope for the best in others!

Phulan touched Shabanu's sleeve and looked into her eyes. "I'm sorry . . ." she began.

"Don't worry," said Shabanu. "I'm happy with just Mumtaz."

"But you would make your husband so happy if you gave him a son. Perhaps you should consult a *hakkim.* . . ."

"I'm very happy with only a daughter," Shabanu said. "Life would have been far more difficult if Mumtaz had been a boy. It's much easier to endure the scorn of the other women than to worry that if I had a son he might be killed."

"Killed!" said Phulan. "Whatever for?"

"Mumtaz will inherit nothing," she said. "It would have been more difficult for Rahim to pass off a son. He would have been a threat to the other wives, and someone would have found a way to get rid of him."

"Still, you should have other children," said Mama as she whirled the last of the *chapatis* into a flat disk and slid it onto the black iron pan over the fire. "You're so healthy! Why have you not conceived again?"

"I *am* healthy," said Shabanu. "So don't worry."

The first time after her wedding that Shabanu had seen her family, Sharma had taken her aside. After the others had eaten, they spread quilts on the ground and slept away the heat of the afternoon.

Mumtaz, a brand-new infant at the time, grizzled halfheartedly, and Shabanu moved away to lean against a thorn tree while she held the baby to her breast. As the infant suckled, Sharma came to sit beside her.

"You've had your daughter for yourself," Sharma said. "But you should have no more children."

"But how can I not conceive again?" Shabanu had asked. She knew what Sharma said was true. "It's too soon after this one's birth for Rahim to demand that I come to his bed. But he will soon. And he wants me to have a son. . . ."

Sharma undid a knot in the corner of her *chadr* and withdrew a piece of dried vine that lay darkly coiled in her open palm like the antler of a black buck.

"Whenever you go to him, you must be sure this is in place," she said. "You will not conceive as long as you use it."

Sharma told her how to insert the piece of vine into the mouth of her uterus, and a great weight lifted from Shabanu's heart. Now, she thought, I will have only Mumtaz and myself to look after.

"You must take control of events before they take control of you," Sharma had said. "If you don't do what you can for yourself, no one else will."

The afternoon wore on, and the heat grew oppressive. The women pulled out their quilts and lay down, dropping unwillingly out of the conversation one by one as they fell asleep.

Shabanu felt as if she'd never left these women whom she loved more than anything on earth. She wished Mumtaz could grow up as she had in the golden warmth of their circle.

Shabanu did not want to waste any of her time sleeping. Mumtaz curled up beside her, and Shabanu sat with her back against the wall of the lean-to, her arms folded and resting on her knees. While she was content just to look at them, she was impatient to talk to Sharma, who moved closer to Shabanu. The older woman crossed her ankles, folded her knees, and sank to the ground beside Shabanu in a single fluid motion.

"So, my little pigeon," Sharma said. "What mischief have the women of Okurabad been up to?"

Shabanu told her about Ibne and the baby camel's foot,

the dead puppy, Zabo's bethrothal to Ahmed, and her promise that she would help her friend. Sharma listened carefully.

"Oh, oh, my pigeon, you must have a good plan!"

"Auntie, listen. We must make a plan for Zabo now. But Mumtaz and I must stay at Okurabad."

Sharma laid her fingers against her niece's lips.

"No. Come to Fort Abbas and live with Fatima and me. Or have you outgrown us and the desert?"

"My life is at Okurabad now," Shabanu said. "As long as Rahim is alive, and perhaps after, I must do my best to survive there."

"Rahim is forty-two years older than you are! You will live a long time as a widow."

"Mumtaz's best chance for survival is to be educated. She can't do that and live in Cholistan. I must do what's best for her, and hope that Rahim lives until she finishes her schooling. Only then can we leave."

"Your daughter climbs thorn trees as naturally as you did," said Sharma. It was as far as Sharma would push her to change her mind.

Have I made a mistake? Shabanu wondered. It is true that Auntie Sharma knows the way of the desert and not the way of the village . . . certainly not the way of the city! But she is the wisest woman I know. Could it be that her wisdom applies to the desert and also to the village and to the city? It was rare that Shabanu's confidence was shaken.

"Once she's been to school, she'll live in the city so she can work," she said, testing.

"Bah!" said Sharma, waving her hand. "You're thinking like a city woman. You must make her tough like you to survive! Promise me you will think about it."

"Oh, Auntie! I've thought of nothing else!" Shabanu said.

"I have promised Zabo I will help her. She can't go through with her marriage to Ahmed unless she knows she won't have to live as his wife. I want to send her to you, to stay in Cholistan. And then someday . . ."

"The time to plan is now," said Sharma, leaning forward, her face barely an inch from Shabanu's. Urgency thinned out her voice. "Times are dangerous. Rahim could be gone tomorrow."

"They watch me so closely that it's hard to do anything without their knowing," said Shabanu. "It's not just Amina and Leyla—even the servants watch and listen. Sometimes it seems the house has eyes and ears!"

"Send word to me when you've come to your senses," Sharma said. "I will be there within a day. So—now we will make a plan for Zabo."

They talked then of how Zabo would get to Sharma just after the wedding, and again Shabanu felt a great burden had been lifted from her. When she was with Sharma she felt somehow hopeful, no matter how impossible the situation looked.

The day went too quickly, and it seemed no time at all before the *tonga* cart returned to take Shabanu and Mumtaz back to Okurabad. Shabanu kissed her relatives good-bye.

She fought unexpected tears when they asked how soon they could see her again. She would find a way to persuade Rahim to allow her and Mumtaz to come again within the next month, she thought. But first she must persuade him that they must come to Lahore.

chapter 7

In the weeks that followed Ibne's dismissal, Rahim was quiet. He no longer mentioned the incident. Shabanu still couldn't tell whether he believed the cook's story—or perhaps he might be trying to protect her from the gossip that had spread through the compound and the village, and no doubt all the way to Lahore.

Shabanu knew what they said about her: that Mumtaz was Ibne's child—or perhaps the product of some other liaison—definitely not Rahim's. She'd heard this from Zenat. Poor Zenat came every afternoon after Mumtaz's nap, dreading Shabanu's questions, then trembling with fear when she returned to the house, where the women gathered to gossip.

They were beginning to say things about Zenat, too— that she arranged Shabanu's assignations and protected her. It was suggested that the old woman put a sleeping draft into Rahim's tea so Shabanu could slip away at night.

Finally Shabanu had had enough of the women and their gossip, enough of wondering what Rahim thought. When she had decided it was time, she spoke.

"Rahim," she said one evening. "Zabo's wedding is just a few months away."

They were in his study. He looked up from his papers. She sat in a small chair opposite his large leather-topped desk, a smock for Mumtaz in her lap. The electric lights flickered. In the distance she heard the whistle and *whump* of a dozen diesel-powered tube well pumps. It was almost time for the electricity to be diverted from the house to electric pumps in other fields.

"I would like to shop with her in Lahore. Don't you have to go there soon to meet Omar?" Leyla's fiancé was due to return from America, where he had spent five years studying agriculture at a university. Shabanu knew Rahim was eager to see him.

Rahim said nothing for a moment, and she kept stitching, her fingers sure and strong with the steady rhythm of the needle.

"If you'd like, you may come with me," he said, and she knew at once it hadn't occurred to him that she might like to help Zabo prepare for the wedding, despite Zabo's having neither mother nor sisters to help her arrange the most significant event of her life. Perhaps he had put Zabo's marriage from his mind, so carefully was it hidden amidst the excitement of the wedding preparations for Leyla and Omar.

Even the lowliest tenant farmer's wife understood that Leyla and Omar's marriage would secure the future of the tribe and their land for another sixty years, and the joy it inspired was no different than that which accompanied each such union over the centuries since the clan had settled in the Punjab.

The cruel pairing of Zabo and Ahmed would go unnoticed, although it was only three months away, following

Leyla's by just a few days. People could talk about the marriage of Omar and Leyla and pretend the other would not happen at all.

"Wonderful!" Shabanu said, and she dropped her stitching to her lap. "I've never been there before, and——"

"But I never knew you wanted to go!" said Rahim. He took off his glasses and set them on the desk before him. She had his full attention.

"I've dreamed of you and me eating oranges together on the roof of the *haveli* and watching the sunset."

She knew well that over the years Rahim had begged his other wives to stay with him in his beloved *haveli*. But they all preferred their modern bungalows in the Cantonment. They hated the pungent smells in the streets outside the ancient courtyard walls—smells of frying bits of meat, cooking fires, and open sewers. He had failed to persuade them to leave their silent, air-conditioned parlors for the clatter of pony carts, the screech of children playing on the roofs and in the lanes, the colors of clothes drying on swaying lines on the rooftops and balconies.

Rahim loved to share with Shabanu the memories the *haveli* held, of himself and his brothers in navy wool school uniforms leaping from the parapet of the flat tiled roof of the *haveli* to the roof of the next house and up to the next roof, flying kites every day after school; of learning to ride bicycles in the narrow lanes, wobbling among the goats, chickens, and small children; of stealing juicy *kinnu* oranges from the stall on the corner and hiding to eat them in the roof niches above the brightly tiled shrines of saints scattered throughout the neighborhood.

But he was never able to extricate his elder wives and their daughters from their tea parties and masseuses, their *darzi*s and hairdressers.

He had never asked Shabanu to go with him. She suspected that since the other women in his life had hated the *haveli* and refused to go there, he thought she also would.

She thought, too, that Rahim would not take her out among Lahore's sophisticated socialites. She wouldn't fit in; she didn't even speak Punjabi properly. Her own clothes were too rustic, and he wouldn't want her to wear the things he'd bought for her to use only in his company. While her social unsuitability was a matter of pride to her, she didn't want it to keep her from going to Lahore.

Shabanu had saved asking him to take her to the *haveli* for the right time.

"You'd make me the happiest woman alive if you'd let me go with you when the assembly is next in session. We could hire a tutor for Mumtaz and me—"

"Wait, wait!" he said, putting his hand in the air. "We're talking about shopping with Zabo, not changing residences!" His brow was creased, and he chewed on the end of his spectacles. "Why do you want a tutor?"

"I want Mumtaz to grow up knowing how to read, and to learn a vocation. And *I* want to learn to read properly, and I want to study music. We can't do that in just a few days' time. But if we went with you for the assembly session . . ."

"Why do you need to know how to read?" he asked.

"I spent my childhood learning about the desert. I know things about Cholistan that you or anyone else would never guess were worth knowing. But that's not my world now. If I can't return to the world I know, then I want to learn about the world I'm in."

He remained silent, and she thought carefully before speaking again. "Things have been difficult for Mumtaz and me since the incident with Ibne. You dismissed him because you were afraid he'd acted improperly. I know Amina laid a trap, but I was her target, not Ibne!"

Rahim did not answer, but he tightened his lips. Shabanu knew he would not tolerate the women speaking against each other. She took a breath and went on.

"They're saying terrible things about us: that Mumtaz is not your child, and that I've . . . misbehaved. I'm telling you this because you deliberately refuse to see things sometimes."

"Why do you think they say such things?" he asked, his voice so quiet it chilled her.

"Because they feel superior," she said. "You never acknowledge it, but it's true. They look down on me."

"And why do you think that is?"

"In part because I'm so much younger; in part because I come from desert people. But most important, because I'm uneducated. I don't know how to read or to speak proper Punjabi, much less English!"

She felt her face grow warm, and lowered her eyes. English was spoken in the parlors of Lahore by the best-educated ladies. Even their Punjabi was punctuated liberally with English words. The fashionable ladies did it for effect. Most of them had never been—nor would they ever go—to England.

"Their families educated them," Rahim said, leaning back in his chair and reaching again for his glasses. "It's part of who they are."

"If you think I *feel* inferior to them, you're mistaken!" she said. "I don't care what they think. I'm afraid for Mumtaz and me . . . if we should lose you. What will happen when you're not here to look after us?"

"Both of you will be looked after," he said curtly. "Soon a husband will be chosen for Mumtaz, and you'll have nothing to worry about."

"*Who* will look after us?" He was startled by the anger in her voice. "I don't question you, Rahim. You have been generous beyond even my father's wildest hopes. But you are forty-two years older than me. When you are gone, Leyla and Omar will be in charge of all the clansmen. Amina and Leyla hate me. They tell the others things so they'll hate me too."

"What things?" he asked.

"They say I steal money from you. That's why I don't want you to give things to Mumtaz and me. They hate every moment of my happiness and every evidence of your generosity. Amina and Leyla will throw us out the second they have the power to do it. The wolves could eat us, and they'd be very happy." She was afraid she'd gone too far, but he listened to her thoughtfully.

"I've always tried to be fair, Shabanu," he said. "What I can't leave you and Mumtaz in my will, I try to make up for with attention. I do love you beyond life itself, and want you to be happy and safe."

"Then let me stay with you in Lahore. Let me try it for a year."

Rahim stood and turned toward the window, gazing out at the garden, where the early summer's dust had begun to settle like pale powder on the mango leaves and rosebushes. It was difficult for him to hear about conflicts among the women. If he kept Shabanu and Mumtaz in a special, safe compartment in his mind, he did the same for the others.

"I thought you would want to be here with Zabo."

"You know perfectly well that Zabo spends the season in Lahore!" He would try everything to dissuade her.

"I thought you enjoyed being here with the others away. If you want to spend the season in Lahore, it will be arranged."

"Rahim," Shabanu said, struggling to be patient. "It's not the season I'm interested in. I want an education for Mumtaz and for myself."

"I don't want to be here without you," he said, interrupting. She could barely see his face. The lights had grown dim as the electricity was diverted to the fields. The dimness helped her to ignore the petulance in his voice.

But her heart sang that he hadn't taken more serious issue with her wanting to be in Lahore!

"Oh, I wouldn't want you to be here without me! I'd only want to be in Lahore when you're there. We'd stay in the women's quarters and not bother you. That's why we would want a tutor for Mumtaz, so she wouldn't have to keep a regular school schedule. And we could return here with you at the end of each session of the assembly."

"We'll see," he said, putting on his glasses again and sitting down behind the desk.

Her heart quivered with a mixture of triumph and despair. This was Rahim's first concession on the subject of her leaving the farm. But she knew he was only giving in to her whim—without a shred of understanding that she desperately wanted a life beyond Okurabad.

chapter 8

As spring turned to summer in Okurabad the courtyard was disturbed with increasing frequency by the excitement of deliveries. One morning a dozen oxcarts clattered through the main gates on wooden wheels that raised showers of thick gray dust. While the large, gentle-eyed oxen drank water brought in brass buckets from the stableyard, tall men in gray turbans—the kind worn by Pathans in the North-West Frontier, where furniture was made—unloaded rosewood tables, chairs, and chests that were carved delicately with Mogul patterns, inlaid with brass, and polished to a warm red finish.

From first light to near dark, the air vibrated with hammering, sawing, and clattering as workers swarmed over the new bungalow that Rahim had ordered to be built for Leyla and Omar at the opposite end of the courtyard from his own house. The wall at that end of the compound divided the ancestral property into what was owned by Rahim and what belonged to his brother, Mahsood, who was Omar's father.

It was said that when the two brothers were dead the

two-hundred-year-old wall between the two properties would be demolished. For the first time since the tribe had settled the Punjab their ancestral lands would be joined. Every landowner and official in the district, every widow and beggar on the streets of the villages of the tribal lands would celebrate the marriage of Omar and Leyla.

In its own way, the marriage of Ahmed and Zabo was also of utmost importance and added to the general air of festivity. Although Nazir's holdings were the least substantial of the three brothers, and despite his having settled in Mehrabpur at the opposite end of the clan's territory, his lands adjoined those of Mahsood and Rahim. Indeed the union of Ahmed and Zabo would be less celebrated than the wedding of Omar and Leyla. It was one of those odd facts of life—a gentle-eyed girl marrying an idiot boy for the sake of reuniting all the ancestral lands for the first time in two centuries. That was all anyone was likely to think of it. And anyone with any sensitivity at all would never mention it to a member of Rahim's family, much less to Zabo herself.

Teams of *darzis* came to Okurabad to outfit Leyla, bringing with them yard upon yard of shimmering silks in turquoise and purple and lime green, and pale georgettes embroidered with sequins and semiprecious stones. The *darzis* took their places each morning on the veranda of Rahim's house. The sun shone through the branches of the neem trees, dappling the clean white cloths upon which the *darzis* sat cross-legged, their small black sewing machines whirring before them. Servants in white turbans and *lungis* came with trays of steaming tea, pink and rich with buffalo milk.

Meanwhile, out behind the stables, Shabanu sat on her *charpoi,* which she'd dragged into the doorway to catch the green air cooled by the canal, embroidering *shalwar kameez* for Zabo in delicate pastel cottons handwoven in India and smuggled across the border through the Cholistan Desert.

Amid the comings and goings in the courtyard, Zabo arrived virtually unnoticed to spend the night with Shabanu before their departure for Lahore. She came in her father's car, barely visible in the backseat between two bodyguards. A third sat in front beside the driver.

Six small boys—all children of servants of the household—stopped their cricket match outside the heavy wooden gates to watch, fascinated by the ugly black snouts of the automatic weapons sticking from the tops of the gray-tinted windows of the air-conditioned sedan.

Shabanu ran to greet Zabo, who stepped from between the gunmen. Shabanu took her hands and looked her up and down.

Zabo was pale and thin, but her eyes shone with pleasure at seeing her friend.

"I'm so happy to see you," Zabo said.

As the servants lifted her bags from the car, Mumtaz came running, her shiny black braid bouncing out behind her. Zabo bent her long slender frame and lifted the child to near shoulder height before dropping her to rest on her hip.

"I won't be able to pick you up this way anymore!" she said, and Mumtaz beamed. "You're too big."

"Auntie Zabo, come see my fawn!" she said, wriggling to be put down again. "She's not growing."

"Where did you get a fawn?"

"Papa brought her from the desert so I would stand still when Uma brushes my hair. Come see!" Mumtaz rushed away again, and Shabanu and Zabo followed.

"She lives for the little beast," said Shabanu. "It was so frail when it arrived. It's still small, but it's grown fat and healthy. It's completely taken over our lives."

In the courtyard, Choti was stealing maize from the bin where the *mali* kept the birds' food.

"Take her away before Mali scolds both of you," said Shabanu. "We'll be out in the garden." She called to Zenat and asked her to bring lemonade.

"You're thin," said Shabanu. Zabo didn't reply. Shabanu took her arm and led her into the shade of the arbor at the end of the veranda. They sat in the covered swing, and still Zabo didn't speak. They listened to the birds calling to each other from their cages, while the flower-scented breeze played around them.

"Tell me," said Shabanu after a while.

"I think of Ahmed often," Zabo said. She looked around to see if any of her cousins were nearby.

"Don't worry," said Shabanu. "They're so engrossed with wedding plans they don't have time to eavesdrop."

"I try to think of how sweet he is," Zabo said. "I try to concentrate on how happy I'll be here with you. But no matter how I try to see his smile, I see him as he really is, with his senseless laugh, hiding his wet chin behind his hand. . . ."

Shabanu squeezed Zabo's fingers, but her own mind carried the picture still further: Zabo lying dutifully on her wedding night beside a quivering Ahmed. The bed would have been prepared with fine white linen, and Ahmed would have been schooled in impregnating her. A shiver of revulsion skipped across Shabanu's shoulders, and she could think no further.

"From now on we will be together," she said. "I pledge it on my life."

The servants lifted Zabo's leather bags into the farm van, which already was half full of luggage that contained Shabanu's and Mumtaz's belongings. Shabanu meant to leave enough in Lahore that they would not have to pack each time they went.

They left early the next morning, their sandals wet from a heavy dew. Their departure went unnoticed but for a pair of green eyes peering from behind the mosquito net of a hand-carved bed that stood beside the window in the top story of the house. Amina sighed and lay her heavy form back against the cushions.

Two of Nazir's gunmen crowded into the front beside the driver. Mumtaz, Shabanu, and Zabo rode behind, and the fawn lay quietly in the back of the van behind the suitcases. She had assumed a proprietary air over every place Mumtaz chose to keep her. Beside the child's *charpoi* at night the little doe slept, her delicate legs folded under her like a bed of twigs. When Zenat came to wake Mumtaz, the deer would stand and lower her head to ward off the old *ayah,* sending Mumtaz into fits of helpless laughter.

Choti lay now on a fine old *kilim* that Mumtaz had folded to make a cushion. The driver had made room for the fawn when Mumtaz had stamped her foot and refused to go to Lahore without her. Choti was unperturbed by the increasing blare of the traffic. She blinked slowly and imperiously atop her cushion.

Zabo talked little during the trip, and Shabanu tried to draw her out by talking about shopping plans. Where would they go? She'd never been to Lahore, and she wanted to know if Zabo knew the shops where the beautiful silks were sold, and where the stones and sequins would be sewn on.

Zabo answered politely a few times, and then her attention drifted away again, seeming to draw her out into the heat-hazed sky over the outskirts of Lahore.

Shabanu turned her attention to the traffic. Enormous trucks hurtled by, loaded so full of cotton that their burlap sides threatened to burst, and small white tufts stuck to the thorns of the acacia branches overhanging the road. The van passed the swaying traffic of wooden-wheeled carts drawn by donkeys, camels, and oxen. These were fewer as the van came closer to the city. Horse-drawn *tongas* crammed with women in city *burkas*, which covered heads and shoulders, and schoolchildren in uniforms—all riding backward—gave way to brightly painted Bedford buses, parting the peace of small villages with blaring horns. Herds of goats driven by small ragged boys with long sticks gave way to minibuses and motor scooters.

Once in the city, they followed the canal, its fecund smell cloaked in the sweetness of early summer flowers and clipped grass. Shabanu and Mumtaz were mesmerized by the smells and the traffic, and more activity than they'd ever seen before. Deeper into the city, wide boulevards lined with splendid old bungalows and manicured gardens turned to ever more crowded and disorderly streets lined with modern public buildings. Shabanu marveled at how perfectly square they were; how white, and how many windows they had!

The streets seemed to grow ever wider until they drew close to Badshahi Mosque, with its red sandstone walls and white marble domes glistening in the sun like enormous translucent onions. Passing through the ancient gates where the modern city ended and the city of the Mogul princes began, Shabanu's excitement turned to quiet anticipation—almost a feeling of familiarity and affection. She felt more as if she were returning to the Cholistan Desert to see her family than making her first visit to Pakistan's grandest city.

Once inside the walled city, the van sat for ten minutes at a time as overloaded *tongas* squeezed past, their sides scraping the walls of the buildings next to the lanes, and hawkers pulled carts piled high with roasted peanuts and fried dumplings out of the way. The bodyguards got out several times and shouted for them to move faster.

The van came to a small square surrounded by very old wooden buildings that looked as if they leaned on each other for support. From here the lanes were too narrow for the van. Above the street, sweating red clay pots kept water cool on platforms behind delicately carved screens that were thick with dust. Women peered out from behind the pots to see what was causing the commotion in the square below.

Here two black lacquered *tongas* with leather bonnets and polished brass carriage lamps stood waiting. The horses were fat, sleek, and well groomed, and bright feathered plumes flashed from the tops of their harnesses as they shook their magnificent heads. The driver unloaded the bags, and groups of urchins and old men gathered to watch. The bodyguards pushed them aside until a large, staring ring formed around them. Not a breath of air stirred, and Shabanu began to wonder how they would be able to move with so many people crowded into the square. The overripe smell from the gray water in the sewers beside the lane grew oppressive. Mumtaz reached up for her mother's hand. Choti slipped her nose under Mumtaz's arm, and the child held on to her pet's neck.

One *tonga* held their luggage and one bodyguard. In the

other, Shabanu sat with Mumtaz on her lap; Zabo held the fawn, and Zenat clung to the back of the seat. The second bodyguard climbed up to ride with the *tonga* driver. The horses' iron-shod feet clattered loudly, and every few yards they passed pyramids of oranges and carts loaded with bright ribbons and mounds of spices, tea, and dried beans.

Deeper they went into the heart of the old city, until it seemed surely they would emerge on the other side. And then the *tonga*s turned in through old wooden gates, their paint visible only as faint blue shadows embedded in the grain.

Inside the thick mud walls they came upon a different world. The fetid stench of open sewers gave way to the joyous sweetness of lime trees and jasmine in bloom in pots under the old banyan trees that crowded the far end of the outer wall. The clatter of wooden wheels on cobble and the shouts of children and hawkers were replaced by the cool splash of water in the blue-and-white tiled fountain at the center of the *haveli* courtyard.

It was a space of graceful proportion. The grand old banyan trees looked like servants kneeling at the feet of the three-storied wooden *haveli*.

Although it was just past midafternoon, the sun set behind the buildings surrounding the *haveli,* casting the courtyard into shadow. An old servant in white placed small clay dishes filled with oil around the fountain and beside vases of flowers set in tiny niches in the mud garden walls. A small boy in a clean but faded *lungi* came behind him and lit the wicks with a thin taper.

Selma appeared wheezing at the bottom of steps that led upward into the midsection of the house, which was open at the center through the balconies of three stories from the ground to the sky.

A white sari draped around Selma's large figure and over one shoulder. White was the color of mourning, and she'd worn it since the death of her husband many years before.

"Come in, come in," Selma said, waving one hand for them to enter. With the other she tucked a silver strand back into the untidy knot of hair at the back of her neck. "Don't stand there loitering like thieves. Who's this? My youngest niece? Come to Auntie Selma," she said, stooping gracefully for a woman of her size for Mumtaz to run into her widespread arms. The fawn followed the child across the courtyard, bucking and dipping her velvety head, as if she too sensed she was home in this oasis of calm in the chaotic and dirty city.

Selma embraced Shabanu and Zabo together, pulling them to her pillowy bosom with her large arms.

"You are as lovely as ever," she said, taking Shabanu's face in her hand. "And you," she said to Zabo, "grow prettier each time I see you." Selma's eyes held Zabo's for a moment.

Zabo's eyes filled with tears, as if the older woman's compassion and tenderness had touched a place she'd kept secret.

"Thank you, Auntie," Zabo said, and lay her head against Selma's comfortably padded shoulder. "It's always so good to see you."

"How wonderful to have beautiful young women and a child here again," said Selma, her voice reassuming its cheery boisterousness. "And Omar's back! We'll fill the place with music and laughter! How happy I am to see you all!"

Selma had lived here alone for many years. She loved the old *haveli,* but had little money to maintain it. While Rahim and Mahsood supplied some funds, it was she who kept it from falling down altogether, sometimes it seemed by sheer will.

Selma took them to their rooms up high in the third story of the old house. Zabo ran her hand along the smooth wall of the stairwell as if she were greeting a dear old friend.

The *haveli* had a feeling of history about it, so that Shabanu felt the presence of generations of happy, well-fed school-children when she looked at the worn treads of the stone stairways and the weathered-smooth wood of the gates and shutters.

The two bodyguards took their places beside the court-yard gates, which they ordered closed. The old wooden gates creaked as two elderly servants pushed them shut.

A servant carried the fawn up the three flights of steps, and it was clear that this house, too, would fall under Choti's spell. Each room looked out over the courtyard and was lit with brass kerosene lamps. Shabanu threw open the ancient wooden shutters at her window and looked out on the winking lights in the courtyard below. They reminded her of the starry nights of Cholistan.

Yes, she thought. We can be safe here in Lahore.

chapter 9

Shabanu stood at the foot of the silver *charpoi* in the center of her room, which seemed oddly familiar, as if she'd dreamed about it without ever having seen it. Apart from the silver bed legs, the room was simply furnished. Stylized vines painted in green intertwined with flowers of red and wound their way around window and door frames, the paint faded in some places but bright in others where cracks in the mud plaster walls had been patched and repainted. Rahim had employed the last painter of many generations whose Mogul designs had graced the walls at Okurabad to restore the *haveli*. The artist, now an old man himself, was the last of his line. He had taught his own grandsons his art, but they had hungered for the city and the chance to earn their fortunes and had gone to work in factories.

A white porcelain pitcher and basin stood on a chest in one corner, and a straight-backed chair was placed beside the window. The windows were without curtains, bare but for scarred shutters of weathered wood. A plain country-made table and two other chairs stood against the far wall. A bowl of oranges sat on the table near the head of the bed.

Gradually it occurred to Shabanu that this was the house she had come to in her daydreams, the house she imagined she and Mumtaz would share one day. There were differences, of course, for she'd never seen these particular rooms before; but she couldn't say what those differences were, and the *haveli* was just as she'd imagined it would be.

Shabanu splashed water on her face over the porcelain basin and went to check on Mumtaz, who was to sleep with Zenat in a small nursery off to one side and opposite the door to Zabo's room. Mumtaz sat on an embroidered pillow, the fawn at her feet. She talked earnestly in a low voice, shaking one fat finger at the animal's black wet nose. Choti blinked serenely, and Shabanu thought of herself in the desert as a child, mothering baby camels.

She sent Mumtaz downstairs with Zenat for an early supper, then knocked on the carved wooden door to Zabo's room.

Zabo sat on the edge of a hundred-year-old *charpoi* with loose strings that sagged in the middle. Her head was bowed, and she stared at her hands in her lap.

"Father is so pleased with the land Uncle Rahim has deeded him, he's given me a fortune to spend on jewelry." She rocked forward, and her hair made a curtain over her face.

"Rahim deeded land to your father? The land that goes to Ahmed is customary, but . . ."

"It was a bribe," Zabo said.

Shabanu was silent for a moment, then she knelt before Zabo, laid her hands over her friend's hands, and looked into her face.

"I'd do anything to keep this from happening to you," she said. "But Rahim won't discuss it with me. 'The issue is closed, Shabanu!' " she said, mimicking his stern formality. "Keeping the family land together is a sacred thing to him. There's nothing I or anyone can do to change his mind."

"I know," said Zabo, and a large tear splattered onto the back of Shabanu's hand. "It's just that until now the idea of Ahmed has seemed so remote. Coming here makes it seem more real." She drew her shoulders forward. "The idea of him touching me, lying with me—that I'm to have his baby!" Her voice caught as she spoke through her tears.

"I've had a nightmare—several times I've dreamed it," Zabo went on, "that a baby is growing inside me. It's not a baby, really; it's a . . . sort of a growth.

"I can barely breathe in the dream as my belly gets bigger and bigger, and I wonder what it looks like. It talks to me. It says terrible things, threatening me and scaring me, and I wake up feeling as if I've just escaped being smothered."

Shabanu sat beside Zabo and held her close. Her own tears fell into Zabo's beautiful black hair. Zabo sobbed for a while, and then was quieter. She took a deep breath, shook out a handkerchief, and wiped away her tears.

"I may not be able to prevent your marrying Ahmed," said Shabanu. "But I promise I will never leave you."

It seemed so little to say, she thought. She remembered how Zabo had made her believe she'd survive when she'd been horrified at the prospect of marrying Rahim, a man old enough to be her grandfather.

But marrying an idiot was far worse than marrying an old man.

There was a gentle rap on the door, and the servant girl Yazmin came in carrying a tray with an old china teapot, two cups, and a plate of tiny meat dumplings and sugary biscuits.

Shabanu made Zabo eat something and sip some milky

tea. Then she made her lie down, and rubbed her temples until she relaxed. Tears seeped through her eyelashes even as she slept.

Zabo was a strong young woman, and the intensity of her unhappiness frightened Shabanu. When Rahim arrived that night he would expect Shabanu to sleep with him. There would be no question of her staying in Zabo's room. She needed to find someone who could help keep an eye on her.

Should she trust Selma? Selma reminded Shabanu of her Auntie Sharma—gentle, wise, and knowing about the ways of men. But she also was Rahim's sister. It took a powerful woman to follow her heart where family loyalty was concerned. Should she trust Selma? Her instincts said yes.

Shabanu lit a candle from the nightstand, wrapped her *chadr* around her shoulders, and found her way through the vaulted hallway. It was dark except for the candlelight glinting from tiny mirrors set into the arches overhead.

She found the back interior stairway and followed it as it wound downward, the shadow of her head bobbing along beside her. She kept one hand on the curved wall to guide her way to the second floor, where Selma's quarters were. Shabanu felt as if she knew her way throughout the *haveli.*

At the landing she turned right and bumped sharply into a tall young man, banging her nose so hard against his shoulder that tears blurred her vision. She looked up through a haze into his surprised dark eyes. Neither of them spoke for a moment, and Shabanu stood with her hand to her smarting nose.

"I'm very sorry," he said, fumbling in his pocket for a handkerchief, then handing it to her. She dabbed at her eyes. When her vision cleared, she was startled by his frank stare.

"*I'm* sorry," she said. "I was watching my feet."

She handed back his handkerchief.

"Oh, you can have it," he said, leaning toward her slightly to peer into her face. She moved backward a step, uneasy at his closeness.

"I don't think it's broken," he said, leaning closer still to study her nose. "It's on straight, and there's no blood."

She took another step backward and nearly fell down the stairs. His face colored.

"I'm Omar," he said, sticking out his hand. She looked at his hand, not knowing what he meant for her to do with it.

"I'm sorry," he said again, and pushed his fists into the pockets of his fitted Western trousers. "In America ladies shake hands. You must be my Auntie Shabanu."

He was formal and uncomfortable-looking. Shabanu laughed out loud.

"My aunties are old and wrinkled," she said, grinning at him. He smiled slowly. She stuck out her hand, and he took it in a firm handshake. She was surprised at the largeness of his hand and the gentleness of his touch.

"Punjabi ladies are supposed to look at the floor when they meet men," she said, still smiling. "In the Cholistan Desert, where I grew up, I would have offered you tea by now, so it would have been fine for you to put out your hand."

He laughed then too, and they set out together to find Selma. Omar produced a small but brilliant flashlight from his pocket. Shabanu's candle seemed dim by comparison, and she blew it out.

"If Auntie Selma doesn't put lights in these hallways, someone will fall down the stairs and be killed," Omar said.

"Why doesn't she?" asked Shabanu. "Is it a question of money?"

"Well . . ." he began, then thought better of what he was about to say. "Maybe she's just old-fashioned."

"You were about to say that your father and uncles can't agree on spending money to keep up this place," said Shabanu. "They want to use it when they're in Lahore, but they're not willing to spend money on it. Poor Selma puts everything she has into running a hotel for them."

"I'm not sure . . ."

"It's true!" said Shabanu, annoyed with him for sticking up for Rahim. "You're just like your uncles and your father!"

But Omar was quick to change the subject.

He explained that he'd just arrived from New York by way of London, and that he couldn't wait to get to the farm. She marveled at how he covered all that distance with just a few words.

He'd been in America nearly six years, with university and graduate school. He'd been back only a few times in those years.

Shabanu listened intently. He spoke in Punjabi, and she kept falling behind what he was saying. He spoke quickly with inflections that moved in strange cadences, as if his words held some meaning that only he could understand.

At the same time she was thinking she'd expected him to be different—haughtier, perhaps. She hadn't expected to like him. Perhaps she thought he'd be more like Leyla—selfish and spoiled. And Shabanu wondered whether Amina and Leyla would poison his thoughts so he too would hate her in a short time.

They found Selma not in her room but in the kitchen,

where a grimy light bulb suspended from the ceiling by a wire supplied the only overhead light. The room glowed with fires from several burners atop the woodburning mud stove, and from flames on the hearth and in the bread oven. The cook, an ancient stooped man wearing a white apron caked with flour, bent over the mud oven, hanging long slabs of bread dough on a rack inside the flames. The kitchen smelled of rich *masala* spices and baking bread.

Shaheen, the toothless old *ayah* who had been with Selma since she was a girl, stood over a pot of dark curry, stirring with a long wooden spoon. A pot of yellow lentils simmered on the stove beside her. Shabanu felt very hungry.

Selma reached behind her to untie her apron and herded them out of the kitchen.

"Mr. World Traveler has come to see your husband," she said, inclining her head toward Omar, "in a motor rickshaw that tooted into the courtyard and nearly ran over my chickens. Never let anyone know when he was coming so he could be met properly at the airport." She adjusted her *dupatta* over her head and shot Omar a look with her eyes half closed.

"Rahim will be here later tonight," Shabanu said, remembering the message suddenly. "He said we shouldn't keep dinner waiting. He had business at Okurabad."

"If Rahim's not killed on the road, he'll work himself into the grave," said Selma. "It's a good thing Omar has come to help."

Selma was wheezing again by the time they reached her sitting room on the second floor, where she heaved herself into a tattered stuffed chair.

The shutters were drawn against the heat from the alley below, and the room was dark except for the pleasant light

of china lamps that threw comforting soft shadows on the
high ceiling. Some of the main rooms had electricity, and
this was one of the few with lights.

In the center of the far wall was a hand-cut crystal fireplace mantel and facing. It was smudged with the soot of
long-ago fires and fingerprints, but still it caught the dim
light from the lamps and cracks in the shutters and flicked
it back in colored pinpoints.

Rahim's great-great-great-grandfather had been prime
minister to the Mogul emperor Akbar, and the house had
been one of the grandest during Lahore's most opulent period. Now there were only ten rooms in use among the
haveli's dozens.

The armchairs and carpets had been stuffed with goose
down once, covered with rich silk brocades. But now they
were lumpy, and the fabric was worn in places to long thin
strands that barely held in the stuffing. The furniture was
sparse, but the shabbiness and austerity were not unpleasant.
Shabanu felt certain that Selma would have chosen to leave
the *haveli* old and comfortable even if she could afford to
have it otherwise.

Selma talked of how happy Rahim was that Omar was
here, how good it was to have young voices in the house
again.

"Of course we'll keep dinner until Rahim comes," she
said. "I've been cooking half the day, and there are six servants in the kitchen now. Tomorrow we shall . . ."

But Shabanu was contemplating how she could get Selma
away to herself, so she might talk to her about Zabo. She
was worried that Zabo might try to run away in the middle
of the night or, worse, that she might harm herself. Perhaps

Selma could send the young servant girl to sleep near Zabo's bed. . . .

". . . flutes, *shenai,* sitar, tabla. . . . There will be music until God know how late," Selma was saying. "So we must sleep early tonight. Tomorrow we'll celebrate!"

Shabanu looked away with a start when she saw Omar's eyes on her. He sat on a sofa beside Selma's chair, where he'd been watching Shabanu intently while his aunt talked. She felt her face go warm. A soft rushing in her ears sounded like a distant river.

When Selma got up to check on the kitchen, Omar unfolded his long frame from the sofa and came to sit in the chair beside Shabanu's.

"Would you like to see the rest of the house? It's like a museum—at least that's how I remember it."

Shabanu nodded. He helped her from the chair, and the touch of his large, soft hand sent shivers through her.

He took the flashlight from his pocket and handed it to her.

"I'm used to candles," she said.

"I brought dozens of these from New York," he said. "You'll need it going up and down the stairs." He pressed it into her hand.

Shabanu walked behind Omar through the door of the parlor into the main salon. She felt acutely aware of the air that touched her skin, the blood that went through her veins, the feel of the floor under her feet. The brightness from his flashlight outlined the hard, angular planes of his shoulders and neck and chin in front of her, and Shabanu realized it had been a very long time since she had even seen a young man.

He spoke to her in his foreign-sounding Punjabi, and she gave up concentrating on what he said just to take in the smooth texture of his skin and the rich timbre of his voice. And the idea that he touched her so easily. She knew her feelings meant trouble—but her fingers still felt his touch.

He turned and shone the light on her face.

"Are you listening?" he asked. She was startled, but she realized she hadn't heard what he'd been saying.

"I'm sorry," she said in Seraiki, which she was sure he understood from having grown up on the farm at Okurabad. "I speak Punjabi very badly."

"Why didn't you tell me?" he asked, smiling at her face in the glow from the flashlight. "I love speaking Seraiki."

She managed a smile.

In the main salon on the first floor a rich silk rug hung on the wall opposite the wrought-iron fireplace. Despite decades of exposure to smoke, dust, and the grime of the city, the vivid phoenixes, dragons, and tigers seemed to leap in the brightness of the flashlights as if they were alive.

Off the courtyard was a bath, with a series of tanks and fountains. The tanks were tiled with interlocking octagons and squares of black and white marble that formed mazes with stars of oxblood stone at the center.

Pitchers of opalescent Persian glass stood in niches in the walls, and Shabanu imagined that in the old days servants had poured scented oil from them into baths for the women of the household.

Dust had collected in the corners of the bathing tanks, and Shabanu wondered how long it was since they'd been filled with water. The bronze fountainheads in the center of the tanks were blue with corrosion, and they looked as if they were too clogged with dirt and white mineral residue ever to run with water again.

Shabanu could almost hear the tinkle of water as it ran into the tanks, which were surrounded by walkways of ancient marble tiles in geometric patterns bordered by tiles inlaid with flowers of lapis, carnelian, and tiger's-eye, and leaves of tourmaline at the center of each design.

The room after the bath was a broad hall that led into the old dining room, where glazed tiles of cobalt and turquoise almond buds, stars, and chrysanthemums reminded Shabanu of the mosques and shrines at Derawar Fort in the Cholistan Desert, where her grandfather lay buried. A low wooden table covered much of the floor.

"How many servants would have served dinner in those days?" she asked Omar.

"Even when I was a child, there were dozens of servants," he replied. "Now there are only four, and three of them are very old: Shaheen, Selma's old *ayah,* who can barely walk; the cook; and Ali, the old one-eyed bearer. And of course there's the girl Yazmin, who is Ali's niece, and there are always boys around to run errands and help Ali. The others in the kitchen are all relatives of the cook who come when they're needed."

"What was Daoud like?" Shabanu asked. "Do you remember him?"

"Oh, yes," said Omar. "He was a wonderful man." Shabanu listened to him talk, and it made her happy to hear his voice and watch his face.

Selma's husband had been an expansive man—generous, wise, and sympathetic, Omar said. He and Selma were happy with each other, despite their having had no children. That was what the others said.

What Selma said was this: "I am only the sister. My children would always be lowest on the ladder. Let my brothers have children! Why ruin a perfectly nice love affair? My life is good *because* there are no children." And, Omar said, Daoud shared her feelings completely.

Shabanu thought Omar talked as if he understood Selma's thinking and would have agreed with her had he been Daoud.

The husband and wife had a picnic dinner in a different room of the *haveli* each evening, Omar said. One night they would sit at the desk in the study, a candle burning over the white linen cloth that covered the green leather writing surface. The next evening they'd face each other over a bench covered with a large banana palm leaf in the courtyard.

Every day when Daoud came home from work they would walk through the *chowk*s to a different part of the old city. One afternoon they would go to Bhatti Gate, which had been the Hindu quarter of the city before the bloody partition of India and Pakistan. There, inside the ancient wooden gates, generations of widows had left their handprints before throwing themselves on their husbands' funeral pyres. Large prints rested beside tiny prints, with marks made by the hands of children in between, as if there had been so many of them rushing to their fiery deaths all at once that they couldn't find enough space for all to leave their marks.

Sometimes they walked to the gates beside the shrine of some unnamed Hindu saint, where women once tacked their sick children's slippers after praying for their recovery in the small neighborhood temples; to the lanes of the sweets makers to buy *kulfi* to have with their tea; to the man who made Selma's eye shadows of powdered lapis lazuli and amethyst, her skin creams from mutton fat, powders of gold and pearl, and perfume, and her eyeliners of charcoal; to the mosque, where they left their shoes at the door and entered for late-afternoon prayers.

If one or the other was unwell, both of them went to the *hakkim,* who sat talking with them about the symptoms, then prescribed some powder or herb to be mixed with milk or brewed in tea for a cure.

They went everywhere together.

"I would like to share a love like Selma and Daoud's," Omar said.

"It's usually not so simple," said Shabanu sadly. "They were unique for their time—perhaps for any time." She was thinking of Zabo and Ahmed and the countless marriages that never had known and never would know joy because they were made for political expediency, or for land, or for some other reason not connected with the suitability of one heart to another.

Omar stood silent and immobile for a few moments, and Shabanu wondered whether he was brooding over his own marriage. Could he be thinking he might share a love like that with Leyla?

"As they walked Daoud would tell Selma about his day in court," Omar went on, taking up the tour again.

Although she had never studied law, Selma's mind was quick, and her knowledge of legal matters was extensive from these shared confidences. Daoud was in awe of the unshakable solidity of her logic and her natural sense of justice, and he sought her advice on many matters.

So Selma had known about the murder of Abdul Muhammad Khan. From the very beginning she had suspected his brother. The men were Pathans, wealthy merchants who had made a fortune in goods transshipped across Pakistan to Afghanistan, so that no duty was due, then turned back at the border and smuggled back into the bazaar at Peshawar to be sold at bargain prices to tourists who came from all over Pakistan.

The brother's defense had been that it would be unthinkable for a Pathan to kill his own brother. They were in business together; the fortune of one man was the fortune of both. It would mean a life of exile and fear, for the sons of the dead man would never rest until they had avenged their father's death.

But Daoud had uncovered a motive: Abdul Muhammad Khan had mortgaged the trucks used to transport the goods to purchase a flat for his mistress, who lived in Lahore. What Abdul Muhammad Khan didn't know was that his mistress was also his brother's mistress.

The entire court was impressed by this motive, once exposed. Yes, perhaps the fortune of one was the fortune of both. But it could never be that the mistress of one was the mistress of both; that would be a blood matter. The defense was in a shambles.

After a short deliberation, the court found the brother guilty. But sentencing was a delicate issue. The government had signaled its intention to increase the powers of the Shariat, or Islamic law. There was some question as to the secular court's finding, and so there had been no death sentence. The brother was sentenced to life imprisonment in Pindi Jail. Selma and Daoud forgot about the case.

But only two years later, through another lapse in the system due to a moment of political vulnerability, the governor of the Punjab had commuted the sentence of the brother of Abdul Muhammad Khan. Unbeknownst to Daoud and Selma, the Pathan was set free.

One premonsoon night, after weeks of nearly unbearable heat, the servants prepared beds for Selma and Daoud on the roof of the *haveli,* where they would catch any breeze that happened past.

The couple talked for a while, unable to sleep immediately in the stupefying heat. But after half an hour, overcome by the exhaustion of days of heat so overpowering it seemed impossible to move their swollen limbs, they fell into unconsciousness without even bidding each other good night.

Selma never forgave herself that moment of neglect that deprived her of saying good-bye to the person she was to love most in this life.

For in the dead heat of that still, dark night, Abdul Muhammad Khan's brother stole up to the roof of the *haveli* and buried his dagger in Daoud's heart with one blow so deft that Daoud died in an instant.

Selma didn't awaken until morning, when the servant came with bed tea. Seeing the haft of the Pathan's dagger protruding from between Daoud's shoulder blades, the servant dropped the entire tray, and the silver serving pieces clattered across the roof's terra-cotta tiles. Only then did Selma feel the stickiness of her husband's drying blood, which had been cooled by the night air.

The Pathan had disappeared, probably into his ancestral village in the tribal lands on the Afghanistan border, where the only law was Allah's.

"None of the servants has ever been to the roof of the *haveli* since," said Omar. "They are certain Daoud's ghost still roams about up there, waiting for his death to be avenged. The door leading to the roof has been locked ever since that day.

"And the most Selma could ask of justice was that Abdul Muhammad Khan's sons would find their uncle in his bed and exercise their ancient right to vendetta."

chapter 10

I expected you to be very different," Omar said. By then they were back in Selma's study, left alone when Selma rushed off to deal with some kitchen crisis.

"You heard I was a country girl," she said, looking at him directly.

"Most country girls do look at the floor," he said, smiling.

"Do you disapprove?" she asked, sticking her chin out.

"No," he said. "I do not."

Shabanu knew what he'd heard: that she ran about barefoot, with her head uncovered; that Rahim had married her for sex—you could tell by the way he looked at her; that she was stupid and couldn't read or write; that she was unrespectable. Omar may even have heard of the Ibne incident.

"Well," she said, "I'm proud to be a country girl."

But Rahim came then, interrupting her, and she was glad. Omar stood and went to him, his arms wide. Rahim embraced his nephew as a father embraces a son, clasping him

by the back of the neck and kissing him on either cheek
before folding him into his arms.

Mahsood came a moment later, and his embrace was
awkward and slightly embarrassed. Perhaps it was because
he knew that his son was fonder of his uncle than of his
father. Mahsood was taller than Rahim and less fit, with a
stomach that showed roundly through his waistcoat. His face
was creased with years of having had to deal with difficult
issues more harshly than his gentle nature might have found
comfortable.

Shabanu left them in the parlor sipping orange juice to
help in the kitchen while the servants put food on the table.
Selma sent Yazmin to fetch Zabo.

Zabo opened the door to the parlor quietly, peering around
the edge of the doorway as Selma gathered everyone to the
table. Zabo greeted her uncles politely with brief little nods.
Omar's face softened when he saw her.

"How is my favorite cousin?" he asked, coming to her.
She smiled briefly. It was the only smile Shabanu saw on
her face all day.

Shabanu was pleased that Omar chose to say nothing about
Zabo's marriage to Ahmed. It showed he was sensitive to
Zabo's feelings—that he really did care for her.

When they were all seated at the long dining room table,
Rahim asked Omar to continue the story of his voyage from
America.

"But the ladies have already heard this, Uncle. Let's hear
news of the farm." Whenever the conversation turned to
things that did not interest the ladies, Omar changed the
subject to something that would.

"We can discuss crops later, Uncle," he said. "How about
the horses? Do you ride?" he asked Shabanu. Again she heard
the faint rushing in her ears.

By the time dinner was served, Shabanu no longer felt hungry. Omar continued to include her and Zabo and Selma in every conversation.

Zabo sat quietly at the table, seldom touching her food. She never spoke once, and Rahim looked at her several times, his mouth in a straight, disapproving line. He looked as if he was trying to catch her eye to scold her.

Selma asked which of the cloth sellers they would visit the next day.

"You must go first to Mahmood," she said. "He has samples, and he'll bring others as he comes to know what you want. He will arrange for the *darzi* and for shoes to match what the *darzi* sews. I will take you myself to the gold bazaar."

The atmosphere around the table relaxed as the women talked together, and Rahim and Omar and Mahsood talked of the farm and politics.

Zabo sat, fidgeting distractedly as she had in the car, then asked to be excused as the table was cleared.

"Can't you even sit politely through dinner?" Rahim asked, banging his hand down so that the teacups rattled. But Zabo stood without answering and left the table.

"Excuse me. I'll go look after her," Shabanu said quickly, and followed Zabo.

"You can't do this," she said, catching up with her on the stairs. She switched on Omar's flashlight, and Zabo turned to her. "You have to at least put up a front, or Rahim will. . . ."

"What can he do to me that's worse than what he's already done?" she demanded, and stalked up the dark stairway, the beam of the flashlight bobbing as Shabanu ran to catch up with her again.

"I'm afraid he'll forbid me to be with you," Shabanu said, catching her on the upstairs landing. "You can see he's angry. . . ."

"*He*'s angry! What have I done?" Zabo turned and ran to the door of her room, swinging it hard behind her. Shabanu caught the heavy door before it could slam. Zabo sat on the wooden edge of the sagging string bed. Shabanu was breathless, the flashlight still bright in her hand.

"I don't think Rahim *likes* what he's done to you. That's why it upsets him to see you unhappy. I'm afraid he'll separate us—that he'll make me go back to Okurabad. Please try, Zabo."

"Help me, Shabanu," Zabo said then, her voice quavery and soft, her eyes frightened in the flashlight beam, which held her face in a tight, pale yellow circle.

"I'm trying," said Shabanu. She walked across the room, and the flashlight beam raced across the far wall as she turned.

"I know of a place where we could go if we had to," she said, walking back and forth, faster and faster. "But I think it's better if I don't tell you where."

"They'd find us in the countryside," said Zabo. "They know where your family is. They'd torture your sister until she told where I was hiding. We have no money, nowhere to hide in the city." Her eyes were little dots of light as they followed Shabanu around the room.

"Whatever we do, we must plan very carefully," Shabanu said. "Your father has made sure the bodyguards are within a few steps of you every second. I don't think we should try anything before the wedding."

"He posts them outside my bedroom at home," said Zabo.

Shabanu continued to pace, and when she turned the light back to Zabo, her eyes were half closed.

"Let's talk tomorrow," said Shabanu.

She helped Zabo out of her clothes and into her night-gown. Zabo was asleep when Shabanu drew the sheet over her, closed the mosquito netting, and returned to the draw-ing room, which was bathed in the glow of electric lamps. The three men sat at one end of the room, and Selma sat alone at the other end, a tea tray on the table before her.

Omar looked up as Shabanu entered. She could see him from the edge of her vision, but she kept her face turned toward Selma as she walked to the chair beside the older woman. She loosened the *dupatta* that lay across the base of her throat, draped over her shoulders and down her back. As she sat down Omar's eyes were still on her. Rahim kept talking, and Omar sat beside him, half listening.

Shabanu ignored them and leaned toward Selma. The older woman held up her hand before Shabanu could speak.

"I know, I know," Selma said, keeping her voice low. "I'd have to be blind not to see she's miserable. It's criminal. There's nothing we can do but distract her until she's used to the idea." Her eyes were weary and heavy-lidded—the eyes of a woman who'd dealt with such problems all her life.

"I'm afraid," said Shabanu. "Can someone spend the night with her?"

"I've told Yazmin to bring her pallet to Zabo's room. She sleeps lightly, and she'll keep an eye on her."

"Thank you," said Shabanu. Selma reached over and pat-ted the back of her hand.

Shabanu looked across the room to where her husband and his nephew sat, engrossed now in their talk, one head dark, the other silver, and she felt a heaviness settle over her heart. She couldn't quite identify the overbearing sadness, but somehow she sensed that their lives had changed forever that day.

Rahim came to bed late, and Shabanu pretended to be asleep. Not wanting to disturb her, he slipped quietly into bed and began to snore almost immediately.

Shabanu stared at the ceiling. She thought of Omar and how his eyes had followed her. She thought of how his large hands moved with ease when he talked; of their surprising softness; and of his sure, strong touch, so very different from Rahim's. She wondered how it would feel to have him touch her body.

The thought made her belly ache, and she rolled over onto her side and rested her head against the inside of her folded arm.

Omar didn't behave toward her as did the other men of Rahim's family. They treated her respectfully, but she could see in their eyes that they regarded her as the woman Rahim kept for his bed. Omar seemed to be interested in what she thought, and . . .

Well, it made little difference. Soon he'd be married to Leyla, and he would take his wife's side against her.

She wondered whether Leyla would be a passionate wife. Of course, there was no *need* for her to be passionate. Shabanu might never have known the depth of her own passion if Rahim's ardor had not been a matter of survival to her. The only need Leyla had was to become impregnated, to produce sons who would inherit the family land.

She thought how terrifying a pregnancy would be for Zabo. Watching her belly grow from month to month, not knowing whether she would give birth to a helpless thing that would live senseless in the world. . . .

She found it difficult to believe that Ahmed could function sexually. But of course Rahim would never have arranged the marriage unless he knew there was a chance Zabo would produce an heir to cement the peace with Nazir. After all, that was the main point of the whole thing. But how Zabo would endure—that was the question.

She thought of the early days of her own marriage. Amina had drawn the battle lines within just two weeks of Rahim's marriage to Shabanu. She asked to see the new bride in the front parlor of the house. It was their first formal meeting, and Shabanu had been unclear as to which of them should be hostess. Shabanu shared Rahim's quarters, but Amina had lived in the house for twenty-four years.

Shabanu had sent Zenat to the kitchen for tea. Amina, a handsome woman of imposing proportion with thick silver hair wound back in a bun, swept into the parlor. She was accompanied by Leyla, who sat and listened with a secret smile on her crimson mouth while her mother told Shabanu how things would be:

"We all help one another at Okurabad," Amina had said, eyebrows arched and lips pursed. "There is always work to be done."

She extended her hand, and a row of seeds strung into prayer beads clattered lightly onto the table.

"And we observe Islamic customs meticulously."

Shabanu, whose family had been religious in their thoughts and deeds, though less so by custom because of their nomadic life, reached out for the string of seeds.

"Thank you," she said.

Then, without another word, Amina had stood, gathered the silken folds of her *dupatta* about her face, and swept grandly from the room, followed by Leyla.

No sooner were they gone than Zenat appeared with a

huge willow basket piled high with clothing from all the women of Okurabad.

"*Begum-sahiba* says you should mend these and return them by tomorrow evening."

Shabanu had not been taken completely by surprise, for her Auntie Sharma had warned that the women of Rahim's household would try to make her their slave.

She didn't even consider telling Rahim, who might suspect her of not wanting to help with the household chores. It was the price she must pay for being the youngest wife, the most lowly born. But she had no intention of being their slave, and she was determined to deal with it in her own way.

She took out her sewing basket and set to work. The first garment was a green silk tunic with broken armhole seams and bodice fabric stressed by the mass of an ample bosom. She mended the seams and disguised the tears with tiny embroideries. She worked all through the night and the following day, mending the clothes with perfect tiny stitches.

The work took longer than it might have, for Shabanu took in the seams of each tunic so that the wearer would find the fit somewhat snug.

Later, Zenat had told Shabanu that the women talked among themselves about the perfection of her work. In the weeks that followed, basket after basket arrived with mounds of mending to be done. Then the women began to appear with cloth from the bazaars to be measured for clothing to be made by hand. They refused to buy her a sewing machine.

Zenat also began to mention an element of discontent in the women's quarters. Arguments broke out at the least provocation. There was much weeping and little laughter.

And then some time later, Amina flew into a rage, telling

her daughters they'd never find suitable husbands if they didn't lose weight and improve their tempers. She fired all the cook's helpers, and a strict diet was enforced throughout the women's quarters.

Still the baskets of mending came day and night, and Shabanu worked continuously until Rahim grew impatient with the toll the mending took on Shabanu's attention, which he regarded his exclusive domain.

When it became evident that Shabanu was entering a late stage of her pregnancy, he ordered the flood of mending to end.

By then the women had dieted until they were gaunt, and still their clothing bound their breasts and pinched their waists.

The thought of it still made Shabanu smile to herself.

The house was completely dark and silent. Shabanu shifted cautiously from side to side on the bed, the strings squeaking softly with each movement. Even the clatter and jingle of *tongas* in the lanes below had been silenced, and she did not want to waken Rahim. She could not respond to him tonight.

There was no chance Zabo would find humor in her life with Ahmed, she thought. If only Zabo could see beyond, to the things she and Shabanu might share.

I need Zabo, she thought, surprised at the intensity of her fear of losing her only friend.

Then she thought again of Omar, and she fell asleep imagining his hands on her face.

In her dreams there were murmurs—throaty whispers that grew excited, then angry. She couldn't see in the dream. Everything was dark, and moans were interspersed with the murmurs. She was frightened, her heart hammering in her ears. She searched for Mumtaz. She could hear her daughter crying out to her.

"Uma! Uma!"

She ran toward Mumtaz's voice, but the women shrieked at her, taunting her and laughing down from the windows of the house at Okurabad.

Then they were still. Wailing began from the windows. "Rahim is dead," they cried. Amina, Leyla, Saleema, and Tahira accused Shabanu of murdering him. They threw her belongings down at her, pelting her with sandals and things from her childhood in Cholistan: brooms of desert twigs, camel bells, small clay jars. Heavy silver anklets and brass camel bells thumped to the ground around her. Gossamer *shalwar kameez* floated over her head, brushing her cheeks as they fell.

They said they would keep Mumtaz to work in the kitchen. . . .

Shabanu sat up straight in bed, shivering and perspiring all at the same time, her heart thumping wildly. Her nightgown stuck to her back. She slipped out from under the quilt. Rahim sighed loudly and she stopped in midmotion, but he remained asleep.

She tiptoed to Mumtaz's door, opening it a crack. Old Zenat's snores chortled through the room, and a *tap-tap-tap* was followed by the cold wet press of Choti's nose against Shabanu's hand.

She tiptoed barefoot to Mumtaz's cot and switched on the flashlight Omar had given her. There was her beautiful Mumtaz, sleeping the sleep of the innocent, behind veined eyelids, heavy lashes, her pink mouth open slightly, her hands, palms up, curled on either side of her face on the pillow.

Shabanu closed the door and stood in the hall, where she

opened the shutter. The sky looked like old dull silver. A faint line of green outlined the domes of the mosque near Masti Gate, where the sun would rise in half an hour.

She didn't think often about what would happen to her and Mumtaz when Rahim was gone. But she had planned her life around the time with meticulous care, as if she were planting a garden that must be harvested all at once.

Down the hall toward the stairway she heard the rustle of skirts, and Zabo came running to her, a shawl drawn around her nightgown.

"Shabanu!" she said, her voice an excited whisper. "I've thought of something! I can't wait to tell you!" Zabo took Shabanu by the hand and pulled her, half running, to her room, their bare feet slapping against the floor.

Shabanu was pleased to hear life in her friend's voice, and she ran after Zabo gladly. Yazmin sat up sleepily in the corner where she'd spent the night.

"Go away!" Zabo said to her, shooing her with fluttering fingers. The servant girl smiled and folded her pallet before scurrying from the room.

"Yazmin told me last night about the fake jewelry in the Anarkali Bazaar. I haven't been able to think about anything else ever since. She says it's made by artists, and you can't tell it from real jewelry. We could buy a few pieces of good gold, rubies, and pearls for the wedding. I'll have a few saris and some *shalwar kameez* made with gold thread, just for the celebrations. The rest will be boxes of fake gold from Anarkali Bazaar and cheap ready-made clothes. What do you think?"

"Wouldn't your father be able to tell the difference?" Shabanu remembered her own father biting into the gold bangles he'd bought for her sister Phulan's wedding.

"Yazmin says they use stones that are almost real, and if you have things made with many stones—and not much fake gold—you can't tell the difference. By the time anyone noticed, we could be gone!" Zabo said.

Shabanu was still thinking of her own father. She thought of how she'd fled into the desert by camel when he told her the time had come for her to marry Rahim.

"I've told you I know a place where we can go," Shabanu said. "But you are your father's only hope of gaining a fortune. Don't you think he'd hunt us down and kill us?"

Shutr keena, Shabanu thought, camel vengeance. It was the rule of the desert, for animals and men alike. It was the rule of all Pakistan, village and city. Each transgression against honor was punishable by death, with no exemptions for the rich, for much-loved daughters, for adored young wives.

"We could go into the desert, to your Auntie Sharma!" said Zabo.

"I have to think of Mumtaz," said Shabanu, feeling a small grain of betrayal fester in her heart. She thought of Mumtaz, still so small and helpless. She had to put Mumtaz first.

"She said you could come to Fort Abbas anytime," Zabo went on, as if she hadn't heard.

"When I left the desert," Shabanu said, "I thought I would die. But I don't belong there now. Mumtaz must be educated and learn to fend for herself. And you—you've been brought up with servants. You would find life in the desert difficult. Do you think you could survive there?"

"I can live anywhere, but not married to Ahmed. Remember how frightened I used to be of the panthers at Dinga? Well, leopards and scorpions and cobras mean nothing to me now." They sat together for a while without saying anything more.

"If you can't live with me in Cholistan, I will go myself. I know you must do what you think is right for Mumtaz," Zabo said, lifting her chin. "Forget your promise to me. Without some hope of escaping a life with Ahmed, having his children, I would kill myself."

The small kernel of betrayal blossomed in Shabanu like a full-blown rose. She wanted to take back what she'd said, to tell Zabo she'd come to Cholistan with her. But a steely voice spoke in the back of her head. "For the sake of Mumtaz," it said. "For the sake of Mumtaz."

At the same time she recognized the warm little pressure at the top of her stomach as being partly fear, partly excitement at the thought of freedom. It was a feeling she'd not had for many years.

chapter 11

The next day was a blur of heat and activity, with Selma at the center of it like a police officer directing traffic from the pedestal in the mall. She gave orders in the kitchen, then dispatched boys in new white *lungi*s and turbans with reminders to houses throughout Lahore that there would be music in the *haveli* tonight. She sent Rahim and Omar to the bungalows in the Cantonment, where Omar was very much in demand.

And she sent Yazmin with Shabanu and Zabo to see Mahmood in the fancy-cloth bazaar. Selma's car was waiting in the lane beyond the courtyard. As Shabanu stepped into the sunlight, glints struck her eye from the mirrors sewn into the black velvet vest worn by the driver, who stood with his back to them holding the sedan door open.

"Ibne!" said Shabanu. The servant touched his starched white turban with his fingertips in a formal, unsmiling salute.

"Good morning, *Begum,*" he said with elaborate dignity.

Shabanu could not keep a happy smile from her face. She stepped into the car, her heart singing to have Ibne back.

They drove through the noisy, crowded lane to the cloth
bazaar, and neither she nor Ibne spoke again. It was as if
she'd seen him only the day before. She wanted to ask how
he'd come to Lahore, but his silence let her know it was
better to forget the extraordinary events of the month before.

She was puzzled by Rahim's capacity for both the chilling
callousness with which he'd imposed a life sentence on Zabo,
and the compassion with which he'd secretly reinstated Ibne—
even promoted him, from white horse to limousine.

Ibne stood outside the door of the shop. As the three
women entered the hot, dark room, Shabanu saw Zabo's
two bodyguards take their places on either side of Ibne. Her
heart took an extra beat—she hadn't seen them all day. But
as the clatter of *tongas* and donkey carts and the white,
vaporous heat receded behind them, Shabanu realized they
had been close-by the entire time.

Mahmood, a tall man with betel-stained lips, greeted them,
bowed deeply, and peered up from under his turban. He
turned on the lights, and a fan began to twirl lazily overhead, stirring air laden with lint from the bolts of cloth
behind him.

Zabo was relaxed, laughing as she and Shabanu sat with
the cloth shop owner sipping tea and poring over silks and
cottons woven by hand in India and smuggled across the
border. Yazmin sat wide-eyed behind them.

"The pale green will be wonderful with this," said
Mahmood, holding up a length of pink silk with diagonal
stripes of the same green. "You must wear a string of ca-
bouchon peridots with it. My cousin has a set . . ."

By noon they were hungry, and Mahmood sent a boy
with a fistful of rupee notes to fetch *pakoras* from the bazaar.
It should have been fun, but Shabanu could not relax with

the bodyguards standing just outside the door. She was glad Ibne also was there.

Zabo selected a red shot-silk skirt for the wedding itself. Shabanu marveled at her calm as she examined the mysterious deep red folds and the heavy border of gold embroidery.

"Rubies are to be sewn here," said Mahmood, touching a tobacco-stained finger to an oval space in the midst of the pattern. "And here," he said, turning the fabric, "and here." The stones were to be a gift from Selma.

The boy came in from the bazaar balancing a round brass tray atop his dusty, tousled head. He set it down, and Mahmood smacked his crusty red lips as he poured more tea and offered the spicy fried dumplings to Zabo and Shabanu. When they had finished, Mahmood wiped his greasy hands on his *lungi* and pulled down more matched pieces of cotton and silk. Zabo selected one more suit and sat back wearily.

"I've had enough," she said.

"But you've selected only four suits," Mahmood said. "That will be enough only for the *nukkah.*"

"You misunderstand," Zabo said, standing to her full height and meeting his eyes. "I have good taste, or I wouldn't be here, but I am not wealthy enough to spend a fortune on wedding clothes."

"But surely an influential family like yours . . ."

"Please have the *darzi* come to the *haveli* tomorrow morning," she said, brushing past him.

Mahmood followed them to the doorway, wringing his hands.

"But *Begum-sahiba* said you should buy at least a dozen suits. . . ."

"At ten o'clock," Zabo said with finality as she stepped

out into the heat and dust of the street. Shabanu could have hugged her.

They spent the afternoon resting in the *haveli.* Shabanu lay on her silver-legged *charpoi,* with Mumtaz curled in the curve of her waist. She tried to persuade herself that if a betrayal was committed in order to save someone's life, it was not a betrayal. For she was convinced that she must save Mumtaz from Amina and Leyla. But her heart would not be still.

Choti lay at the side of the bed, her delicate hooves tucked under her. Not a breath of air moved in the room, and the mosquito netting hung dry and limp around them without a promise of relief from rain or breeze.

Shabanu heard a soft groan as the door moved slightly, and she raised her head. Zabo pulled up the netting and settled at the end of the bed, her slender brown arms hugging her knees. Small strands of wavy black hair had come loose from the ribbon tied around her head, and the tendrils framed her face softly. Her eyes danced.

Shabanu propped her head on her hand.

"What are you plotting now?" she asked.

"How can we get away from Selma? If she takes us to the gold bazaar . . ."

"Shhh . . ." Shabanu whispered, looking over her shoulder at the door, which still stood open a crack. Zabo climbed out from under the netting and closed it.

Choti raised her head and followed Zabo with her bright eyes. Mumtaz stirred but remained asleep, and the fawn lay her head down again and closed her eyes when Zabo climbed back under the netting and settled beside Shabanu.

"Selma's sympathetic," said Shabanu, still speaking in a whisper. "But we can't risk telling her. Perhaps she doesn't

know how much money you have to spend. Maybe you can
tell her you have less. But stop looking happy. She'll suspect
something!"

Zabo laughed, covering her mouth with both hands.
Shabanu put her finger to her lips. "Zabo, we must be careful of the bodyguards. I have the feeling they're always within
listening distance."

"They're ax murderers," Zabo said, hunching her shoulders forward.

"They certainly look it."

"No, truly! I saw them come back with bloody axes after
my father accused some poor farmer of taking water from a
canal that didn't belong to him." She lowered her voice
further. "They found him months later, stuffed into a well!"

Shabanu shuddered. She wondered whether the farmer
was Lal Khan, Phulan's brother-in-law. His wife had found
him in a well, with his embroidered slippers pointing toward
the sky. How many farmers could Nazir have killed? She
leaned closer to Zabo.

"God help us," she whispered with a shiver. "We will
have to be so careful." Mumtaz woke up and squirmed to
get beyond the heat of her mother's body.

They talked then for a while of normal things in normal
voices, while Mumtaz played with the fawn.

Yazmin called them early to tea, and Zabo arranged her
face somberly. She said little and ate less.

"Come, child," said Selma. "You have to eat. You'll be
sick, and that won't help anything." Zabo sighed and nib-
bled at a biscuit. She was masterful! She didn't overact—
she was simply somber and restrained.

She's probably starving, thought Shabanu.

The next day Ibne dropped Shabanu, Zabo, and Selma at

the edge of the jewelry bazaar, its narrow alleys lined with shop after shop of velvet-cushioned glass cases.

Before some of the long, glistening cases sat customers, wealthy women whose strong European perfumes over-powered the bazaar's scent of spices, wood smoke, and roasting nuts. Behind the cases sat prosperous-looking men in clean white shirts, who offered tea and effusively proclaimed the virtues of their jewelry. The customers acted dramatically unimpressed, pointing out the flaws in the stones and faults in the designs.

The shop owners who were without customers busied themselves arranging and rearranging velvet display stands beneath the polished glass. Gold chains the thickness of a single strand in a spiderweb glinted among displays of dome-shaped earrings encrusted with emeralds and rubies that, in their brilliance, rivaled the feathers of Rahim's caged birds.

A group of women wearing hand-dyed *chadr*s draped over their heads stood before a case of gems that shone more palely than the others. The youngest, a girl of twelve or thirteen, stood on one bare foot, the toes of her other foot rubbing her shin above a heavy silver tribal anklet.

Shabanu thought of the day she'd gone with her father to the gold bazaar at Rahimyar Khan to buy Phulan's jew-elry. They'd been simple desert folk like these. She'd been this girl's age, and the sum of money her father laid on the counter had staggered her. It represented nearly half the proceeds from the sale of their finest camels, half the fami-ly's wealth. But it also had represented her sister's life in-surance. A good dowry should ensure a girl's future with her in-laws. Phulan was lucky—her husband's family would have been kind to her regardless of the dowry. She won-dered how it would be for this girl.

When they reached Selma's favorite shop, the man behind the counter stood and bowed formally.

"Asalaam-o-Aleikum, Begum-sahiba," he said in formal greeting. This man was not obsequious, as Mahmood had been. He seemed genuinely happy to see Selma. His eyes crinkled easily as he spoke, and his smile was natural.

"This is my niece," said Selma, and Zabo kept her head bowed. The man nodded. "She'll be married in just a few weeks, and we need to see a nosepiece and chain, earrings, a head ornament . . ."

The shopkeeper brought out several purple velvet boxes and opened them under their eyes. The head ornament was suspended on gold chains that would be pinned to the hair. It was a gold disk the size of Shabanu's palm, set with pigeon blood rubies and diamonds, and enameled with ground emerald, pearl, and ruby. Tiny pearls were suspended on chains the thickness of hair from its outer perimeter, and a longer chain was attached to a nose ring of sculpted gold with diamonds and rubies outlining it like a halo.

Zabo reached out from under her *chadr* and touched Selma's arm.

"I beg your pardon, Auntie," she said in a shy and tremulous voice. The shopkeeper stepped back to give them privacy.

"I don't believe women should spend their fortunes on jewelry like those poor desert women," said Zabo. She kept her voice low, but it had grown in intensity. She looked into Selma's eyes and tightened her grip on her arm. "It's not right to put a price on a woman's head. This marriage will happen, with or without jewelry."

Selma watched Zabo closely as she spoke, her lips parted slightly. She then looked at Shabanu, who stood holding her breath and watching her friend with admiration. Selma looked back at Zabo's unflinching eyes.

"I see," said Selma, and Shabanu believed she really did understand. Everything. Selma turned to talk to the shopkeeper.

Shabanu slid her eyes toward Zabo, who continued to look straight ahead, her face earnest, while the shopkeeper folded away the velvet boxes and took out others that were smaller.

They settled on an intricately molded gold hoop with a single clear ruby that lay just against the nose. Zabo chose an enameled pendant on a red silk cord to wear around her neck. She couldn't decide on earrings.

"Never mind," said Selma. "I have a lovely pair from my own wedding, and you may wear them. It will be a wedding gift to you."

Zabo looked up at the older woman with glistening eyes.

"Thank you," she said, and Selma squeezed her hand.

That evening Selma served a grand dinner. From the bazaar she'd borrowed cook pots large enough for Mumtaz to hide in and servants from all the neighboring houses.

Rahim's other wives and daughters came from their bungalows, dressed in silk and sequins, their jewels glittering from behind pale georgette *dupattas* drawn demurely across their faces.

After polite greetings murmured at the front gate, Shabanu and Zabo strayed to the kitchen, beyond the range of the other women's scornful eyes. Rahim, Nazir, Omar, Mahsood, and all the other male cousins and nephews sat together, talking earnestly of land and politics.

It was a time of few intrigues for the men, and they were able to relax. The sealing of the brothers' children's wed-

dings and the reuniting of their lands signaled to their enemies that they stood undivided and strong. No rival would
dare challenge them in their time of strength. Shabanu caught
glimpses of Rahim; he smiled often and openly, like a king
secure on his throne.

It was after eleven when the musicians began to tune
their instruments in the courtyard. Everyone moved outside.
A thousand tiny *divali* lamps surrounded the fountain, gleaming from the ancient tiles and burnishing the brick walls of
the outer perimeter of the courtyard; copper oil lamps glowed
from niches spaced every few feet. Dozens of jewel-colored
carpets had been spread over the paving stones of the courtyard for people to sit on. Mirrored and embroidered bolsters
were placed like large kabobs about the courtyard for the
listeners to rest against for the long night ahead. Tuberoses
perfumed the air, and the night seemed to have been planned
by fairies.

The musicians sat on a raised platform decorated with
flowers in tall crystal vases, fine red Persian carpets, and a
shower of tiny electric lights on a velvet curtain behind them.

A man in a plain white *lungi* raised a bamboo flute to his
lips, and a clear melody floated out over them, reminding
Shabanu of the shepherds of her childhood calling their flocks
out to graze in the desert. She could almost hear the animals
respond with a soft symphony of muted bells as they moved
off among the dunes.

Two other men joined the flute player on the platform.
Silver rings gleamed from a pair of hands that kneaded and
coaxed the skin head of a tabla, making the drum speak
eloquently, as if it had several tongues. Beside the tabla player,
a man in a turban that glowed with silver threads had been
tuning a sitar, sending out shimmering notes from string

after string. When he and the instrument were ready, a chord fanned out like the tail of a peacock, and several voices from the men's side of the courtyard murmured, "*Bismillah!*" The audience was lost in a *raga*.

Shabanu leaned back against her bolster, her feet curled under her. It was one of those rare times, she thought, when parts of the ancient world of beliefs and customs and art came together to heal modern troubles with their harmony.

Across the courtyard sat Omar, dressed now in a white silk *shalwar kameez*. He looked more at ease out of his Western trousers. In the loose dress of his childhood, he was long and lanky, his form graceful and natural.

As Shabanu appraised him, he looked away from the musicians and turned his gaze directly on her. His eyes held hers powerfully and tenderly, and suddenly Shabanu knew that this was what her heart had been searching for all her life.

chapter 12

In the days that followed, it seemed all of Lahore was caught up in preparations for the wedding of Omar and Leyla, which was to be in only six weeks.

Although Amina and her coterie were far away in the Cantonment, *tongas* clattered into the courtyard of the *haveli* every afternoon piled high with gifts; *darzis* delivered clothing, and Pathans brought new pieces of furniture to be stored. A row of rickshaws and scooters waited in the narrow lane to make deliveries, setting up a constant clamor and impenetrable screens of dust and exhaust that were trapped in the airless alleyways.

As the heat of the dry season advanced, the glossy leaves of shrubs in red clay pots around the courtyard turned a powdery white with dust, despite twice-daily washings by the *malis*, who moved ever more slowly by the day.

Apart from the wedding activity, life in the *haveli* was as close as it ever came to a standstill. Servants knocked rather than bring tea unasked; meals were left uneaten on rough tabletops in the shade of the banyan tree, as if they'd been brought for ghosts. The flies hovered so lazily they didn't even buzz. Everyone shuffled through the halls and common spaces of the great house, bound for or just returned from naps. Even the children who lived in the lanes were quiet, their play subdued as if there'd been a death in the neighborhood.

Shabanu relaxed far away from the other wives, who were busy socializing in the Cantonment. Even Zabo's bodyguards seemed less vigilant.

Shabanu often felt in those days as if her mind hovered in the driftless air above where she and Zabo sat for long hours talking quietly, sewing and planning. Part of her was there, listening to Zabo plan their trips to the Anarkali Bazaar and describe the kind of imitation jewelry she would buy.

"I do like rubies," she'd say. "But emeralds are very nice. And we must have everything clustered with diamonds." She'd reach forward and lay her hand on Shabanu's.

"This is more fun than real shopping," she'd go on. "I do love jewelry. But if this were real, I'd feel as though I was being bought and sold!"

Which, of course, she was. But Shabanu never said it.

They never discussed the money. It was as if Zabo had entrusted that part to Shabanu, as she had entrusted her with seeing that she would get away from Ahmed and her father, as if that was all that really mattered. Both of them knew she would not be able to endure marriage to Ahmed.

As for Mumtaz and Shabanu, they were safe as long as Rahim was alive. When he was gone they must be ready to step into a new and completely different life, far from Okurabad, far from Amina and the others in the Cantonment. It must be laid out and ready to take on, perfectly prepared as a bride's wedding dress. On those hot and airless days in the *haveli* they felt no harm could come to them. But Shabanu thought about it constantly.

Zabo did not want to discuss anything beyond her plan for the jewelry. But Shabanu knew that having the money accumulate secretly and safely where it would remain until they needed it was as necessary to Zabo as the oxygen she breathed.

There were many obstacles to overcome. But the most difficult of all for Shabanu was one she had not foreseen.

For an important part of Shabanu dwelt on the glimpses she caught of Omar as he came and went from the *haveli* with Rahim, or in the company of his cousins and friends. If he happened to see her, he would stop and watch, his eyes softening at the corners. He sometimes smiled. It made her heart race, and for the rest of the day she found it difficult to concentrate on anything. Her fingers were sore with needle pricks. She went on with her embroidery, although its quality vaguely displeased her.

She knew she was in a dangerous drift, but she had no power to bring it to an end. All she could do was take on projects that made sense to her—to deal with things she could preside over, and wait for a time when she would be able to end the domination of her wild emotions.

So she spent each morning helping Selma screen prospective tutors for Mumtaz. This was something she'd dreamed of and worked toward since Mumtaz's birth, and it occupied her mornings completely. It was real and immediate—not something looming in the future, vague and only half-promising—and she pursued it with optimism.

Several of the women they interviewed needed full-time work. Others were humorless, with hard lines for mouths.

When Shabanu was beginning to fear they'd never find the right teacher, a small, dark Christian widow came to the door and explained that she lived in the *barsati* on the roof across the alley with her two children.

She had enormous energy. Her eyes were bright, her skin dark, her voice high and sweet. She looked like a small brown bird. Her son was a year older than Mumtaz, small, calm, and serious. The daughter was two years younger than her brother, with a lightness of spirit that matched her mother's.

There was much excitement in anticipation of the lessons. Selma ordered an old nursery cleared on the second floor, and a table and chairs were produced. The shutters were mended; reed mats were hung at the windows and doused with water to keep the room cool. The drying reeds smelled like the grass that spilled from broad mowers hauled by oxen around the garden at Okurabad on summer mornings.

Ibne returned from the bazaar one day with a large chalkboard and seven different colors of chalk. Selma and the widow discussed at length the books they would use.

On the morning of the first reading lesson, Shabanu squeezed her knees under the oblong table she shared with Mumtaz and the widow's children. She was enthralled with the smells of the classroom: the chalk dust, the ink on the books, the oil in the wooden floorboards.

"I am taking you to a wonderful new world," said the widow, whose name was Samiya, standing before them for the first time. "Once you've learned to read, adventures you've never even imagined will unfold. You'll visit places you never knew existed. There will be no secret you cannot unlock."

Shabanu's spirits lifted with the thought that knowing how to read could give her a new and extraordinary power over the events of her life.

Samiya turned to close the classroom door. Choti, who

couldn't bear to be shut out of a room where Mumtaz sat, butted her head against its thick wooden planks and had to be taken down to the courtyard and tied beneath the banyan tree.

In the days that followed, Mumtaz proved to be a quick student. Samiya praised her, rewarding her with hugs and boiled sweets in bright cellophane wrappers. Shabanu sat in on every lesson, and within a few days she had finished the children's reader. Samiya brought more advanced readers for her, and Shabanu began to practice her script for a letter to her father. Her father was one of the few men in all of Cholistan who could read. He would be so proud of her!

Rahim was busy with the provincial assembly. And, as usual, it seemed half his constituency had followed him to Lahore. They gathered in the courtyard of the *haveli* each morning, just as they did at Okurabad, hoping to have their petitions presented that day and action taken on their cases. Omar sat beside him quietly, learning and establishing himself in the eyes of the tribesmen as heir apparent.

One day Shabanu sat with Zabo on the balcony above the courtyard, sewing and sipping tea in the morning sunshine, watching the petitioners mill about as they waited for Rahim to appear. Mahsood stood in the doorway, keeping watch and establishing the order in which cases would be presented.

The crowd quieted, and Zabo leaned over the balcony to watch Rahim and Omar enter. Behind them came Ahmed, Mahsood leading him by the hand. Omar sat beside Rahim on the dais, and Shabanu tried not to stare at the square line of his cheekbone, the black fringe of his lashes against his fine light skin. Mahsood settled Ahmed on the floor beside the dais and sat next to him.

Ahmed's hair was still wet with comb tracks. His skin

was soft, and his eyes dark; he looked almost pretty, like a young girl. Mahsood leaned over his shoulder and whispered into Ahmed's ear.

Ahmed managed to sit quietly for a few minutes. But then he began to squirm, and his chin grew shiny with saliva. Mahsood led him from the room. When Ahmed arose from the cushion upon which he'd been sitting, he left behind a wet stain.

Zabo gasped and clapped her hand to her mouth. Shabanu slipped her arm around Zabo's waist and led her from the balcony.

It was the only time Ahmed appeared at the *haveli,* and it took Zabo a week to recover.

For the first time in the years since Shabanu had married Rahim, he spent his nights not with her but across the city in the Cantonment, where dinners and sporting events were arranged by friends to honor him and his brothers and Omar on the approach of this most significant of weddings.

In other times she might have worried about Rahim's shifting attention. Now she was simply grateful to have the time to think of other things, but mainly to untangle the jumble of her feelings.

Also in the Cantonment, a mad whirl of tea parties, shopping, and gossip occupied the women of the family. Shabanu and Zabo were never invited, and Selma would return from the teas and luncheons with tales of the behavior of her spoiled nieces and their in-laws.

"You'd think the only subjects they'd ever studied were jewelry and clothes," she said. "Or who was planning the most enviable holiday. And food. Their expensive educations have been wasted!"

In the *haveli* Shabanu and Zabo and Mumtaz were far

removed from the others. Each morning after Samiya had dismissed her class, Ibne drove Zabo and Shabanu to the furniture maker or the drapery shop or the cloth bazaar, where they searched for fabrics that were hand-printed or handwoven, which they regarded as superior in beauty to the heavy silks that Amina favored for Leyla and which cost only a small fraction of the price.

From inside the shops Shabanu and Zabo watched over their shoulders for the bodyguards, who arrived silently behind them and stood with their guns at their sides.

The women grew impatient for the day they would not appear, when Shabanu was certain Ibne would help arrange for them to visit the Anarkali Bazaar secretly to find the makers of the jewelry that was less than real.

Shabanu spent her evenings decorating *shalwar kameez* for Zabo, Mumtaz, and herself, embroidering each with loving stitches. As her fingers flew over the handwoven fabric, her mind would drift to Omar, regardless of how she'd try to discipline it. While she was stitching a mirror into the intricate patterns she'd made, suddenly his face would appear, and her fingers would be still for a moment.

Thoughts of Omar settled over her days like a sweet haze of sadness, and her nights were filled with longing so that she was constantly in a heightened emotional state. She was easily alarmed, and easily moved to tears. She felt as if her skin had been scalded; she was aware of the faintest movement of air around her.

Then one hot and humid afternoon, a day in which the limp heat seemed to portend the first monsoon rains, Shabanu sat in a swing at the edge of the courtyard. She looked up to see Omar loping along beside Rahim, across the garden toward the *haveli*. His walk was graceful as a shepherd's now that he was accustomed again to wearing *shalwar kameez* and sandals. She went back to her sewing, but her fingers trembled.

A while later, Rahim came looking for her.

"Come have tea with Omar and me," he said. Shabanu looked down. She was not dressed as Rahim liked. She wore her desert clothes: a rough, hand-loomed cotton *shalwar kameez,* a silver ankle cuff, and no shoes. He was never at the *haveli* during the day, and she felt free to dress as she liked.

"Don't worry," he said. "You look like the twelve-year-old girl I first met. Just come."

She slipped her feet into a pair of embroidered leather sandals and followed him into the house. Rahim had never asked her to join him and another man for tea. At Okurabad, Amina was always asked, but never any of the others. When he was in Lahore, Rahim had taken to entertaining in the Cantonment. Shabanu was not his proper Punjabi wife, and everyone was more comfortable with Amina presiding. Shabanu felt tongue-tied and uncomfortable, like the country girl Omar must have thought she looked.

Rahim and Omar talked easily, and neither of them seemed to notice her discomfort. But before the servants even brought the tea tray, Rahim's secretary came into the parlor, where the curtains were drawn against the hot afternoon sun.

The secretary bent from his waist to whisper into Rahim's ear. His large pleated turban hid Rahim's face. The ceiling fans whirred overhead, stirring the hot air lazily. Cobwebs drifted back and forth in the corners, where the hottest air was trapped. High above, the mirrored ceiling winked down at them.

When the secretary straightened to leave, Rahim was frowning.

"Excuse me," Rahim said, standing.

"Shall I come, Uncle?" Omar asked, standing to follow.

"No," said Rahim. "It's Nazir. He will be annoyed if you come. You go ahead and have tea." He left before the secretary, who held the door for him.

"What is Nazir up to now?" Shabanu asked. She looked up, and Omar's eyes were steady on her.

"Nazir is acting beyond his authority," Omar said. "He has befriended the commissioner who took over after Uncle Rahim became a member of the provincial assembly. And now he thinks he can do as he pleases. He is moving the edges of his land into the land of his neighbors, including Uncle Rahim. Everyone is angry with him."

"It hasn't taken long for Pakistan to reclaim you," she said. "You were so exotic, so foreign, when I first met you." They looked at each other for a moment without speaking.

"I have always been a Punjabi in my heart," he said. He spoke with a soft intensity, and for a moment she thought he might touch her. She felt as if she were being pulled along by a strong current toward a place she didn't want to go. But she had no power to resist.

"Tell me about America," she said quickly, breaking the silence.

"In America," he said, "you can be poor one day, living on the street, and the next you can be wealthy. Money doesn't grow on trees, exactly—but nothing is impossible. It's a wonderful place. But I don't mind shedding my American ways. And in one way I've changed forever. I will never again regard women in the old way."

She thought about his habit of including women in conversation and looking into their eyes when he spoke. It was the Cholistani way, and it felt right to her. It was one of the things that drew her to him.

"Do women in America look men in the eye when they speak?" she asked.

"Of course," he said with a small surprised laugh.

"I'm told it's not done in polite society here," she said. "But it's not something I thought of when I was growing up. I never learned not to do it, and it gets me into trouble at Okurabad."

"Yes," he said, still smiling. "I can imagine it does."

"And do women interrupt men in their conversations to give their opinions? I've heard this is so."

"Well, yes, they do . . ."

"Amina told me once that I was brazen as an American," she said. "I thought that was what she meant."

Omar threw back his head and laughed. He had the most wonderful laugh, deep and rich and warm.

"I like it that you're different from the others," he said. "Are you like your father and mother? And your sister?"

"It's very strange," she replied. "My sister and I were born of the same mother and father, even within the same year. We grew up doing exactly the same things, year after year—learning the exact same lessons about cooking and sewing and about the desert and the animals. Phulan thinks as my parents do about most things. But my whole life has been a struggle to appear to be doing what's expected of me while I continue to think as I please."

"And does that also get you into trouble?" he asked.

She nodded.

"Don't ever stop," he said. "It's one of your great charms."

They talked about other things, Shabanu interrupting to ask questions and feeling surges of joy at the simple freedom of being able to speak openly with him. He *is* different from Rahim and his father after all! she thought.

But a loud wail interrupted them, and Shabanu put her hand to her mouth. Mumtaz called to her from the hallway outside the parlor. Shabanu ran toward the sound of her voice. It was high-pitched with alarm. Omar followed.

In the dark corridor, where the air was cooler, Mumtaz struggled to free herself from Zenat, who held her by the wrist. When Mumtaz saw her mother, she broke loose and ran to her.

"Choti is gone! We've looked all over, and she's nowhere. Uncle Omar, help me find her!" She took Omar's hand and tugged him toward the stairway. He stooped and picked up the child in his arms, quieting her for a moment.

"Where have you looked?" he asked Zenat.

The old *ayah* explained that they had searched every room.

"The roof?" he asked.

"Nay, *Sahib,*" Zenat said gravely. "No one will go to the roof. The door is locked, so how could Choti get in?"

Shabanu's heart raced. How could she have relaxed her vigilance, even here in the *haveli*? She felt such a fool! While she was lost in thoughts of a man who could never return her affection, Amina had ordered someone to plant yet another of her evil seeds!

Omar sent Zenat to get three other servants. They were to help search the lower floors of the house again—systematically this time, he admonished. He asked Selma for her huge silver key ring, which she kept tied to her waist at the fold of her sari. The ring held the keys to every door and closet in the house, but Selma handed it to Omar without hesitation. Then he and Shabanu took Mumtaz to the roof to begin a search downward from there.

"I know this house better than any of the servants," he said as they climbed through the still, hot air in the stairway. "I lived here with Auntie Selma and Uncle Daoud when I studied at Aitchison. They were always after me to do my homework, so I found places to hide."

As they got closer to the roof the stairway was narrower, and the air grew closer and warmer. At the top of the last flight, hot white sunlight seeped through the cracks of the locked door that had contained Daoud's ghost for more than fifteen years. One board had been torn loose, leaving a hole big enough for the fawn to slip through.

"Choti's probably up here having a nice chat with Uncle Daoud's ghost," he said. "You aren't afraid, are you?"

Shabanu shook her head, but the hair prickled along her spine all the way up her neck. She did believe in ghosts, but she was sure Daoud's would not harm them.

Mumtaz ran up the last few steps and squeezed through the hole. She turned to peer through at them as they climbed to the top. Her upper lip was misted with sweat, and her chin quivered.

"Uncle Omar, you're wasting time," she said, gulping so she wouldn't cry.

Omar unlocked the door and handed the keys to Shabanu to hold while he pried open the rusty hinges. Shabanu stepped through the old doorway, and it felt as if she'd left behind her a world of trouble for one of . . . of secrets and benevolent ghosts!

"There are many rooms that lead from the roof," Omar said. He dropped to one knee before Mumtaz and put his large hands on her shoulders. "We must start here to look for Choti. It's important to know how the rooms are arranged. We'll go around this way."

From the stone parapet around the large square hole in the center of the roof they could see the courtyards of the floors below, where laundry hung ghostly and limp in the faintest of breezes, and small speckled chickens pecked at bits of grain left over from the *mali*'s morning rounds.

A feather floated over the parapet as a pigeon fled at their approach. Otherwise the roof was completely abandoned, left untouched since the morning of Daoud's death a decade and a half before.

Four floors down, the water in the fountain at the center of the courtyard sparkled and splashed. Only the loudest clanks and rattles were audible from the lanes outside in the walled city.

"We'll all go together. I know every room, and if Choti's here she'll come when you call her," Omar said to Mumtaz, taking her hand again.

He led them through the first doorway to the left of the one that descended into the stairwell. A dim room lit only by a small square window covered by a lattice screen just under the eaves was mounded high with dust-draped shapes that looked like furniture piled on furniture. Their eyes grew accustomed to the light that shone in from the doorway onto painted wall scenes from Mogul courtyards. In them, the bodies of men and women were intertwined amid cushions flecked with gold. Shabanu's breath caught at the beauty of the paintings, and a small sound came from the back of her throat.

"Oh," said Omar, turning toward her. "Maybe you'd rather not look at these." Women should be protected from such lurid scenes.

"No, no," said Shabanu. "They're very beautiful."

She took out the flashlight Omar had given her to ex-

amine the paintings more closely. The scenes had a flat quality to them, but the detail of the figures' hair and fingernails
and eyelashes was minute and intricate.

"I forgot they were here," said Omar. "This is where
Grandfather entertained. . . ." Omar's voice stiffened with
a self-conscious correctness that touched her. She smiled to
herself.

She switched off her flashlight, and they moved on to the
next room.

Mumtaz ran ahead, calling, "Choti, you naughty girl. Please
come. Ple-e-ease!"

Each room was different. The walls of one were covered
with an intricate pattern of mirrors that soared into the
domed ceiling overhead. Omar took the flashlight from Shabanu and aimed it at the dome. Each small piece of mercur-
ated mica tossed the light back at them.

Mumtaz was wild with impatience, and ran always ahead
of them, constantly calling.

Then they reached a very special room, half-hidden behind a mound of debris from some long-forgotten construc-
tion project, and Shabanu thought the heat was playing tricks
with her mind. As they entered she had the sensation that
she'd been there before—the same feeling she'd had when
they'd first arrived at the *haveli*.

It was a garden room, its walls made of sandstone and
marble lattices cut in starlike patterns. Even on this hot and
airless day a breeze blew gently through it, and the air playing lightly through the stone screening sounded like the eternal
breezes of Cholistan.

"This is the summer pavilion," said Omar. "Auntie Selma
and Uncle Daoud used to come here on summer evenings.
Just outside is where they slept the night he was killed."

"Well, if his ghost is here, it's a very pleasant ghost," said Shabanu. "This place is like magic!" Omar laughed.

"I too used to think it was magic. I fled to the roof one day to escape my tutor. To my amazement, someone actually came to the roof looking for me. This was the only place I could reach in time to hide. I was afraid they'd see me because it's so open. From inside it looks as if there are no walls at all. But from the outside you can't see in!"

At that moment Mumtaz came around the corner of the pavilion looking for them, turning her head this way and that, frightened that she too was lost. She went past without seeing them, and Shabanu ran out to her.

They found Choti in a plain room with boxes of papers and disintegrating fabric stacked to the ceiling. The fawn was tangled in an old lace curtain, which had wrapped about her delicate legs. Her face was smeared with torn cobwebs, but her eyes were placid, as if she'd been waiting for them to find her here all along.

Mumtaz threw her arms around Choti's neck.

"Thank you," Shabanu said, looking from Mumtaz to Omar. "Now that Choti has learned to climb the stairs, we must keep her tethered so we don't lose her!"

Omar was watching her, and she was grateful for the duskiness in the room, that he could not see her face color. "Heaven only knows when we would have found her. . . ."

"Just tell me I can visit you in the summer pavilion," Omar said quietly, and Shabanu felt all at once as if her prayers had been answered and that she'd set off on a dangerous and uncharted journey.

chapter 13

Omar's schedule continued to be filled with lavish entertainments arranged by relatives and friends wishing him well in his approaching marriage.

Shabanu heard of caravans of thirty vehicles, carrying as many tents, and fifty servants for week-long hunts for the bustard and other rare birds of Cholistan; of wooden barges rafted six across floating down the Indus River, carrying bands of musicians and tables mounded with food; and of lavish dinners under billowing *shamiyana* with embroidered walls of primary colors in geometric patterns, silver candelabra, and whole oxen roasted outside under the stars.

Shabanu began to guess that Omar had been caught in the moment—that he might have intended to visit her in the summer pavilion but was too busy celebrating his approaching marriage. For more than a week she felt bereft. Then she was angry that he had made a promise he had no intention of keeping.

Overriding her dizzying feelings was a sense of danger. If this went any further, she thought, there would be no turning back. If she and Omar met and Rahim found out—the thought made her shudder. For as kind and gentle as Rahim was, the law of the land prevailed: Shabanu's sin of desiring another man was punishable by death at the hands of her husband.

She knew she must stop thinking of Omar. Still, the thought of him made her emotions swirl within her so that she began to wonder whether she'd lost her senses.

She filled her time with lessons, Zabo's plans, play with Mumtaz, and a secret project.

One still evening when Zabo had gone to bed early, Rahim was out, Selma was going to a reception in the Cantonment, and Mumtaz was asleep, she had supper alone in her room. She was not hungry and was anxious to go to the roof and see what the summer pavilion would need to make it habitable. But she ate anyway, because it had become a habit at Okurabad, where rumors would circulate if a meal tray was returned to the kitchen untouched.

There was a light tap on the door. Selma stuck her head in.

"I wanted to see you a minute before I go out," she said.

"Come in!" said Shabanu, looking up from her dinner. "I'm just finishing." She patted the *charpoi* beside her. She wondered whether the turmoil she felt had found its way to her face and if Selma, who missed nothing, had seen it.

"I don't want to disturb you," said Selma. "I'll stay only a minute."

"I'm finished," Shabanu said. She poured water over her fingers into a small basin and wiped them dry. A servant came and cleared her dishes. This seemed to take a very long time.

"What is it?" she asked, for Selma's brow was furrowed and her hands were clasped before her so tightly that the skin on her knuckles was pale and shiny.

"Has Nazir spoken to you?" Selma asked.

"To me? He's hardly ever spoken to me. Why?"

"Well, it's very odd. I was out behind the kitchen helping Shaheen pluck chickens. Her poor old hands are so arthritic. . . . And I heard Nazir talking to his bodyguards. It seems he wants them to keep watch over you. All this time I thought it was Zabo they were watching. But he said to them: 'If you let the little *Begum* out of your sight, I'll have your ears!' "

"But I don't understand," said Shabanu.

"Listen," said Selma. "Nazir has always coveted what is Rahim's—his land, his house, everything. You are Rahim's youngest and most beautiful wife. Why shouldn't he covet you?"

"If Rahim finds out, he'll have Nazir's head, never mind his ears!" said Shabanu. "Selma, did you know that my father gave me to Rahim because he settled a land dispute between Nazir and my sister's in-laws?"

"Oh, oh!" said Selma, the crease between her eyebrows deepening.

"Nazir tried to kidnap my sister and me. He killed Phulan's fiancé. And then he tried to steal her in-laws' farm! Rahim stepped in and made peace. My father gave me to Rahim to thank him."

"Oh, oh!" said Selma again, plucking at the folds of her widow's white silk sari. Heavy emerald globes hung from her ears, earrings of her great-great-grandmother from the days of the last Mogul emperor. Shabanu recognized them as the earrings Omar had called "Auntie's pigeon eggs."

"So this is the wound to Nazir's pride that will not heal."

Shabanu's heart raced. She should have been paying closer attention to Rahim's troubles. Her preoccupation with Omar had clouded her judgment.

"Oh, Selma!" she whispered. "How do things get so complicated?"

"My brothers bring it upon themselves," Selma said wearily. "These feudal grandees have more pride than sense. They inherit more land than they can take care of, and then they want more. They fill their houses with women and call it duty. The Koran says men should take more than one wife to protect their brothers' widows. But these fellows take as many wives as they want to serve their pleasure! They end up causing mountains of woe."

"I've tried to get along with Amina and the others," Shabanu said.

"I know, child, it's impossible," said Selma, shaking her large gray head. "There are so many good and simple people in the world. But the wealthy make life very difficult for them."

"Perhaps the younger ones, like Omar . . ."

"Bah!" said Selma. "He will end up just like them—or else he won't survive."

Shabanu felt as if she were caught in a hill torrent, the kind that swept down out of the mountains of Baluchistan and wiped out villages and farms and cattle and roads.

"If Mumtaz and I need a place someday . . ." She swallowed hard.

"You and Mumtaz are always welcome here," Selma said, reaching to lay a hand on Shabanu's arm.

When Selma had gone, Shabanu climbed to the roof. It was just as they'd left it, except for the lock, which was missing from the door.

After they had found Choti, Shabanu had slipped the key to the roof from Selma's key ring and tied it into a corner of her *dupatta.* Omar had relocked the door by snapping the old brass lock shut; it did not require the key. She was certain no one would notice that the key was missing from the ring, which had more than three dozen other keys on it: keys to the spice cabinets, the soap cabinets, the food cupboards, the jewelry cupboards—keys to every cupboard and every door to every room in the house. Selma kept the large ring tied at the waist of her white sari at all times.

After Omar had gone and the rest of the household was napping, Shabanu slipped back up to the roof and removed the lock, reattached the key to its ring, and fastened it at her own waist for safekeeping until she could return it to Selma. She replaced the lock with an identical one that she'd brought from Okurabad for her trunk. She wore the key on a chain around her neck.

The last amplified strains of the muezzins calling the faithful to prayer at neighborhood mosques hung in the air. It was just sunset, and the light was still golden and pink around a wide margin of the sky. The fat domes of Badshahi Mosque still glistened at the edge of the walled city through the early evening haze.

Yes, she thought, I must remember. There are so many good people in the world. Mumtaz and I can survive. But we must get away from Amina and Saleema and Tahira and Leyla. And Nazir. And Omar.

The *haveli* looked down over the rooftops of several houses in the immediate neighborhood, and Shabanu could see many dramas of family life unfolding in the dusk below. Some electric lights came on, and many oil lamps flickered to life. Women brushed the hair of little girls, cleaned vegetables, bathed babies in large buckets; cats stretched on waking from naps to hunt mice among the grain cupboards; and men in close-fitting crocheted caps squatted in twos and threes in doorways, smoking *hookah*s.

One day Mumtaz and I will have a normal life like these people, she promised herself.

Her plan to furnish the pavilion took on new urgency. She felt powerless over the other events in her life. A battle between desire and the certain knowledge that loving Omar was too dangerous to contemplate ground on within her endlessly. No wonder she was exhausted. With her every ounce of will she vowed again that she would keep him from her mind.

She sat and watched until it grew dark, then took out the flashlight Omar had given her and went to the room where shrouded furniture was piled to the ceiling. She searched through the dusty piles for small treasures to furnish the summer pavilion.

"For the sake of Mumtaz," she murmured to herself over and over as she worked in the pavilion.

In a week's worth of evenings searching through musty rooms filled with draperies and cushions and broken pieces of furniture, she found several beautifully embroidered pillows and bolsters from which she pounded clouds of ancient dust. She arranged them in the corners of the pavilion as places where she might read and play her flute and think. In one corner she placed two carved and enameled *charpois* where she and Mumtaz might sleep in their summers together in the *haveli*.

Perhaps, she thought, next she would clear the room beside the pavilion for them to sleep in during the winters.

She uncovered low, carved chairs and tables from the Valley of Swat that she rubbed with oil until they shone darkly, and placed them together. She found a small, low writing table and a cushion to sit on, where she could write to her father and where Mumtaz could do her lessons.

And she unearthed and polished four old brass lamps with

cut-crystal chimneys. She asked Samiya to bring her scented oil from the bazaar so that she might stay up and study while the rest of the *haveli* slept. And she filled the lamps in the pavilion so she could come there to read and write.

The activity made her feel she was doing something to protect herself and Mumtaz and Zabo in case of trouble. Her notion of what exact form that trouble might take was dim, but nevertheless she perceived it as a concrete threat.

She arranged the furniture in clusters, with no particular divisions within the pavilion, so that the chairs and tables looked as if they had floated and perhaps come to rest at random. She liked their inadvertent harmony.

When she finished at the end of the week, she looked around with satisfaction. It was what she had always wanted: a place of her own. And no one else even knew about it. She loved Selma for offering her a place at the *haveli* without asking questions. Selma knew that Shabanu and Mumtaz could never stay at Okurabad or in the Cantonment if anything happened to Rahim.

By day she concentrated on her work, on her plans with Zabo, on her books—on anything but Omar, or Rahim's troubles with Nazir. If Omar appeared unsummoned before her mind's eye, she banished him quickly with the thought that in just a few weeks he would be not merely unavailable to her as he was now; as Leyla's husband, he was likely to be her enemy.

Being surrounded by danger made it easier to keep from hoping to talk to Omar or from seeing his face in her sewing.

She imagined Omar as an enemy until she could not hear his name or catch a glimpse of him without seeing also the hot green glint of Leyla's eyes, the crimson flash of her pampered fingernails, her languid repose after executing one of Amina's evil tricks.

As Omar's image was suffused with Leyla's evil, it became habitual for Shabanu to regard him with a certain remoteness. She concentrated on the evil aspects, the danger Omar represented to her and to Mumtaz, and hoped that her feelings for him would subside altogether.

Her immediate world was inhabited by slow—and often suspended—motions. Very little happened in the *haveli* in early summer. The lazy cadences of waking, studying, eating, gossiping with Selma over amusing anecdotes about life in the Cantonment, and Rahim's increasingly occasional visits were punctuated by brief, rapid, secret exchanges with Zabo about a series of planned visits to the Anarkali Bazaar.

Still she didn't tell Zabo about the pavilion. The danger Shabanu perceived also included Zabo, who remained unwilling to concentrate on anything in the future except for the task she now had before her. Shabanu could hardly blame her.

Zabo had researched the subject of the almost-real jewels meticulously. She had been cunning with her confidences—and had won not only the acquiescence of Selma and Ibne in her scheme, but their complicity as well. So great was their faith in her, they helped her find the places she sought without once asking why.

Shabanu marveled at the skill of her friend. Zabo, whom Shabanu had loved for her directness in their world of shamelessly manipulative women, had worked together the strands of her bravery, the cruelty of her betrothal, the sympathy of the only trustworthy souls in the *haveli,* and a knowledge of the process of making disingenuous jewels into a plot so fine and seamless that Shabanu imagined it couldn't fail.

With an innocence as pure as Zabo's bridal linens, Ibne had scouted out the finest jewelry establishments in the bazaar. He brought samples—both real and less than real—for Zabo's approval, until she was satisfied that there was no discernible difference between them.

"These days even the finest experts need electronic instruments to pick a red zircon from a row of rubies," Zabo explained. "They even make them with the tiniest flaws . . ."

She held up a ruby necklace with a jeweler's monocle for Shabanu to inspect the stones.

"See how toward one side of the large stone it turns slightly cloudy? The stone has been cut so that the facets sparkle around the cloudy plane. The stonecutter must have been a master!"

Shabanu saw only blood-red glitter through the eyepiece. "Well, even if the stones aren't real, the work of such a master would make this very expensive. . . ."

Zabo clapped her hands with delight and laughed. "That's just it! The stone maker turns out thousands of stones with this same imperfection. But there are enough counterfeiters these days that the jewelers have a huge selection of fake stones and can match them with zircons of similar cut and color. They're just imperfect enough to seem real."

"But the gold must cost . . ."

"Don't be silly! It's rolled gold," said Zabo. "Bite into it and see."

Shabanu tried to find a piece of the setting large enough to test with her teeth. The piece was so encrusted with stones that there wasn't enough gold to bite into. Zabo clapped her hands and put them over her laughing mouth. She took

back the necklace and handed it over Shabanu's head to
Ibne.

"Well done," she said. "I think we're ready to discuss
prices."

Ibne nodded, then hesitated a moment.

"I believe your father's guards will be taking their guns
to the gunsmith tomorrow afternoon," he said gravely. "It
seems someone dropped sweet tea into the mechanisms. Your
father would not be happy with them for being so careless.
I've assured them that I will take full responsibility for your
welfare, and I've promised not to breathe a word about their
misfortune."

"Thank you, Ibne," Zabo said. "Perhaps tomorrow would
be a good day to visit the Anarkali Bazaar?"

"Yes, no doubt," he said. "Will that be all?"

"Yes, thank you," Zabo said.

Shabanu felt her eyes grow wider as she looked from one
face to the other. After what Ibne had been through because
of Amina and Leyla, Shabanu was amazed that he would
dare to take part in Zabo's elaborate scheme!

That same evening Rahim came to spend the night with
Shabanu. She had thought several times about how seldom
he came to see her, and that somehow she should be more
concerned that Tahira or another of his wives had rekindled
his interest. Or, worse, there might be someone new—
someone he'd met in the Cantonment, perhaps. But she'd
been so wrapped up in thoughts of Omar and Zabo's plans
and in learning to read that she'd welcomed the diversion
of his usually earnest attention.

That evening, however, she took special care with her
makeup and wore a new turquoise and purple *shalwar kameez*
that brought out the blue-green flecks in her gray eyes. She

served his favorite mint tea and tried to amuse him with talk about Mumtaz's progress and the antics of Choti—things that ordinarily would have charmed him.

Her heart was not fully in her chatter, but Rahim never noticed.

His mood was grim and fretful, and he fell asleep without even holding her in his arms. As she lay on her side with her back to him, Omar crept into her thoughts again. She pushed him away, but his face appeared in her mind, and regardless of her efforts to keep him away she could not. It made her dizzy with a sense of failure, and she was relieved that Rahim was not interested in her.

Once again she conjured up images of the danger that meeting Omar posed. Still she could not stop the desire for him that welled up and left her feeling hollow with longing. She stayed awake the rest of the night so that he could not creep into her dreams.

Very early the next morning, Shabanu heard Zabo's rapid light tap on her door. She moved quickly out of bed and to the door, grabbing her shawl from the nightstand and wrapping it about her shoulders in one motion.

She held her finger to her lips and opened the door just an inch, to where she knew the old iron hinges would begin to groan. Zabo was dressed, and her long slender fingers fluttered in frustration when she realized Shabanu was not alone. She formed the words "Anarkali Bazaar" with her lips, drew a necklace around her neck with her fingers, while her eyes danced, then pointed to her delicate wristwatch to indicate that they would leave in one hour. Shabanu raised her shoulders and eyebrows to say she wasn't sure she could be ready. Zabo nodded, then went away.

Rahim was just turning under the linen bed sheet when

she came back, and as she sat down on the bed he got up from it heavily, as though he too had not slept.

"What is it, Rahim?" she asked. "What's wrong?"

He waved his hand at her to be still, not impatiently, and shook his head as he wrapped his dressing gown around his middle.

"Nothing for you to worry about, my dearest." His hearty formality again—he used it like a mask. Shabanu took a deep breath.

"Rahim, you haven't been in this bed for two weeks," she said. "And when you do come, you might as well be sleeping alone in any other bed in the world."

He stopped for a moment, and when he turned back to her he smiled faintly, as if he'd forgotten how.

"Whose bed did you think I'd been in?" he asked.

She lowered her eyes and didn't deny that it had occurred to her that he might have a new love interest. Or perhaps that he'd tired of her. He seemed to forget his worries for a moment to delight in her display of jealousy. But for the first time Shabanu identified her feelings toward her husband as being more daughterly than wifely.

"There will be plenty of time for us later," said Rahim with a small, soft laugh. "It's just Nazir. His little demands keep increasing by the day. He's trying to make this bloody wedding of Zabo and Ahmed into a more prominent event than Omar's wedding. He's a terrible nuisance!"

"Rahim, I've never seen you so disturbed," she said. "Surely it's not just Nazir's demands over the wedding . . ."

But he pushed past her and dressed without another word, not even about breakfast, and was gone by the time the servant came to the door with a bed tea tray for both of them.

*   *   *

Shabanu had grown so accustomed to the cool, quiet world inside the *haveli* that leaving it was a shock. She felt like a jackal coming out of its lair after the winter and finding the world inhospitable—bright, hot, dusty, and noisy. She pulled her *chadr* over her face, and Zabo did the same as they left by a heavy wooden door that usually remained closed to a small and particularly filthy side lane outside the mud walls.

The *tonga-wallah* was waiting with his horse and cart where Ibne had said they'd be, outside the gate and down the lane toward the small tiled shrine at the corner.

Shabanu watched her feet, for the lane was littered with fruit and vegetable peels, goat droppings, and filthy gray water splashed up from the slimed gutters on either side of the mud paving.

The *tonga* was worn and dusty, as was the pony, which stood with its head down like a flower wilted in the merciless sun. The *tonga-wallah* clucked, and the poor gray pony reluctantly raised his head and, in a shuffling trot under cracks of the whip, made his dusty way from Bhatti Gate to Lohari Gate, where Zabo took out a small map drawn by Ibne to guide them on foot through the maze of lanes to the Anarkali Bazaar.

The map led them under canopies; past shops selling wedding garlands strung with tinsel, rupee notes, and flowers; past posters with pictures of sinister-looking politicians plastered on the walls beyond Bhatti Gate; past the icicle-shaped stone Hindu temple, long since abandoned and fallen into disrepair; past the bustling Bannu Bazaar, where they had bought Zabo's real gold jewelry; and into the Anarkali Bazaar, where counters overflowed with audiotapes and plastic buckets, and Western-style rock music blared over loudspeakers.

As they picked their way down ever narrower lanes, Shabanu thought of Anarkali, the young harem girl in the court of the Mogul Emperor Akbar.

The emperor's son, Prince Salim, fell in love with Anarkali, who was named for the delicate beauty of the pomegranate blossom. One day Anarkali returned Salim's smile, sending Akbar into a jealous rage. The emperor ordered Anarkali buried alive. When Salim became the Emperor Jahangir, he built a magnificent tomb in her memory.

I have been like Anarkali, thought Shabanu, buried alive all these years. And I never knew it until I fell in love.

Passersby and shopkeepers stared at the two young women, some of the tradesmen leaning over their counters to watch them walk past. Dozens of pairs of eyes followed their shrouded forms as they floated through the chaotic lanes. For although their bodies were covered, their gold bangles clinked on their slender arms as they gestured, a cloud of floral scent trailed after them, and their high, soft voices sounded like bells on the hot summer air.

chapter 14

It was just less than a month before Omar's wedding, and still he had not come to the pavilion. Shabanu refused to think of him. She had prepared a small speech to deliver to him—if ever he should appear—about the risks she faced by meeting him, and how it just wasn't possible. . . .

Still his face appeared unbidden before her as she sat, late into the summer nights, embroidering clothes for Mumtaz, Zabo, and herself, and coverlets and bolsters for the pavilion.

A soft breeze blew through the stone screens, and Shabanu knew with certainty that here, high above the stench of the gutters and the dusty alleys, blew the only cool breeze in all of Lahore. But the thin wicks of the lamps burned straight and true behind their crystal chimneys, and the pavilion glowed like her old Auntie's brass water pots in Cholistan's winter sun.

She reached into her sewing basket, which she'd used to carry up her belongings, the things she'd brought as a child from the desert and carried to Lahore, then over the last two weeks, one or two at a time, to the summer pavilion. She took from it a pile of rupee notes, wrapped in white cloth and stitched at the edges in a thick oblong bundle. She placed it on the table.

Zabo had handed it to her with her eyes closed.

"I don't know how much there is, and I don't want to know," she'd said. "I don't want to know where you keep it. Just keep it safe."

Three intermediate Urdu readers were stacked on Shabanu's desk beside a newly sharpened green pencil and a tablet of rough white paper with gray lines. Beside that lay another bundle of handmade paper upon which Shabanu intended to write her father.

On the low lacquered table lay her most prized possession—the small wooden flute carved by her grandfather, a warrior in the army of the last of the Abbasid princes. She could see him clearly, his large white turban nodding as he worked beside a fire of *khar* twigs, its acrid smoke twisting like a blue ribbon toward the stars.

In the corner of the room stood a large red clay milk jar, an important part of a Cholistani girl's dowry. It had stood empty all these years at Okurabad, and she'd had Ibne bring it back when he took Rahim home for one of his tribal meetings.

Shabanu took her scissors from the sewing basket and snipped slowly and deliberately at the threads that bound the money. She unwrapped the muslin. Inside were not one but two stacks of notes—not ten-rupee notes but five-hundred-rupee notes, all blue and crisp from the bank, still stapled at one end. A *lakh*—one hundred thousand rupees—enough for them to live on for years!

Zabo had never said how much Nazir had given her to

spend on the dowry. But she had already spent tens of thousands, and this was only part of what he'd sent to pay her bills. Shabanu remembered Rahim's bribe of hundreds of acres of land and knew he had made Nazir promise to be generous with Zabo, who was his only daughter.

She rewrapped the notes and restitched them carefully into two bundles that would fit into the milk jar. She was about to cross to the corner of the room where it stood when she heard a quiet footstep outside. Her heart flew into her mouth, and she moved quickly to the tall jar. She laid the bundle in the bottom and was just replacing the lid when a shadow fell over the doorway.

"Who is it?" she asked. "What are you doing here?" Her voice was calm, but she felt tense and strong, ready to defend her aerie.

"It's me. Omar. May I come in?"

Shabanu's heart hammered, and the back of her throat was so dry she was unable to say anything.

"Forgive me," he said, looking through the doorway to see her standing with her hands crossed over her chest. "I wanted to talk to you."

"You *frightened* me!" she said. She sounded angry but relieved. She ran her hands through her hair and then clasped them in front of her.

"Do you want me to go?"

"No . . . no," she said. "It's just . . ."

"I understand you don't want anyone to know about this place," he said. "I didn't want to intrude on you, but I had to see you."

"No, I was going to say I'd expected you—but . . ."

"I meant to come sooner, but I thought . . ."

"Selma's been telling us about the parties and hunts and

dinners." The speech she'd prepared fled from her mind, and she couldn't remember anything she'd meant to say to him.

"I haven't been able to get you out of my mind since the day we first came here. I've had to fight myself not to come looking for you. The risk is enormous, especially with Uncle Nazir's guards following every move you and Zabo make."

He watched her intently while he talked, as if to see whether she understood what he was saying.

Shabanu felt weak and trembly as a newborn camel. She didn't trust her voice, and so she nodded. She was grateful that he understood the seriousness of their meeting. Again she thought of Anarkali, of Akbar's rage, and of the horrible price Anarkali had paid for love.

Omar looked past her shoulder and into the room.

"Would you like to come in?" she asked then.

He looked at the old-fashioned furnishings and the mirrored embroideries that cast light from the oil lamps in little fairy dots all over the room.

"It's a room only you could have made," he said.

They crossed the golden pools of light that the oil lamps made on the stone floor to the Swati chairs and the low lacquered table. Omar reached out and picked up her bamboo flute.

"Can you play?"

"I used to," she replied. "That's how we called our animals in the desert. But it's too sad to play and not hear their bells as they move among the dunes. . . . I haven't played since I left Cholistan."

Shabanu adjusted her *chadr* around her shoulders and looked across the table at Omar. Now, she told herself. Tell him now that he can't come here anymore, that he can't meet you anywhere, or speak to you. The lamp on the desk lit the fine straight line of his cheek from behind, like a halo.

"I have loved being back in the Punjab," he said. "Until now I haven't thought about America at all."

"And what makes you think of it now?" she asked.

"I've told you anything is possible there," he said. "It makes people think differently. Here so much is not possible, and people learn not to think of what cannot be. I know I should think that way about you. But I can't."

His words were accompanied by the graceful gestures of his large, smooth hands. She remembered the feel of them on her hands. His hair was glossy, his skin smooth, his voice deep, the planes of his cheek and chin and shoulder straight— all of his textures were clean and strong. They made her ache with longing and sadness.

Stop it! she said to herself. Stop it now!

As she sat watching his lean figure folded gracefully into the small Swati chair, a warning came to her from her Auntie Sharma: "Don't ever fall in love," Sharma had said. "It will ruin your judgment."

Now she knew what Sharma meant. Here she was with everything at stake, and all she could think of was how it felt when Omar touched her. She'd never expected her heart to be so stubborn about having its way. She prayed to Allah to give her the strength to discipline her feelings.

For the sake of Mumtaz, she said to herself. And that time it caught hold, and there was no turning back.

"I have learned to live with what is possible," she said quietly.

"I don't believe you," he said.

She couldn't look at him for fear she'd tell him what was in her heart.

"You are the girl who could never obey. You are too direct to hide your feelings from me. You can't tell me you don't care for me."

She could not let him know how she felt. He would try to persuade her to give in to her feelings, and she couldn't do that. She had to lie.

Allah, give me strength, she prayed. For the sake of Mumtaz, for the sake of Mumtaz.

"You are wrong," she said, looking directly at him. "In America do men respect the wishes of women?"

He looked at her with disbelief.

"Do they?"

He nodded.

"Then take the best of what you learned of duty in Pakistan and of respect in America, and leave me in peace." Her voice was firm and steady, and she knew she was convincing.

Without speaking, Omar stood and left. She didn't look up until he was gone. She saw him pass the outside wall of the pavilion and heard his footsteps recede into the stairwell.

When he had gone, she bowed her head and let the grief engulf her. Her heart crumpled and shrank, like a ball of paper set on fire.

chapter 15

Shabanu didn't see Omar the rest of that week or the next, as the social whirl surrounding the weddings increased to what seemed to her a maddening crescendo.

She had been right, she told herself again and again. Omar would have jeopardized all her plans—for Zabo, Mumtaz's education, her marriage to Rahim, their very lives. And there was no possibility of a future. But there was no comfort in being right.

She tried to keep busy, but each afternoon she was drawn into the courtyard or up into the pavilion, where she sat still as a pool of water. It was as if she feared she'd fly into a million pieces if she moved.

Late each afternoon the women of the Cantonment, still dressed in their finest *shalwar kameez* from lunch or early tea, piled into their air-conditioned limousines to be driven to watch matches at the Lahore Polo Club.

One day Selma insisted that Zabo and Shabanu join her.

"I won't have you two moping about," she said.

They sat at the end of a row in the section reserved for

Omar's team. The field was green and cool-looking in the late-afternoon sun. A breeze played over them, ruffling their hair and clothing, refreshing them.

Amina and Leyla sat in the middle of the row of women like two large roses in sunglasses. They were surrounded by their relatives and friends, eating chicken on gray paper napkins and sipping lemonade.

The men sat separately, most of them dressed in riding clothes, their handmade leather boots gleaming in the late sun.

On the playing field, Omar sat tall and straight on his bay mare, his green shirt matching the mare's leg wraps. The horses thundered up and down the field. When the bell sounded to end the chukker, he rode with his mallet on his shoulder at a trot past the women and tipped his cap. When he got to the end where Shabanu sat, his eyes went straight to hers.

Her heart leaped into her mouth. She loved him totally, without hope. The rest of the afternoon she sat still as a stone.

After the match, Omar returned to the end of the field where his team celebrated their victory over the very best army team. He did not play in the next match. He came to sit in his boots and his green shirt and white jodhpurs, looking painfully handsome and at ease amid the giant roses of Okurabad.

Not once did Shabanu look in their direction. But she heard peals of feminine laughter as Omar teased and joked with his cousins, among them his bride-to-be.

It was a very modern notion, almost scandalous, a betrothed pair socializing together so close to the wedding. They spoke in Punjabi, and Shabanu understood little of what was said. But it sounded very sophisticated, very foreign to Shabanu. She imagined this was how young people in America socialized.

She felt like a bird with clipped wings. She felt thoroughly excluded from their camaraderie—like an outcast. Omar's voice sounded as if it were the voice of another person, one totally unknown to her. While it sounded relaxed, it also sounded formal; where it expressed humor, it lacked the warmth and gentleness that she associated with him. It sounded somewhat cruel. Suddenly she sensed the enormous distance between herself and Omar, and the gulf felt like a physical illness.

"Are you unwell?" Selma asked. "Your face is pale."

Shabanu managed a nod.

"I must get out of the sun," she replied.

Shabanu left with Zabo and Selma before the next match. Amina and Leyla leaned forward in their seats to watch as they walked down the long row of spectators.

"Shabanu is ill?" someone asked. "Why doesn't she cast a spell and cure herself?" And a small titter of wicked laughter followed them the length of the stands.

Had she heard Omar's laugh among them? She thought perhaps it was her imagination.

In the days that followed at the *haveli,* darkness tortured Shabanu's heart. She had hoped to find comfort in the small motions of everyday life: Samiya's arrival for lessons, trips to the bazaars with Zabo, naps with Mumtaz in the oppressive afternoon heat, tea with Selma, and evenings spent writing in the summer pavilion. But every move required the utmost concentration of effort.

She tried to find hope everywhere, but it eluded her until

she fell into an almost paralyzing torpor. This was how Anarkali must have felt, Shabanu thought, suffocating in her tomb.

When Mumtaz asked a question, she had to force herself to concentrate on every word, and then to think hard to find an answer.

During their morning lessons Samiya would ask Shabanu to read aloud. Often Shabanu did not hear and was unable to find her place in the book. Samiya cocked her little head and looked at Shabanu quizzically.

Selma clucked over her at meals, and Shabanu forced herself to eat. Zabo seemed not to notice.

Shabanu felt she'd been caught up in a rush of time that ran for someone else, most certainly not for herself. She felt life was passing by without her. And yet the hours crawled past so slowly she thought she would never reach the end of each day. She felt better when she was alone in the pavilion in the evenings. At least there she didn't have to pretend to anyone.

Then she decided she must do something to shake herself out of this state of paralysis. She began to keep a diary about everything except Omar in the hope that the appearance of normalcy would gradually become reality.

"Zabo's stash of money has grown enormous," she wrote. "This week two more bundles of rupees lie in the bottom of my milk jar. We now have more than two *lakhs*—enough, if we live modestly, to keep us for more than ten years."

Still she told no one about the pavilion. And as time passed she grew more confident that no one would ever invade the roof and see her haven. Zabo slept early each night, tired by the heat and the fervor with which she pursued her plan to purchase clothing and jewelry that made it appear she had spent the entire fortune her father had given her on an elaborate dowry.

Every time Shabanu heard a whistle outside in the courtyard, she would steel her heart and think, I won't die if I see him. Each time she heard a footstep in the hall she pretended she'd heard nothing at all. She saw him once from Zabo's window, which looked out over the courtyard. She felt as if she were on fire, but he didn't look up. She barely survived, utterly without hope.

Then one day Rahim came unannounced into the parlor at the *haveli* after Samiya's lessons were finished, and said they would return to Okurabad the next morning.

"You should be packed and ready to leave by seven," he said brusquely, then turned to leave. It was the first time Shabanu had seen him in more than a week.

"Just a moment!" Shabanu said, her words hard-edged. "Why, may I ask, are we leaving?" She was tired of allowing herself to be buffeted about by her feelings. She was tired of doing what everyone else wanted, of meeting the demands of others, of being without hope for herself. The anger felt good, as if it released the flow of blood into her veins again.

The air in the room was still as everyone stopped what they were doing to look at her. Mumtaz, who had been working to prepare for the next day's lesson, sat with her pencil poised in the air, her eyes round with surprise. Selma's rocking chair stopped suddenly in midmotion, appearing to defy gravity. Zabo, who had been gazing distractedly out the window, suddenly paid attention. Even Choti's ears and nose were still.

Rahim stopped in midstride and turned back toward her, astonishment briefly displacing the lines of worry that had occupied his face for so long.

"Will you excuse us, please?" Rahim asked, and animation was restored in the room as Selma herded Zabo and Mumtaz out the door and upstairs to pack.

"Why didn't you give us warning, instead of ordering us about like so many sheep?" she asked, the tension still high in her voice. "What's so important that we should interrupt Mumtaz's progress with her lessons and shopping for Zabo's wedding?"

"Zabo and Ahmed will be married in three days," Rahim said quietly, avoiding her eyes.

Shabanu let out her breath in a rush, as if someone had kicked her in the stomach. She must get word to Sharma!

"But . . . why?"

"Because Nazir won't agree to the wedding otherwise. What difference does it make? Selma says Zabo is ready."

"Yes, Zabo is as ready as she ever is likely to be," she said. Why would Nazir insist on changing the timing? And why would Rahim agree? Of course, she thought, the wedding *would* be less conspicuous in the country, where the family and all clansmen would rejoice. There really was no need for a big city celebration. . . .

Rahim turned and left before she could say anything else, and Shabanu ran into the dark, hot hallway to find Zabo. Selma caught her there and held her by the arm.

"I've already told her," Selma said. "She's not happy, but she's resigned. Samiya will come with me to help at Okurabad. Don't worry. Zabo wants to see you. She's in my sitting room. I'll be along in a minute."

It was the first time in a week that Shabanu felt something other than grief. It was as though she had wakened from a deep sleep.

She ran to the second-floor sitting room next to Selma's bedroom. Zabo looked pale and stunned, but she came to Shabanu and hugged her.

"Don't worry," Shabanu whispered fiercely. "I am going to Aab-pa the *hakkim* now to send word to Sharma. She will come as soon as it's safe. We have a plan, and it will work. But we must be cautious. I'll leave the money hidden here. It's too dangerous to carry it. Don't worry," she whispered again, holding Zabo at arm's length and giving her a gentle shake.

"Someone will find it!" said Zabo.

"No," said Shabanu. "It's hidden where no one has been for fifteen years. I am the only one who knows the place."

"Everything will be fine," Zabo said softly. "I trust you. I won't worry."

Mumtaz was the only one happy to return to Okurabad.

"Choti needs fresh air," she said, stroking the fawn's ears. Choti blinked serenely.

"Mumtaz, please go with Auntie Zabo to pack," Shabanu said. "Tell Zenat to be sure to get all Bundr's clothes. I'll be there in a minute."

Zabo took Mumtaz by the hand, and Choti followed them. Before Zabo turned to go, Shabanu looked her in the eyes. Her friend smiled faintly, and Shabanu smiled back. They would make it, she thought. Somehow she had to keep her wits about her and, God willing, they would all survive.

Selma came in then and dropped herself wearily into one of her threadbare chairs.

"I've been worried about you, child," Selma said as soon as she'd caught her breath.

"I've been very strained," Shabanu replied carefully. "But I'm feeling better now." She was certain Selma knew untruth as well as she knew truth, and Shabanu didn't want to make the older woman suspicious and set her to guessing.

"The hard times are just beginning," Selma said as she clicked open her rosewood fan and moved it back and forth in front of her large, pale face. "You mustn't lose heart now."

Shabanu felt a twinge in her chest, as if the great, gaping blackness inside her had begun to contract, as if her heart was healing.

"Why is the wedding to be now?" Shabanu asked.

Selma sighed and smoothed the ever-unruly wisps of gray hair into the bun at the back of her neck.

"I only know that was Nazir's demand," Selma said. "It fills me with foreboding." She clicked her fan shut then and hefted herself to her feet. "It's time we got ready," she said.

Shabanu went to her room. First she reached into her cupboard for her worn canvas suitcase and filled it with the *shalwar kameez* she'd been embroidering for Zabo's wedding.

Then she went to the stairway that led from the courtyard to the roof. The *mali* was scattering one last handful of maize for Selma's spotted courtyard chickens before wandering off for his afternoon nap. His thin ankles were the last part of him to disappear into the hard-edged shadow of the first-floor balcony. When he was gone, Shabanu ascended out of the lazy afternoon heat through the stifling, cobwebbed stairway up to the pavilion, which sat shimmering on the roof.

In the doorway Shabanu paused for a second to savor the cool, calm interior that she had created. She crossed to the milk jar, which stood in one corner of the room. She removed the lid and lifted out a tray of thread spools, a bundle of letters from her father, her diary, and a flat piece of round baked mud that made a false floor in the jar, which stood as high as Shabanu's waist. Under that were the bundles of five-hundred- and one-thousand-rupee notes, all stitched neatly in muslin bundles.

She counted more than enough for Mumtaz, Zabo, and herself to live into their old age in the desert with Auntie Sharma.

She folded the treasure back into the jar and replaced all of her other treasures with a silent prayer: "Allah be praised," she whispered. "With this wealth waiting for us in Lahore, we will make our plan work and stay in Cholistan until it is safe to return."

Then she put an old black *chadr* over her head and climbed back down to the courtyard. She took off her sandals and held them in one hand as she ran lightly as a breeze to the back gate. It was deep into the time for afternoon naps, and she heard loud snores from the servants' quarters. She had no trouble going unseen out the rear gate into the small alleyway behind the *haveli*.

Shabanu bent to put on her sandals and picked her way through the alley, the *chadr* wrapped around her face loosely in folds that covered all but her eyes.

At the intersection of the lanes she stopped and untied the corner of her *chadr*. She withdrew a many-times-folded paper on which Sharma had drawn a map. It led her down an alley where shirtless men sat stirring large kettles of milk over open fires as if in slow motion, and down another alley where men sat hammering sheets of copper into flat pans for making *kulfi,* and down another where men sat before machines that clanked and whirred, and down yet another where men welded small bits of metal over gas jets.

In the midst of this lane she stopped before an open doorway. The green paint that identified it as the place she wanted was worn to a faint tint embedded in the wood grain. She knocked lightly.

"Come in," said a sweet, soft voice.

She stooped through the doorway into an unremarkable brick hut with a roof of corrugated metal that seemed held on more by hope than gravity. It was surprisingly cool and dark inside.

"Come in, come in," the voice said again, from a room beyond a black curtain. "I won't bite." The voice was mild, with a humorous, kindly impatience.

Shabanu pulled back the curtain and bent to pass through the tiny doorway; she entered a small room with a high window that admitted some of the hot white light from the lane without letting in any heat.

Aab-pa sat in the center of the room on a red satin-covered cushion surrounded by fat embroidered bolsters. The opulence of the fabrics seemed oddly out of place against the smooth dirt floor and the rough brick walls. Strewn about him were yellowed, curling charts, unrolled and anchored with bits of broken pottery and pieces of stone, teacups, and amulets.

He was a rotund little man in a white *lungi* with a robe thrown across his shoulders. He wore an angelic expression on his face, which was so smooth and round it looked like the face of an infant, except for startlingly wise and compassionate eyes that peered out from under a loosely wound turban.

The walls of the small room were lined with jars and bottles of various colors, sizes, and shapes. Overhead a canopy of dried plants gave off a musty smell.

He asked Shabanu to sit, and with one foot he pushed a small flat cushion toward her so she wouldn't have to sit on the bare earthen floor.

"I've been expecting you," he said before Shabanu had even said who she was. "I can get a message to Sharma tonight."

"Please let her know that Zabo will be married at Okurabad in three days," she said. "It's much earlier than we'd expected. Please tell her we need her before the time we'd agreed on."

"It will be done," he said simply. He had neither written down what she'd said nor asked questions.

The *hakkim* then shifted his whole attention to Shabanu for the first time since she entered the room. He asked about Mumtaz and about Choti. He questioned her closely, as if the small deer somehow was the key to solving a very serious problem.

Then just as abruptly he stopped asking questions and took out an old wooden box and lifted its lid. He removed small round bottles with square bases and glass stoppers that were filled with different-colored liquids, powders, and grains. He arranged the bottles in a cluster before him.

He withdrew a long, clear crystal on a fine gold chain from the fold at the top of his *lungi* and twirled it in slow circles, letting out the chain bit by bit as it swung over the vials. He concentrated on the crystal and the vials, eliminating them one by one until only two stood from the cluster, one containing a white powder, the other grains that looked like lavender sand.

"The stars show trouble for you and your daughter," he said finally, his rosy cheeks pouching as he pursed his lips. Even his voice was childlike.

"What kind of trouble?" Shabanu asked quietly. Something in his eerie high voice and his ethereal looks made her believe there was a special connection between the *hakkim* and the world of the unknown—something to be regarded with gravity. She trusted him.

"I cannot be one-hundred-percent sure," he said. "It may be that both of you will fall ill." He leaned over the vials again and poured a bit of the contents of each onto small white squares of paper and folded them into two neat packets.

"Mix these with your tea. The white in the morning, and the lavender in the evening. Divide them into equal portions, one for each of the next five days. Both of you drink this without fail. When you return to Lahore, come back to see me."

"Can't you tell me the nature of the danger? Perhaps I could be more vigilant. . . ." she said.

"Just do as I say, child," Aab-pa said, working his lips over his small, even teeth, which were stained red with betel juice. "Keep the child with you. Sleep with her. Don't let her out of your sight. And her pet deer, too. And tell nobody about any of this. These are dangerous times."

Shabanu was alarmed. Her heart thundered. He had helped her without her having to ask. She must concentrate only on keeping herself and Mumtaz safe.

She hurried through the lanes on her way back to the

haveli. She wanted to be back before she was missed at tea-time. She felt light-headed and slightly ill as she let herself in through the back gate.

It's good we're going, she thought. It's time for a return to reason.

But reason was not so easy to come by.

On the drive from Lahore to Okurabad, Shabanu, Zabo, and Mumtaz sat in the back of Rahim's European sedan. Rahim drove, and Omar sat in the front seat. The air conditioner cooled the air to a frigid stillness, keeping out the smells and sounds of animals and vehicles on the roadway. The bodyguards rode in automobiles in front, clearing the road as they went. The other servants followed in the van behind.

Omar and Rahim were engrossed in talk of politics and crops. Zabo stared out the window, and Mumtaz begged Shabanu to play a game of cat's cradle with her. Shabanu concentrated very hard on the string in order to keep her eyes from Omar.

There was a loud thump, and Shabanu felt a jolt to the side of the car. Rahim jammed his foot on the brake, and Mumtaz was thrown against the front seat with the suddenness of the stop.

A woman standing at the side of the road threw out her arms, and horror twisted her face. She raised her hands fluttering to her mouth.

On the roadbed beside and slightly behind where the car had come to a stop a child lay sprawled on his back, his arms flung wide. Blood gushed from a terrible wound in his head. A young man rushed to the child, and a crowd gathered around him. A moment later another man sped off down the canal path on a bicycle.

Rahim slapped the wheel with impatience. The bodyguards emerged from the car behind with their guns, and
the crowd moved back a step.

The crowd fell silent. People stood beside their animals,
carts, and bicycles along the roadbed, some staring at the
child, others at the bodyguards.

A few moments later the bicyclist returned with a *beldar*,
still wearing the red turban from his job as tender of the
canal, behind him on the seat over the rear wheel. The *beldar*
jumped from the bicycle before it stopped and ran to the
boy. He knelt, gathering the small form against his chest.
When he stood, the boy's arms dangled lifelessly from his
shoulders. The man looked up and walked toward Rahim's
car, his bare chest heaving with sorrow. The bodyguards
stepped forward to stop him, but he brushed past them,
tears wetting his face. His wife wailed and struggled against
the women who restrained her.

Rahim stepped from the car. Shabanu opened the back
door to go to the mother. All she could think was how
grief-stricken she would be if the dead child were Mumtaz.

"Stay in the car!" commanded Rahim, and Shabanu froze
for a moment, then pushed the door open wider. Rahim
whirled around.

"Get back inside," he said, his voice flat and hard.

Shabanu looked at Omar, who sat immobile in the front
seat. Slowly she got back into her seat. Omar did not turn
around, nor did he return her look. A muscle twitched in
his cheek.

Mumtaz sat with her nose pressed to the window.

"What happened, Uma?" she asked.

Shabanu picked up Mumtaz and resettled her on her lap,
hugging her close.

"It's okay," she said. "Papa's taking care of it." Mumtaz

looked up, and Shabanu realized that she had spoken with such bitterness that even the child recognized it. She rolled down the window to listen.

Still Omar sat facing forward, saying nothing.

Rahim reached into his breast pocket. He pulled out a packet of five-hundred-rupee notes and, unfolding it, counted out two bills. He leaned forward and held out the thousand rupees toward the man.

"Will this bring back my only son?" asked the man, his voice cracking. But after a moment he reached out and took the money, which no doubt was more than he'd ever seen at one time.

The crowd dispersed silently, Rahim returned to the car, and they drove off again with nothing more said.

Shabanu's heart raced with anger. She could keep silent no longer.

"How can you be so callous?" she asked, her voice breaking. Rahim didn't so much as look at her in the rearview mirror. A blush crept up the back of Omar's neck. He too remained silent.

"Don't you realize that people like the *beldar* and his wife live simple lives? The death of an only son is the loss of their greatest treasure!"

Rahim's silence could only mean he was angry. Zabo reached out and put her hand over Shabanu's.

"It would have been better to offer sympathy than money!" she said, and then through a monumental effort managed to say nothing more.

The car flew over the sun-dappled pavement, the overhanging acacia branches sheltering the roadway.

chapter 16

Back at Okurabad the focus shifted to preparations for Zabo and Ahmed's wedding.

Mumtaz was cross because Shabanu would not allow her out to play with Samiya's children. Samiya and Zenat kept watch outside Shabanu's room, where Zabo stayed with them during the day. At night Zabo went with Selma to the house.

Choti also remained in the room with them, according to Aab-pa's orders, and she liked the confinement as little as Mumtaz did. She stood in the doorway tossing her head and tapping her small hooves on the floor.

After lunch Zabo, Shabanu, and Mumtaz napped in the room beside the stable, under the limp mosquito netting, their breathing shallow and slow in the afternoon heat. They awoke slowly, their eyes still hot, and folded back the mosquito netting. Shabanu opened the shutters, and the harsh white sunlight was painful to her eyes. There was no breeze, and the air outside was as hot and stale as the air inside the room.

From under the *charpoi* Zabo dragged two large trunks.

She and Shabanu shook out the pieces of Zabo's dowry and arranged them about the room, examining each piece minutely.

The top of every table and chair, the floor, the cupboards were covered with elaborately embroidered and jeweled saris, *shalwar kameez,* and shawls.

Sitting atop each article of clothing—several suits for each day of the celebration of the wedding—was the jewelry Zabo would wear with it.

Mumtaz stood beside a pink and shimmering yellow-green silk *shalwar kameez* fingering rows of tiny peridots strung on golden threads and earrings of peridots clustered with diamonds. Beside it a silver silk sari woven with a maroon paisley border was offset with deep, mysterious crystals of wine-colored garnet set in platinum. Choti stood immobile beside her, as if she too were in awe of such finery.

"This is the real test," said Zabo as she lifted two identical lamb suede sacks and dumped their clinking contents onto the coverlet on the bed between her and Shabanu. The red sack in her left hand contained solid gold bangles; the one in her right held imitation rolled gold of exactly the same color and design, created by the finest jeweler in the Anarkali Bazaar. As the bangles mixed together on the coverlet, they were impossible to tell apart.

"Guess which are real," said Zabo. Shabanu picked them up and turned them in her fingers.

"They weigh the same," she said. "And they're exactly the same color." She hefted them, one by one, in her palm. "I can't tell," she said.

"Let me see," said Zabo, bending her head over the gold circles in each of Shabanu's outstretched palms. "I can't tell either."

Shabanu was about to test the two gold pieces with her

teeth when the door to her room banged open, and there stood Nazir, his globular frame outlined by the harsh light from the courtyard.

"Why are you hiding in here?" he asked, his voice booming in that still, small room, which until this moment had never reverberated with a man's voice. "What are you doing? Looking at your dowry? Why haven't you shown me? I sent you a fortune. . . ."

"Father! I was just organizing it to display in Uncle Rahim's house for you to see," Zabo said. A small red dot high on Zabo's left cheekbone was the only sign that betrayed her fear. Her voice was calm and normal.

Nazir came in without asking or being asked, his breath wheezing in a rattle through his overfat chest.

Shabanu and Zabo sat immobile with shock on the bed, and Shabanu's shoulders twitched with wanting to hide the bangles away. But she knew Nazir's suspicious nature and sat still, the gold—was it real or fake?—still sitting in her open palms.

Nazir bent over Shabanu to peer into her hand. His breath was sour with the aftersmell of tobacco and whiskey, and floating over the stench was an overwhelming cloud of expensive perfume. He reached out and picked up the bangle in Shabanu's right palm. A large diamond gleamed from a gold ring on his pudgy pinkie finger.

Shabanu's breath caught in the back of her throat, and Zabo shot her a searing look, but Nazir appeared not to have heard. Neither of the women moved.

Nazir sidled over to the doorway and turned to look at the bangle in the unforgiving sunlight. Shabanu reached out for Zabo's hand and gave it a quick squeeze, then she stood and walked to the doorway.

"Aren't they beautiful?" Shabanu asked him.

"How many ounces are they?" he demanded.

"I . . . I'm not sure," said Zabo.

"I sent you enough money that each one should weigh at least two ounces," he said.

"I don't believe in buying heavy bangles," said Zabo, standing to face her father with resolution. "I think it's vulgar."

Shabanu sensed that Zabo, who never disobeyed or questioned her father, wanted to engage him in a discussion of the jewelry to distract him from testing it.

Without warning, Nazir's arm lashed out. The back of his hand caught Zabo full in the mouth, sending her flying backward onto the floor. The diamond ring had caught her lip, and a thin line of blood trickled down one side of her chin.

Choti bucked and bolted from the room with a skittering of tiny hooves, and Mumtaz shrank back against the wall. Shabanu hurried to help Zabo to her feet. Mumtaz ran over and hid behind them.

Nazir turned back to the sunlit doorway, ignoring them, and lifted the bangle to his teeth.

Allah have mercy, please let that be a real one, Shabanu prayed to herself as she dabbed at Zabo's now profusely bleeding lip with the end of her *dupatta*.

They couldn't see Nazir's face, for his back was turned to them, and that moment seemed to last forever. The spot between Shabanu's shoulder blades twitched wildly.

Then Nazir turned.

"At least it's good twenty-four-karat gold," he said. "You shouldn't have more than eighteen-karat gold in a bangle. This will bend. Still, it's better to err on the side of heavier gold, even though it's softer. . . ."

He went around the room then, bending over to examine

every article of clothing and every piece of jewelry that lay with it. He held each piece of jewelry up to the light and turned it to see the facets gleam. He touched the silks and embroideries tenderly, with the only affection Shabanu had ever seen him display.

Zabo clung to Shabanu, but he seemed not to notice he'd hurt his daughter, or indeed even that the two women and Mumtaz were in the room.

Shabanu thanked Allah each time Nazir put down a piece of jewelry. He tried to bite into every piece, but there was too little gold in each of the settings, and Shabanu thanked Allah doubly.

Soon he wearied of criticizing—and sometimes praising—the stones, and left the pile of real and less-than-real gold bangles, chains, and pendants untouched on the bed.

"Is this all?" he asked.

"Nay," said Zabo. "There are still things to come from Lahore."

"I want to see the rest when it arrives," he said, and without another word he turned and waddled through the door, leaving it open behind him.

Shabanu took a deep breath when he was gone. Mumtaz still had her face buried in Shabanu's tunic.

"It's all right, pigeon," she said to the child, prying her away and dropping to one knee to look into her face.

"I don't like Uncle Nazir," Mumtaz said. "I don't want to see him anymore."

"He gets angry easily," Shabanu said. "You must stay out of his way."

Zabo still breathed unevenly.

"It worked," she said, smiling, then wincing. Her lip was swollen and bruised.

"Yes," said Shabanu. "But we're lucky. There is little privacy now, with so many people coming and going. The times are strange, and we are just lucky your father picked up the right bangles. We must be more careful."

Shabanu called out into the stableyard for Zenat, who appeared immediately, her eyes cast down at her feet. She had heard Nazir, Shabanu thought.

"Yes, *Begum*," she said softly.

"Please take Samiya and her children out to find Choti. Then it's time for Mumtaz's supper."

"Yes, *Begum*," Zenat said.

"And keep a close eye on Choti. Don't let her out of your sight," said Shabanu, fixing an eye on the old servant.

Zenat nodded gravely and muttered softly to herself as she walked away.

"Now it's time to talk about our plan," Shabanu said, turning to Zabo.

ahim did not send for Shabanu that night. She went to bed with Mumtaz and fell asleep immediately, her eyelids like lead. In the banyan tree at the edge of the stableyard the peacocks wailed mournfully, as if their clamor would call in the monsoon.

Sometime in the stillest part of the night Shabanu awoke, when the entire household was sleeping—even the animals, including the mosquitoes and flies—and the silence was palpable.

She was certain she'd been awakened by a sound, but now she heard nothing. Then there was a faint tapping at the shutter near her bed. The strings of her *charpoi* groaned as she got up and reached for her shawl. She wrapped it about her shoulders and crossed quickly to the door, her bare feet silent on the earthen floor. She stuck her head through the doorway.

"Who is it?" she asked in a whisper.

A shadow pulled itself in against the wall, then moved toward her.

"Who is it?" she asked again.

"Did you think it was a fairy?" said a deep and throaty female voice, the voice of her Auntie Sharma.

Shabanu ran to her and pulled her inside the room, closing the door behind her. She hugged her tightly. She smelled Sharma's clean desert smell, and her small lurking fears fled like goblins.

"I was afraid you wouldn't come! How did you get inside the gate?" Shabanu said, her words tumbling over each other. "Where are you staying? Did you come alone? Where is Fatima?"

"Never mind," said Sharma. "The fact is I am here, and none too soon."

Mumtaz and Choti awoke, and Mumtaz squealed "Auntie! Auntie!" when she recognized Sharma's voice, and Choti pranced on her delicate hooves.

Sharma held the child on her lap, and soon she returned to sleep, her breathing even and quiet. They lay Mumtaz on her *charpoi* and moved over to the small sitting area at the end of the room.

Shabanu didn't want to take a chance on lighting her oil lamp, and so they talked in the dark. Shabanu asked first about her family. Sharma assured her they all were well.

"And what has caused the change in wedding plans?" Sharma asked.

"Nazir demanded it. And everyone is very nervous."

"And why should that be?"

"There is much tension among Rahim and Mahsood and Nazir. No one knows what is in Nazir's mind. And then other things . . ." She told her what Aab-pa had said about Mumtaz and Choti and about how the weather had made everyone tense.

"The best time to take Zabo away is the time of Leyla's

wedding," Sharma said. "There will be a great deal of activity. It should be easy for her to get away unseen then."

"But that's two weeks at least! What if she conceives in the meantime?"

Sharma lay a finger aside her nose. She reached into a belt she wore under her tunic and withdrew a piece of vine just like the one she'd given Shabanu after Mumtaz's birth.

Shabanu tied it into a corner of her *chadr.*

"Poor Zabo," she groaned.

"It's the only way to be sure," Sharma said. "She must be certain to use it, or she may be sorry the rest of her life."

Then they talked of the details of how Zabo would come to Sharma. When they were satisfied, Sharma hugged Shabanu to her.

"There is much danger in the air," she said. "I hope you are being careful. And wise."

"I'm trying," said Shabanu. "But it's difficult. Amina is always watching for a chance to do some mischief. And Rahim will not talk to me."

"You can only do your best and trust in Allah to attend to the rest."

"Thank you for agreeing to help Zabo, Auntie," Shabanu said. "I thank Allah for you and ask His blessings on you a thousand times."

Sharma waved away her thanks.

"It's just that it puts you in as much danger as we are in," Shabanu said. "It's one thing to face danger because it's thrust upon you, but to choose it for another is very brave."

"You mustn't worry," Sharma said. "If everyone is calm and does as agreed, we cannot fail."

"God willing," said Shabanu. "We will be ready."

Sharma left as silently as she'd come, making herself as
still and dark as the stableyard shadows. When she was gone,
Shabanu lay awake on the *charpoi*. In her sleep Mumtaz sensed
that Shabanu was near, and the child curled herself into the
curve of her mother's waist.

Shabanu had perfect confidence in their plan. She felt no
fear. In the face of all that had been forced on her and all
that had been forced on Zabo, what they risked—death—
did not seem so unattractive.

It was the first night in many weeks that Omar did not
steal into Shabanu's waking thoughts or dreams.

The muezzin climbed into the minaret and began the long
low wail that signaled the call of the faithful to prayer before the sun rose.

"Allah-o-Akbar!" he chanted in his beautiful thin voice.
"Allah-o-Akbar!" But Shabanu was asleep by the second call.

Selma and Samiya busied themselves with a thousand tasks:
supervising the removal of the modest furniture Zabo had
selected to the rooms she and Ahmed would occupy at
Okurabad; seeing that the *darzis* who made the drapes had
tea; making sure that the relatives' children were fed and
that the kitchen had plenty of food; finding more pots and
kettles for the wedding preparations and more servants to
help with the extra work load.

And there were dozens of children. Samiya's son and
daughter played with Mumtaz. They stayed with her, loyal
despite Shabanu's insistence that Mumtaz stay within her
sight. The boys played cricket in the empty space between
the garden wall and the canal.

The girls watched with reverence as the final preparations
were made, and helped with tea and fittings, then slipped

away to try out their aunties' eye makeup and rouges on one another.

Shabanu followed the *hakkim*'s advice meticulously. In the morning she mixed the powder into her tea and Mumtaz's, and she measured out the crystals for the evening. She was with Mumtaz every moment, and the child loved the attention.

They took long walks on the towpath with Choti, who followed obediently, as if she sensed there was danger. The deer kept her head high and her eyes watchful. Mumtaz grew impatient because Choti wasn't interested in their usual game of running together along the path and jumping over logs and rocks.

Mumtaz climbed trees and made houses of mud on the canal bank. She and Shabanu stopped to watch boys wash the dust from their water buffalo in the canal. The buffalo lolled appreciatively, only their big gentle eyes and round nostrils protruding from the surface of the water. Their black skin shimmered like oil when the dust was gone.

At midmorning Zenat pulled the shutters against the searing white light, but the air was as hot inside as it was out.

In the afternoons the wind picked up, hurling eddies of dust against the mud-brick walls of the buildings. This was the beginning of the daily premonsoon windstorms. Afterward every quilt, every item of clothing on the shelves, every bolster and cushion billowed with dust.

The men hunted deer in the desert. They returned at sunset, their jeeps loaded with the tiny deer of Cholistan. The servants hung them upside down by the rear legs out behind the kitchen to skin them. In the evening clansmen came from all over the desert area to eat venison curry in the dining room.

Later Rahim, Omar, Nazir, and Mahsood were occupied with village elders, politicians, and others who came to offer and seek advice and to extend congratulations.

But if Selma was any indication, there was no reason to think the tensions between Nazir and Rahim had eased. She paced about the house and garden sighing and speaking sharply to her nieces and sisters-in-law and cousins and friends and friends of friends. They were used to Selma's being that way, and made extra space for her as she swept through the rooms of the women's quarters. Otherwise they paid her little attention. But Selma was gentle and kind with Zabo.

Rumors flew about the compound like a plague of locusts. They even reached Shabanu's sanctuary behind the stable, where idle gossip was not only unwelcome, but where it seldom seemed to find its way. The first important rumor came by way of Zenat, who avoided gossip as she had avoided bees since the day of Khansama's trick.

"It's said that the astrologer is troubled because the stars of the bride and groom are not compatible," she whispered, pressing her dry lips up close against Shabanu's ear. "It is said that he is unable to choose an auspicious time for Ahmed-*sahib*'s wedding. It is said that the stars portend evil!" Zenat said the latter with a shiver of fear.

Shabanu pulled back to look at the old *ayah*. There was no malice in her eyes, and Shabanu could see she really was afraid.

The day before Zabo was to be married she was spirited away to the main house, where the women insisted she must stay until the wedding. She went bravely, spine straight and eyes dry, as if there were no tears left in her.

Shabanu knew better: Zabo drew strength from the bundles of money that Shabanu had hidden in the bottom of the milk jar in the summer pavilion high atop the *haveli* in Lahore, and from the plan Shabanu had forged with her Auntie Sharma months ago behind a dune in the Cholistan Desert.

Shabanu wanted to be with Zabo, and so she had to go to the main house, where so many cousins and aunts and friends had crowded into each bedroom and guest room that there was no room to sit, no privacy to talk. Fans turned lazily overhead, but the smells of perfume and so many bodies were dizzying in the heat.

The noise and activity drew Shabanu outside of herself, and she began to feel that her feet had reasserted themselves beneath her, and that she was part of the world after all.

Leyla was nowhere to be seen. Was she nursing her resentment at the attention being lavished on Zabo these two days, when her own wedding was only two weeks away?

Do not relax your vigilance, Shabanu told herself. And that also helped to keep her from thinking of Omar. When she did, what she thought of was how like Rahim he'd become, how committed to duty and the family, how unconcerned he'd been for the life of the *beldar*'s small son.

Whenever she was about to relax, the crimson flash of lips and fingernails jolted her out of her complacency, and she was grateful for the suspicion that lurked within her.

When Shabanu went to help Zabo organize her clothing for the wedding, an ominous feeling seemed to have settled like a fog over the courtyard and the house. The sun was blistering, though it was not fully up in the sky, and the light was so white it almost seemed there was a mist in the air.

The birds on the veranda blinked from between the bars of their bamboo cages, but were silent. Even the peacocks had stopped summoning the rain from their perches in the banyan trees. The leaves rustled as they shifted their weight from foot to foot, and the branches swished as they jumped from one to another. But their familiar wails were eerily absent.

Shabanu and Zabo had no privacy to talk. Dozens of cousins pressed near, talking about the *mahendi* that afternoon. Zabo squeezed her hands together and smiled.

Afterward, after the dust storm had subsided, Shabanu and Mumtaz went out to walk beside the canal. Choti refused to graze. She held her head high and her ears forward, watchful and alert to danger.

The canal was a muddy brown. Usually it flowed swift and clear through the meadows of Okurabad. This day it seemed so sluggish as to be standing still, except for little whorls and backwashes that sucked around the banks.

Mumtaz walked along the towpath kicking up puffs of dust with her feet. Even she, with her irrepressible energy, seemed subdued.

Shabanu tried to tell herself that the hot white light that seared her eyes, the feeling of oppression in the air, the oddly silent birds were all part of the premonsoon tension. But the people who walked along the towpath, even the schoolboys, moved slowly and were silent. Even the staccato beat of the hooves of donkeys carrying loads of bricks and cement was oddly muffled.

A loud crack sounded overhead, as if a large tree limb had succumbed to the weight of the heated air, and Choti bolted.

"Choti! Choti!" Mumtaz cried.

"Choti! Come back!" Shabanu called.

But the little deer was gone, her small dark hooves kicking up high and tucking under her chest as she cleared fallen trees.

Mumtaz darted after her into the wooded area beside the path away from the canal, but Shabanu overtook her in less than a dozen bounds, caught her by the arm, and lifted her into the air, kicking and crying.

"Uma! Let me go! Please! Choti! Choti!" Her voice broke and she cried, at first in anger and frustration.

Shabanu set her down on her feet and held her tightly. Mumtaz cried, her breath coming in chokes and gasps between small wails. Shabanu let her sob for a minute.

"Mumtaz, listen to me! Listen!" she said, shaking the child by the shoulders. "Choti probably will be waiting for us when we get home. We should go now. If she is not, she will find her way back to us. Now be quiet and come with me."

Something about the calm, intense way Shabanu spoke to Mumtaz always made her listen and obey, and she quieted. She held her mother's hand as they walked quickly back to the gate into the courtyard.

Shabanu was not surprised when Choti was not there waiting for them, but Mumtaz went through the gate into the garden without arguing. Shabanu and Zenat stayed with Mumtaz the rest of the afternoon, but the child would not sleep. She sat up to wait for the fawn, leaving the garden only when it was time to dress for Zabo's *mahendi,* the beginning of the wedding celebration.

Finally Shabanu could bear it no longer. She sent Zenat for Samiya and told the two of them to lock the door behind her and to stay in the room with Mumtaz until her return. They were not to leave the room for any reason.

She went bareheaded in her desert nomad's clothes to

the yard in back of the kitchen, where the servants sat in groups gossiping between serving courses of a large mid-afternoon banquet to the men in the dining room.

They fell silent as Shabanu darted through the yard, their starched and fanned turbans still, their waxed mustaches un-moving; even the gold fringe on the shoulder boards of their red uniform jackets did not jiggle.

Shabanu didn't care who saw her, who might take plea-sure in her pain. She went straight to the neem trees at the outer edge of the yard, where the late sunlight gleamed from the open eyes of the deer killed in the day's hunt. They hung from the lowest branches of the trees, their heads pointing toward the ground.

There among them, smaller than the rest, was Choti, eviscerated, blood dripping from her nose in a thick ribbon to the ground. Shabanu thought almost absently that Choti was the only one that still dripped blood. She must have been killed after the others were already hung.

The pink silk cord that held her little brass bell had been cut from her neck, and left an imprint in the fur.

Shabanu had half believed that Choti would come back— or had she only hoped for Mumtaz's sake?

She lay her hand on Choti's flank, stroking up along the grain of the fur. The servants in the kitchen yard looked at the ground.

They knew, she thought. She turned without looking at them and walked back slowly to dress for the *mahendi*.

A deep anger burned in Shabanu the rest of the afternoon as she thought of what to tell Mumtaz. She felt nothing but contempt for the people of Okurabad. Nazir's greed had pushed everyone beyond the edge of worry and suspicion. Where his evil was forthright and seemed therefore less menacing, it was as if he'd laid the field for the evil that was hidden within each of them. It was as if they all had played a part in Choti's death: Rahim because he refused to see the evil Amina and Leyla cast about carelessly; Omar because he had proven to be so like Rahim; the servants because they were always persuaded to do Amina's bidding; the men because they killed the beautiful animals of Cholistan, when they had no need for the meat; and Amina . . . well, Amina would come to justice one day. If Allah could be trusted—and Shabanu had no reason to doubt He could—Amina would be repaid.

Mumtaz stood quietly to have her hair brushed and braided. She willingly put on her newest *shalwar kameez,* a pale pink silk with small white embroideries across the top. She held on to her mother's hand throughout the afternoon, as if it were her only link to safety. She did not cry, but Shabanu felt her shudder occasionally, and squeezed her hand.

On the table were large samovars and silver ewers and Chinese porcelain cups and small cakes decorated with bright-colored frostings on milk white plates. Zabo appeared without makeup and jewelry, and she received her guests with restrained dignity and grace. Her face was solemn and pale. All this was customary for a Punjabi bride.

But Zabo's gravity was not an act, as often was the case. Shabanu knew she was not only sober and sad but also frightened. Suppose something went wrong with the plan? Would she have to stay with Ahmed forever? Even one night was too long!

Three dozen women were arranged about the room like so many dollops of fruit sorbet, all wearing pale georgettes and gold strapped sandals and heavy ropes of amethysts and peridots and rose quartz that glittered in the same colors as their clothing.

The *mahendi* was like a very formal tea party. Zabo distributed gifts to Amina and Leyla and to Ahmed's other relatives. The *mahendi* artists—local women wearing worn hand-printed *chadr*s and silver bracelets in rows on their slender arms—solemnly bent over the women's out-stretched hands, painting delicate patterns on them with sticky gray mud.

As usual on such occasions, attention shifted to the end of the room where Amina and Leyla talked loudly to a co-terie of admirers. They had come late to the *mahendi,* their first appearance since Shabanu and Zabo had returned from Lahore.

The other women, who had been gossiping and laughing in small groups, hushed so Amina and Leyla could speak uninterrupted. It was not that they had anything special to say; it was more that they were used to commanding the attention of any roomful of ladies. On this occasion they were intent on not allowing Zabo to steal the limelight from Leyla.

One of the rumors that flew about the compound was that Amina was annoyed with Rahim for allowing Nazir to arrange Zabo's wedding first.

The shift of attention allowed Shabanu and Mumtaz to sit quietly with Zabo. Privacy was nowhere to be found. Even the bathrooms were occupied by women in numbers. It was the way with families in times of weddings.

It seemed the house had eyes and ears, all watching and listening for something to report to Amina. But Shabanu waited patiently until the women laughed at something Amina said. She leaned close to Zabo and whispered in her ear. "Don't be afraid," she said. "You will be with Auntie Sharma soon—at the time of Leyla's wedding."

Shabanu and Mumtaz slipped away early. The sky had

darkened, but the clouds were thick and gray, and there was no movement of air. Mumtaz had been brave. But no sooner were they inside their room than she began to cry again.

Shabanu pulled Mumtaz onto her lap and held her, letting her cry for a while.

"You know, little one," she said, as if telling Mumtaz a bedtime story. "Choti has gone back."

"No, Uma, she was very happy here. She wouldn't want to go back to the desert and leave us."

Shabanu held the child close to her.

"I mean that she's gone to where we all go when our lives are finished."

"When will she come back here?" Mumtaz asked. She stopped crying and looked into her mother's face.

"She won't come to us," said Shabanu. "God gave her to us for just a little time. And now He wants her back."

"I want her to come back to me," Mumtaz said, and she began to cry again.

Shabanu pressed her daughter's head to her shoulder and stroked her hair.

"It will hurt when you miss her for a little while," she said. "But soon when you think of her you'll think of the happy times you had together. She'll be yours forever that way."

Mumtaz put her finger into her mouth and sat still, thinking about Choti until she fell asleep. Shabanu lay her on her bed, pulled off her silk *shalwar kameez,* and covered her with a thin cotton shawl. In her sleep Mumtaz shuddered slightly from her day of crying and trying not to cry.

On the day of the wedding, the monsoon broke. The rain poured in sheets so thick that Shabanu could not see through them. Occasional gusts of wind knocked the rain sideways, and water came in through the shutters.

Usually the monsoon's arrival was cause for celebration. The rain after months of overbearing heat was like salve to a wound. Children played outside in the driving rain, running with their heads back, catching water in their open mouths.

Monsoon weddings should ensure many sons. But rain on the day of the wedding meant unhappiness—perhaps disaster—and the house at Okurabad was filled with foreboding as the final preparations were made.

Everything was late. The sweets makers had to carry huge pans from their shops in the village bazaar in the back of *tonga*s, and the *tonga-wallah*s had to be coaxed out of their houses on such a day. And *tonga*s were to bring tuberoses that were to come from Kashmir by train, but the train never arrived, and no one seemed to know why or whether it would come at all. And the borrowed servants who were to come by bicycle were not able to ride their bicycles through the muddy ruts of the road.

A dozen men were gathered from the village to help erect the huge *shamiyana,* a tent of red, green, yellow, and blue canvas panels sewn in geometric patterns, in the garden where the wedding and the banquet were to take place. The men stood under the overhang of the stable, watching the rain stream down before them. The *shamiyana* was rolled on poles in the corners of the yard with plastic tarpaulins protecting it.

The gentry of the Punjab had been invited to the *nukkah* and the feast following it in the evening. But the monsoon often brought with it hill torrents, flash floods that struck without warning when the hills could hold no more water, carrying away roads and buses and cars and entire villages. With the monsoon so late and this such an inauspicious event, who could tell what would happen? Many people just did not want to drive the distance in such terrible rain.

It was amid the downpour, when Shabanu was bathing Mumtaz before her nap, that the second important rumor made its way to the stableyard.

There was a knock on the wooden door to the bathhouse. It was Samiya. The widow scurried around trying to help, fetching a towel, more water, flitting like a sparrow before and after Shabanu, chirping the entire time.

"Please, Samiya!" Shabanu said after a while, barely able to contain her annoyance. "Surely there are other things you might be doing."

Instead of being calmed, Samiya fluttered ever more persistently until Mumtaz was in bed, the sheet clasped beneath her chin.

"*Begum,* you must listen," she whispered when Mumtaz had drifted off to sleep. "There is talk in the kitchen. Please listen. It is something you should know. Amina is starting an apprenticeship program for the children of the house servants. She talked about the children getting into mischief, not having supervision, not having a school. Mumtaz's name was mentioned."

"Mumtaz? A servant's apprentice? You must be mistaken." She had the terrible, familiar feeling of having let her guard down and giving those who never stopped watching a chance to hurt her and Mumtaz.

"They asked if I would teach," Samiya went on. "They were counting how many children there might be, naming them. Mumtaz is one they named. This is how the talk came to me."

"Samiya, stay here," she said. She took a tattered old *chadr* from the hook behind the door and threw it over her head.

"Lock the door after me and don't let anyone in—not anyone—until I come back. Do you understand?"

Without waiting for an answer, she slipped out. All she could think of was the servant children in other households who lived by their wits like animals, and whose veiled eyes saw only opportunities to steal. These children were never children, really, with no time for play or learning about what is good and beautiful in the world. Their lives were confined to their masters' houses and the nearby bazaars. She pitied those children when she saw them, and she would see beyond certainty that her Mumtaz did not become one of them.

Shabanu walked purposefully through the rain to the main house, where Rahim was celebrating over tea with the few relatives and close friends who had braved the storm and a few who had come the day before for the wedding. Her *chadr* was soaked by the time she reached the veranda, but she never felt the rain. Two bodyguards stood at attention outside the door.

"Please," she said to one of them. "Please tell Rahim-*sahib* that I wish to see him."

The bodyguard stood still for a moment as if he hadn't heard. Insolent, she thought. But then he turned without speaking and went into the hallway and repeated her message to Rahim's secretary, who came out on the veranda.

"Begum," the secretary said unctuously, his hands folded over his broad belly. "Is there something I can . . ."

"No," she replied. "I must speak to Rahim-*sahib*." The secretary's eyes were narrow slits in a fleshy face covered with a black stubble of beard, as if he couldn't be troubled to open them to look at her.

"But he's busy. He's having tea now. . . ."

"He's been having tea for three months," she snapped, and the secretary's eyes opened a bit wider. "Tell him it is a matter of much urgency."

The secretary turned to go back inside, and Shabanu stepped in front of him.

"I shall wait in the hallway," she said, entering the house.

The secretary went into the parlor, and a billow of cigarette smoke escaped with a buzz of male voices in the instant the door was open. A few moments later Rahim emerged, looking tired and cross.

He greeted her with a faint nod and crossed the hallway to the study, holding the door open for her to enter first. The study was gloomy, even with the heavy velvet drapes opened wide.

Rahim's shoulders were stooped, and he looked for the first time, she thought, older than his years.

"Is it true?" she asked.

"Is what true?"

"That Amina plans a servants' apprenticeship and that Mumtaz is to be included?"

Rahim shrugged his shoulders. "Amina handles these matters," he said.

"A servant's apprentice," said Shabanu, "is only a small servant, and Mumtaz should not be treated like a servant."

"I'm sure you're mistaken," he said, holding up his hands to quiet her. "Amina probably just wants Mumtaz to be included in a school program. Of course she won't be a servant's apprentice."

"Since Amina has asked Samiya to teach, does that mean she won't be teaching in Lahore any longer?" Her heart was pounding with anger. But she spoke calmly and carefully.

"Perhaps," he said. "If this teacher is talented, perhaps her employment should benefit many children, not just Mumtaz. And there are many more servants here than at the *haveli.*"

"We won't be going back to Lahore?"

"Of course! You can visit whenever you like. . . ." His exasperated tone of voice let Shabanu know he did not believe Amina would rob Mumtaz of her freedom.

"Rahim," she said. "I don't mind if Mumtaz studies with the servants' children. But I will not—"

"Good!" he said. "The matter is settled." He turned to go.

Shabanu knew she could not dissuade him now. But she must get Mumtaz away.

"Rahim," she said. "Before Mumtaz begins school I'd like to take her to Cholistan to visit my family."

"Why not?" he said. "Now I must get back." He turned again to leave, but Shabanu spoke his name once more.

"I've hardly seen you at all," she said softly, and she was surprised at the emotion in her own voice.

"There will be time for us after these weddings are over," he said, and pulled her close enough to kiss her lightly on the top of the head. And then he was gone.

Shabanu was not comforted. She was very angry with Rahim for going back on their agreement that she and Mumtaz could stay in Lahore. He would allow Amina to treat Mumtaz like a servant. And not least of all he'd dismissed her—his wife!—like a child. But she said nothing. The important thing was that she had his permission to take Mumtaz away.

Shabanu's mind was aswirl with so many worries they bumped into each other and melted together, each becoming part of the other. Choti's death threw an ominous gloom over all. Amina's plan to put Mumtaz into apprenticeship was dangerous. Shabanu was not fooled by Rahim's reassurance. Once a servant in that household, there was no escape. She was certain of that.

Sending Mumtaz to her family was risky. Rahim would object when she came back without her. She thought of what she might say to him: "Mumtaz will never fit in here. She will always be the daughter of a gypsy, even if she studies and becomes an engineer. I want her to know her own people so she can be proud of them, as I am."

Shabanu worried that having Mumtaz safe in Cholistan would forever ruin plans for her education. And the thought of living without her daughter, her jewel, filled her with an unbearable sadness.

Floating in and out among her concerns was Omar, though she managed most of the time not to think about him. For while she did keep him from her consciousness, he lurked beneath its surface. Her longing and sadness made all the other worries seem worse.

But Shabanu was not one of those helpless women who wrung their hands and walked about moaning "What to do? What to do?"

At the moment there was only one thing to do, and she set about doing it. The rest she would trust to Allah.

Shabanu was Zabo's only attendant for the wedding. The rain had stopped, but the sense of foreboding and gloom that had engulfed the house earlier remained. Zenat dressed Mumtaz while Shabanu dressed. No one spoke.

Shabanu chose a plain *shalwar kameez* in a deep blue that reminded her of the desert night sky. She knew her dress was hardly suitable for a wedding; instead it suited her mood. She wore no jewelry except for a pair of silver nomad's earrings and her heavy silver bangles that she had worn to a burnished mellow glow. She and Mumtaz went together to the main house, where Zabo was to dress.

They met in the parlor. Servants bearing trays and last-minute flowers and dishes scurried through the room.

Zabo looked pale, and her eyes had deep dishes beneath them, as if she hadn't slept in days. But she was calm. She wore a plain cotton tunic. She smiled and bent to hug Mumtaz.

"Did you sleep?" Shabanu asked in a whisper.

"A bit."

Shabanu longed for the friend to whom she'd once told everything—who understood and comforted her and offered advice. But these days, with Zabo so preoccupied with her own troubles, Shabanu felt from time to time that she'd never been more alone. In these moments her sense of solitude deepened.

Selma came to announce that she had laid out Zabo's dress in Rahim's bedroom. She looked at Shabanu's plain dark *shalwar kameez* but said nothing.

Selma held out her arms to them. Both of the women went to her and bent forward to accept kisses on their foreheads. Shabanu held Mumtaz up to be kissed. They climbed the stairs together slowly, waiting for Selma, who wheezed on the landing.

"The others wanted to come," Selma said. She sat heavily in the chair inside the door and waited for her breathing to return to normal. "What you did not need was a gaggle of women in here gossiping and worrying you about omens." Zabo stepped out of her clothes.

"Who could expect good omens for such a match under the best of circumstances?" Zabo asked with a small, thin laugh.

"You have been courageous, child," said Selma. "I hope Allah has given you the wisdom to know how to deal with your father as well as your husband."

Selma looked around, found her purse, and, to Shabanu's immense relief, moved toward the door again.

"I'll leave you to dress. But I have a special gift for you," she said. "I'll see you downstairs."

When she had gone, Shabanu untied the knot in the end of her *dupatta* and pressed the darkly curled piece of vine into Zabo's hand. She explained what it was for and how to insert it to keep from being impregnated. Tears filled Zabo's eyes, but she breathed deeply and wiped them away.

"You will be all right for two weeks." It was partly a question and partly a statement. "Selma says Leyla's wedding should be around then, though the *imams* have not yet fixed the exact day."

Zabo nodded. She stood still for a moment, as if gathering

her composure. She pulled the red satin slip over her head, and her hands paused for just a second as she smoothed the silk over her waist, where it curved in to fit snugly.

"As long as I know Sharma will come without fail," she said. But there was a quaver in her voice as she reached for the beautiful wedding skirt with pigeon blood rubies sewn into its Moguli pattern.

"The plan is very simple. She'll meet us in Lahore. With the wedding, there will be much confusion. And in case something goes wrong, the assembly will be back in session the following week, so we are sure to be there. I'm to tell Sharma through Aab-pa if we must suddenly return to Okurabad. We'll work out the final details then."

She looked at Zabo in the red satin slip, the straps draping against her slender shoulders, the silk molding her lovely round breasts. What a tragedy to waste her beauty, her loyalty, her wonderful gifts for love and laughter on an idiot boy!

Again Shabanu was overcome by anger: at Rahim for making this happen; and at Nazir for being greedy, cruel, and unreasonable. Even Selma in the end had acquiesced. But Shabanu knew she should harness her rage—save its energy for when she needed it. So she ignored the sharp prickles that ran up and down her spine.

Zabo raised her arms, and Shabanu slipped the gold-embroidered red silk tunic over her head.

Zabo crossed to the dressing table and sat before the mirror, her eyes level on her reflection. Shabanu fastened the enameled pendant's red silk cord at the back of Zabo's neck and pinned the ruby and emerald *tikka* so that it hung low on her forehead, the tiny fake diamonds sparkling for ten times all they were worth just above her eyebrows. Zabo attached the end of the ornament's chain to the slender gold nose ring, the *nath*—which means "caught"—and the single real ruby glittered against the rim of her nostril. Selma's gold-domed earrings with ruby and emerald drops did not diminish the sparkle of the less-than-real stones, and Zabo examined the effect with satisfaction.

She then set about applying gold powder and kohl to her eyes, and rouge to her cheeks and lips.

"How do I look?" Zabo asked, turning her shimmering eyes to meet Shabanu's in the mirror.

"Like you paid a *crore* of rupees for your trousseau," said Shabanu. "And you look very beautiful," she added, bending over to hug Zabo's shoulders.

Zabo busied herself for a few more seconds, adding more powdered gold to the creases of her eyelids. Then she snapped her makeup and jewelry cases shut deliberately and slowly, inspected herself a final time, and stood.

Shabanu took her hands, and they stood facing each other for a moment until Zabo turned to unfold the red silk and fake gold-embroidered *chadr*. She handed it to Shabanu to arrange over her head.

Selma met them at the foot of the stairway. She had in her hands a velvet box. She opened it, and inside was a ruby-and-diamond bracelet that glittered on its gold satin cushion. Zabo looked up into Selma's face.

But Shabanu's anger swelled in her chest and throat. She wanted to throw the bracelet to the marble floor and smash it with a hammer and tell them how unfair this was to Zabo.

"Daoud gave it to me on our wedding day," Selma said softly. "May it bring you peace."

Shabanu realized then how fully Selma had understood all along what Zabo was going through, and what she and Zabo had been up to with their endless days of shopping in Lahore. As suddenly as it had come upon her, her anger toward Selma evaporated. Her deep affection for the older woman returned, and the knowledge that she could be trusted settled over Shabanu for once and forever.

She took one of Zabo's arms, and Selma took the other. Samiya brought Mumtaz, whose thick hair flowed down her back. Her face was composed and solemn. She looked very grown-up in the cobalt blue silk tunic and long skirt that matched her mother's. She trailed along behind Zabo, holding her auntie's skirt and tunic up so that they didn't drag on the carpets that had been laid over the muddy grass.

Zabo walked slowly and deliberately, her head bent, making the traditional, hesitant, fearful bride's march to the dais where Ahmed was to join her.

The wedding guests—only a couple of dozen relatives and nearby neighbors had braved the floods—sat under the *shamiyana,* its brightly quilted walls billowing in the stiff breeze.

The rain had stopped about an hour before, but the sky boiled and menaced. The air was cool and damp.

In another chamber of the tent, the men were exchanging the marriage documents and congratulating Ahmed.

The female guests talked quietly of the rain and the unhappy marriage it portended.

"It's uncivilized to have a wedding in such weather! It's going to pour again at any second," said a sister of Amina, leaning across a half-occupied chair to speak to a woman whose ample bottom spilled over to fill part of the chairs on either side of her. "My brother-in-law has taken leave of his senses."

"Hush," said Amina, leaning her elaborately coiffed head back from the row ahead. "My husband has his reasons. . . ." Her voice trailed off in a tragic sigh. Her eyes were lined with sparkling powder, which glittered from the corners like a rivulet of tears.

Most of the women wore georgette *shalwar kameez* sewn with iridescent beads and sequins. The younger ones, whose bodies had not yet expanded, wore the magnificent clothing of their own weddings—unpacked from trunks and unwrapped from tissue paper each year, as long as they fit, for the wedding season.

Many wore jewels brought all the way from Damascus and Baghdad at the time the ancient caliphs left to spread Islam throughout the world. One wore jade disks the size of rupee coins, which had been carved in China by the emperor's jeweler; another wore a diamond pendant that looked like a paperweight. All wore strings of gems in their hair, diamonds sewn into the folds of their clothing, and gems in their noses and on their fingers.

They moved slowly and languidly, fanning themselves with bored movements despite the coolness of the evening, and gossiped furtively behind their fans. The breeze blew oppressive clouds of mingled expensive European colognes about the *shamiyana*.

"What would you expect?" asked one cousin. "Marriage to the daughter of Nazir cannot bode well for anyone."

It struck Shabanu as ludicrous that they should be more concerned for Ahmed's happiness than Zabo's! Zabo's face was completely covered, and her shoulders trembled slightly under the weight of her tunic and skirt. She looked like a proper Punjabi bride, all tremulous and lovely.

Shabanu and Zabo made their way to the dais through the women, who hushed their gossip briefly as they passed. The dais was draped with garlands of jasmine and marigolds. The tuberoses never did arrive.

In the front near the center aisle sat Leyla, her hair swept up dramatically and caught high above one ear in a comb set with diamonds. Her eyes were heavily made up, and her mouth and fingers flashed a brilliant wet crimson.

When Zabo was seated on silken cushions piled on a carved chair, Ahmed entered through the rear of the tent from the men's chamber, and the women hushed as he walked down the center aisle to take his place beside Zabo on the dais, where he sat still for a few minutes and then began to squirm. He looked frail in his knee-length *sherwani,* with its fitted waist and high collar, which made his neck look vulnerable and childish.

Amina made her cumbersome way down the aisle to the flower-festooned dais. Leyla helped her as she climbed the steps to the wedding party. When she turned to sit, Amina's face was florid, nearly matching the brilliant pink of her sequined *shalwar kameez.* She and Leyla sat on either side of Ahmed, amid heavily embroidered bolsters. Amina handed Ahmed a glass of sweetened milk. When he had drunk from it, his mother urged him to give it to Zabo. She took a small sip, in an act of ceremonial obedience to her husband.

From within the folds of her *dupatta,* Amina produced a gilt mirror. Shabanu watched quietly as Amina slipped the mirror into Zabo's lap, under her downcast eyes. Amina said something to Zabo, who hesitated a moment, then curled her fingers around the edge of the mirror. Amina took Ahmed gently by the back of his thin neck and steered his gaze toward the mirror.

As the bride looked at the reflection of the groom, at the reflection of her husband that was to become the very essence of herself, the mirror clattered to the floor. Zabo's hands went up under the *chadr* to her face.

Shabanu put her arms around Zabo's shoulders. At the

same instant, Leyla grabbed Zabo's hands to pull them from her face. Shabanu leaned forward, inserting her body between Leyla and Zabo. After an absurd moment of resistance like a silent shoving spree, Leyla moved aside and allowed Shabanu to comfort her friend.

All this happened in the space of a minute, amid the chaos of relatives fluttering to get a closer glimpse of the bride and groom and gossiping among themselves, and the male relatives drifting in from the tent area where the formal wedding documents had been exchanged.

And before anything could be made of the incident, the wedding party was whisked away to reassemble for the banquet.

Shabanu and Mumtaz stayed with Zabo as the guests gathered on the lawn, under the *shamiyana* and cascades of tiny white lights. People stood in clumps, the ladies twinkling with jewels, and watched servants in white jackets and white turbans heap the long tables with silver platters of lamb on skewers, steaming tureens of curries, baskets of fresh steaming *roti,* and a sweet *biryani* rice with raisins and nuts.

Shabanu kept a firm hold on Mumtaz's hand. She caught sight of Omar several times, but she pretended she didn't see that he was looking at her. Her heart felt as if it were encased in glass.

The thought of giving up Mumtaz to her family had opened her heart wide again to the pain of loss. It made Omar's loss seem very far away, as if it had happened years ago. She kept pushing away panic at the thought of living without Mumtaz, telling herself it was only temporary. She'd be able to join Mumtaz and Zabo and Sharma and Fatima one day. They were the people she loved and trusted most on this earth. The thought of all of them living and working together should comfort her. But all of her plans for Mumtaz's education, for the two of them to live in Lahore at the *haveli,* were shattered.

Mumtaz was caught up in her own loss, and she willingly clung to her mother's hand. Since Choti had disappeared she'd taken to carrying Bundr with her, and she had him hugged to her chest with her free hand. The other children her age drank Coca-Cola and ate fistfuls of sweets, and while the adults stood around talking after the dinner was served, the youngsters chased one another pell-mell, like rabbits, through the rows of chairs and under the tables.

Mumtaz and Shabanu floated among the other guests, congratulations and wisps of gossip and the shrieks of the other children parting around them as they passed like bits of cloud.

Shabanu and Mumtaz went to see Zabo in the big house the day after the wedding and found the apartment she and Ahmed had occupied only the night before in chaos. Servants ran from room to room gathering pieces of clothing and wrapping them in tissue paper, hauling trunks from storage and filling them to the brim.

Zabo had chosen simple furniture, and she'd moved many of her hand-embroidered bolsters and cushions from her father's house. Strewn over them was more evidence of planning for a long journey: shawls and scarves and a bag of biscuits; silk pouches filled with jewelry; a box of writing paper; and a bottle of water. And Zabo stood prettily in the center of it all, looking rested and pleased.

"Where are you going?" Shabanu asked. Zabo came to her and hugged her cheerfully.

"My father is taking Ahmed on a hunting trip," she said. "I'm going to Mehrabpur."

"But why don't you stay here?"

"Because my father wants me at Mehrabpur. Afterward we're going to Lahore. And soon you'll be there with me!"

Shabanu linked her arm through Zabo's and walked her out to the garden, a thousand questions threatening to burst from her lips before they were in a private place.

The garden had been cleared. The *shamiyana* was rolled and carried away, the carpets lifted, and there was no sign a wedding had taken place except for the compressed, muddy grass.

It had rained earlier, and now steam rose from every surface in the hot sunlight. Crows hopped across the ruined lawn, their heads cocked, looking for earthworms that had emerged the night before under the carpets.

Zabo looked behind them.

"Where's Choti?" she asked. Mumtaz looked stricken. Zabo glanced from Mumtaz to Shabanu and back.

"She's gone away," said Mumtaz. "She's not coming back."

"Oh!" said Zabo. She bent and hugged Mumtaz, who stood still and clutched Bundr tightly against her. "I'm sorry."

She stood and took Shabanu's arm again.

"What happened?" she asked softly. Shabanu shook her head.

"She's not coming back," Mumtaz said again, and Shabanu could have cried for her.

They walked along arm in arm, not talking for a while. Then Shabanu could wait no longer.

"You look well for the day after the worst night of your life," she said, and Zabo laughed her old tinkling laugh. It lifted Shabanu's heart.

"Last night," she began, "Father gave Ahmed some whiskey."

"Oh!" said Shabanu.

"Ahmed fell sound asleep. And today they leave for the hunt as soon as we arrive at Mehrabpur."

"We mustn't tell Rahim!" said Shabanu. Her husband was a devout Muslim who disapproved of liquor.

"Certainly not!" said Zabo, her old spark returned for the first time in months. "Listen! This is a reprieve! Uncle Rahim would not only disapprove of the liquor. He would want the marriage consummated as soon as possible. The sooner he has a grandson, the sooner the rest of the family lands are consolidated."

"But what an odd thing for your father to do!" Shabanu said. "Why shouldn't he want you to become pregnant too? He benefits most of all, because it gives him an equal claim to the family holdings."

"I don't care what the reason is!" Zabo said, tossing her head. "If it means Ahmed stays away from my bed until I can get away with Sharma, I want it that way."

"But if your father is up to something, it could be dangerous for you!" Shabanu said.

"You think I care about danger!" Zabo's eyes flashed. "Promise you won't tell Rahim." It was a demand more than a request.

Shabanu hesitated. If she promised not to tell Rahim, she would be violating her oath of loyalty to him for the first time. And she had a strong sense of some terrible impending danger.

"Promise!" Zabo insisted. "Promise!"

"When will you return from Lahore?" Shabanu asked.

"Promise!" said Zabo, refusing to yield.

"All right, I promise!" said Shabanu. "But Sharma will be ready for you in two weeks."

"Father is going to Lahore early to please me," Zabo said. "We'll still be there for Leyla's wedding."

Zenat came then to tell them that Nazir was ready to

leave and that the others had assembled for the traditional farewell.

Zabo's eyes sparkled, and she did look like a bride departing for her honeymoon, almost like a bride in love, as she waved good-bye to the assembled household. Everyone stood under umbrellas, for the rain had begun around noon and was growing steadily heavier. There was traditional wailing among the female members of the family, but it all seemed acted, except for Amina, whose tears for once were real as she kissed Ahmed good-bye.

The car was loaded and waiting as they left in the early afternoon, with Nazir and the bodyguards all squeezed into Nazir's sedan. Shabanu's last glimpse of Zabo was through a circle she'd wiped in the fog on the window, waving good-bye to her and Mumtaz as the car splashed through the rain.

In the main house life returned to normal very quickly. It was as if Zabo and Ahmed never had been wed. The pots and pans had been returned, the extra servants had gone back to their own households, the lights and flowers and tables were gone. Even the ruined lawn had begun to recover in a thick thatch of new growth prompted by the rain.

Shabanu sat in the doorway of her room watching the rain, which fell gently now, *plipping* in the stableyard puddles. She felt she had crossed a precipice into a new and dangerous territory. She had actively violated her oath of loyalty to her husband.

But she was not sure which was more dangerous: telling Rahim or not telling him what Nazir had planned for Ahmed. She knew Nazir well enough to expect the worst of him. She knew he wouldn't hesitate to risk Zabo's life.

But she had already broken one promise to Zabo, and she

would not break another. What sealed her decision was this: If Rahim knew that Nazir had delayed the consummation of Ahmed's nuptial vows, he would be angry. If he knew of the hunting trip, no doubt he would intervene. And no doubt he would require Shabanu to go to Mehrabpur with him to keep Zabo company.

And that would delay her departure for Cholistan. Shabanu could not let anything interfere with her taking Mumtaz to safety.

That same afternoon Shabanu sent word to her sister that she would be coming to visit at the farm near Mehrabpur. She asked Phulan to let Sharma know. The message expressed all of her excitement about a visit to her family. But there was an urgency to it, lent by the short notice of just two days. These family gatherings normally took up to a month to arrange. Shabanu's mother and father must be summoned from the desert, and Phulan could never be certain where Sharma might be found.

Back in her room, Shabanu began to gather Mumtaz's clothing and books. She took from the cupboard only those *shalwar kameez* that were newly made and sturdy. She wanted them to fit her for as long as possible. The silks and fragile lawn clothes she left in stacks on the shelf, as if Mumtaz would soon return. And when that was done she sat on her bed. Mumtaz had been watching her silently.

Late in the afternoon the rain let up, and Selma came to see her before leaving for Lahore. She reported that the wedding plans for Omar and Leyla had run into delays.

"Amina has demanded that Rahim postpone the wedding," she said. "She thinks it's barbaric to have a wedding celebration in such terrible weather." Selma twisted a wisp of hair back into the bun behind her head.

"You mean it won't be in two weeks as planned?" Shabanu felt her panic rise.

"No, I'm sure Rahim will win this argument," Selma said with a small, weary chuckle. "He wants it all over and done before the assembly meets. He wants Omar ready for the elections. It's just more aggravation for him."

"Poor Rahim," Shabanu said, but her mind and heart had already fled to the desert. She did not have the energy to worry about Omar's wedding.

She kissed Selma good-bye and went back to getting ready for her trip to Cholistan.

That evening Shabanu had an early supper with Rahim. They ate quietly, talking little.

Shabanu, who knew that her ability to be untruthful with him would be limited, did not want to discuss anything that might give him a hint that Mumtaz would stay with Mama and Dadi in Cholistan. Any question from him that would force her to lie would be a disaster. She also wished to avoid any discussion of Ahmed, for fear she'd break her promise to Zabo and tell Rahim about the whiskey and the hunting expedition.

"When will you return from Cholistan?" he asked.

"In a week," she said, concentrating on her plate. "And you?"

"I'll stay here until you return. We'll all go to Lahore together, the week before the wedding."

Rahim also seemed preoccupied. After dinner he kissed her good night and sent her back to her room early, even before Mumtaz was asleep.

It seemed forever until morning. Shabanu could not sleep, and she listened all night to the rain outside. She listened to Mumtaz's soft breathing on the small *charpoi* beside her own.

How she would miss her! Shabanu helped her with her lessons every day, and they read books together and walked together beside the canal. She must see to it that Mumtaz continued to read and write. Shabanu would ask Mumtaz to keep a diary so she might read what her daughter did and thought about every day.

How would she fill the hole in her heart that Mumtaz would leave? And how would she fill the empty hours?

At first light Shabanu awoke with a start, without ever realizing she'd been asleep.

They were ready to leave by the time their bed tea came on a tray with fried bread and milk. Zenat had to coax Mumtaz to swallow just a few bites.

It was a fine morning, the air washed fresh and clean of dust by the heavy rains of the days before. The big leaves of the leathery saal trees in the courtyard waved and flopped, bidding Mumtaz farewell. The birds in the banyan twittered and chirped as if an evil cloud had passed and the courtyard was safe once again.

Shabanu's heart lifted. But she cautioned herself not to let down her guard until they were safe in Cholistan.

The *tonga* that waited outside the gate for them was clean, and the horse was spry, lifting its head to sniff the air. The *tonga-wallah* greeted them cheerfully. It seemed the whole world was buoyed by the break in the rains and the heat.

The servants loaded their bags and bundles of gifts for Shabanu's family into the carriage, and the horse took off at a lively trot.

They passed through the village without slowing down, sending chickens and small goats fleeing into the narrow drains on either side of the lane. It was prayer time, and several shops were closed. Old brass padlocks glinted on rough wooden doors as a sign that their devout owners had gone to the mosque.

Old men squatted on their haunches in doorways, their white turbans gleaming in the sunlight. Some nodded, others watched bicycles and scooters wind through the lanes, their bells jangling and horns tooting. Cats walked along the parapets of shop buildings, and a herd of donkeys seemed to wander aimlessly, their backs piled high with grass to take back to the desert, their owner probably at his prayers.

Overhead, laundry hung on a pole that stretched from the roof of one house to the roof across the lane, which was so narrow a woman reached out her arm and handed a cup of sugar across to her neighbor on the opposite roof.

A few women in *burka*s floated like ghosts from shop to shop buying vegetables and milk and yogurt and spices and lentils.

Behind the village the road stretched out between two rows of trees that gave way as they left the irrigated lands of Okurabad to more delicate desert shrubs and trees.

Keekar trees spread their lacy branches over the road, and stands of tamarisk floated light and fine on the gentle breeze.

As the *tonga* horse trotted along, Shabanu told Mumtaz of all the wonderful things they would find in the desert at monsoon time.

"There will be *kumbi* that appear like magic among the dunes when the rain ends. They are small and white, growing very close to the ground. They taste mysterious and dark and must be picked before the sun climbs into the sky to dry them—they're that fragile. And perhaps Auntie Sharma will have killed a chicken to eat them with!"

They had brought a crate of mangoes with them, the

most important treat of the summer. It always made the hot season worth surviving at Okurabad. Mumtaz and Shabanu shared one, the sticky yellow juice running down their arms.

The *tonga* turned off the main road to a smaller road that ran beside a canal, and then onto two dirt tracks that ran beside an even smaller canal, and finally onto a path made by the feet of the farmers who lived at the end of the smallest irrigation ditches.

They passed some shabby farms no larger than the courtyard at Okurabad. Their walls were crumbled. In the hopelessness of poverty, people sometimes made the mistake of failing to repair their walls each day, and before long their roofs collapsed.

The goats had trampled little fences of brambly branches that protected yards where clothes dried and kitchen gardens grew. The gardens were as overrun and barren as the ground outside the fences, except for a few spindly cornstalks.

When they arrived at Phulan and Murad's farm at the edge of the desert, at the very end of the irrigation system, the whole family had assembled to greet them. They looked like a small bouquet in the distance, and the desert spread out behind them like a gentle gray carpet.

At Murad's farm the walls were perfect and straight. The roof was freshly thatched, and the kitchen garden was bright with peppers, corn, and squash. The fields were neat and square, and the tiny irrigation ditch had been dredged and kept clear. The earthen dowels that ran along either side to protect the fields from overflow were straight and even. The farm gave Shabanu the feeling she'd had as a child that there was order in the world and all was well. It was not until they reached the farm that she allowed herself to relax.

Mumtaz jumped up and down on the hard *tonga* seat when she saw that her grandfather had with him several baby camels, standing with their heads held high to inspect the cart and its passengers. It was the first real enthusiasm she'd shown since Choti had left them.

Shabanu hugged Phulan first. Her sister's belly was round with a fifth child. The fourth son was still an infant, and the other three boys crowded around their cousin Mumtaz, anxious to have a new playmate. Mumtaz stood on tiptoe to pet the baby camels, who ducked their heads shyly and blinked their long-lashed eyelids.

Dadi held the mother camels back so the children could pet them for a few minutes, and when he turned the mothers loose they rounded up the babies, ducking their heads and sniffing each one until they found their own.

Shabanu's mother, father, sister, and aunt crowded around her, all talking at once.

"Why have you come with such little notice?"

"Is anything wrong at Okurabad?"

"How long can you stay?"

"Tell us about the wedding!"

Sharma and Fatima did not arrive until after dark. Their animals came with them, their bells gonging softly, plinking lightly, rattling and plunking as they made their way among the dunes. As always, Sharma was greeted with much chatter and laughter.

Phulan's in-laws had come with supper from the adjoining farm and *jelabee*s from the village. They sat before the fire eating the sticky sweet fried pretzels and gossiping about Shabanu's cousins, several of whom had sent their children to school in the city of Multan.

Shabanu felt divided. Part of her was hollow with the

thought that Mumtaz would not be educated if she stayed in the desert. A larger part of her was filled with the certainty that Mumtaz would be safe here. There would be no more looking behind to see who might be watching or planning a trick. Mumtaz would be loved by good and decent people who would continue to teach her right from wrong. She would learn to love the things in the world that no one can take away—sunsets and rainstorms, birdsongs and the sound of water running in the canal—but for which the people of Okurabad had little regard. And there was always the hope that one day it would be safe for them to return to the *haveli* and live with Selma, and Mumtaz would be able to go to school.

After they had eaten, Phulan's mother-in-law, Bibi Lal, produced a surprise. She had invited a drummer and bagpipe player from the village, and Murad's cousin Kharim marked rhythm with a pair of metal tongs. Two other cousins produced their flutes with little coaxing.

The flames leaped as the women danced, their bare feet slapping the rain-packed sand under the starry sky, and here among her own people Shabanu's doubts about leaving Mumtaz to grow in the desert melted away.

That night Shabanu crept between two quilts spread on the desert floor where Mumtaz already slept. Sharma came and sat beside her.

Shabanu sat up and looked beyond the orange flicker of the dying fire, to where Mama, Dadi, Auntie, and her cousins slept.

She leaned forward to hug her Aunt Sharma, and a sob escaped her throat. Sharma held her close, and Shabanu told her of Amina's plan to make Mumtaz a servant.

"So I must leave her here with you," Shabanu said.

Sharma held her at arm's length and then wiped Shabanu's face with the end of her *dupatta.*

"You're doing the right thing," Sharma said.

"I have no choice!" said Shabanu.

"No, pigeon," said Sharma. "You always have a choice.
And that is why you act wisely. Because you choose."

"I can't bring myself to think of living without her," Shabanu said, her voice choked.

"The only thing we have in this life is time," Sharma said,
taking her by the shoulders. "And we never know how much
of that we have. The good things that happen in the time
we have foretell what will be in the next life. The bad is
only a trial to be endured. You will be with Mumtaz again."

As she fell asleep under the stars Shabanu thought of all
that she had left behind: her impossible love for Omar, her
husband whose life was a series of struggles to hold on to
power, the troublesome women of Okurabad—and she was
certain that Sharma was right.

chapter 20

The next morning Shabanu awoke to the smell of a fire and roasting bread. Mumtaz had slipped out from under the quilt before sunrise to find the baby camels at the edge of the *toba*. The night before she had fed them sugar from her hand.

Shabanu rolled their quilts and joined her mother beside the fire. Her mother handed her a tin mug of sweet milky tea. She felt warm and happy and relaxed in a way she'd forgotten it was possible to feel.

"Ah, it's so good to see both of you," her mother said, and Shabanu prepared to listen with patience to the familiar plea that she have more babies.

But before her mother could go on, they were interrupted by the distant roar of a four-by-four station wagon making its way down the track from the main road to the farm. As it came closer, still miles away, the engine ground as the vehicle labored through sand that was damp from the recent rains.

In the distance, behind the *toba,* the camels milled about, the mothers gathering the young into a circle in the midst of the herd.

The car passed the farm and continued down the track to the edge of the desert. Ibne drove, and Rahim and Omar sat in the back, both of them straight and silent. When they came to a stop, Rahim got out.

Again Shabanu was struck by how her husband had aged. In fact, she thought, it was more than age; his face looked creased and gray, as if he'd fallen gravely ill.

"*Asalaam-o-Aleikum,*" Rahim greeted her father, who came running from the *toba.* There was a brief exchange of greetings among Omar, Murad, and his cousins, and Rahim addressed Shabanu.

"I'm sorry to interrupt your holiday," he said. "But I must ask you to come with me."

"What is it?" she asked.

"There's been an accident at Mehrabpur," Rahim said. "We're on our way there now to find out what happened. Ahmed was involved. You must come to stay with Zabo."

"What happened?"

"I don't know anything except that there has been an accident, and that Ahmed was involved," he said.

Shabanu and her mother flew into action, gathering her things from the courtyard. Mama called to Mumtaz, but Shabanu lay her hand on her mother's slender brown arm.

"I want Mumtaz to stay here," she said. The intense way she spoke had the same effect on her mother as it did on Mumtaz, and there were no further questions. "I'll go say good-bye to her."

Shabanu ran to the *toba,* calling "Mumtaz! Mumtaz!"

There, behind where the sun glittered on the water, Mumtaz ran over the top of a dune, the loose sand pulling at her bare feet, her hair blowing out free behind her, as if she'd never lived anywhere else on earth.

Shabanu ran to her and held her close. She smelled the sweetness of camel's milk on her breath.

"I'll be back soon, pigeon," she said, and Mumtaz broke away from her and disappeared behind the nearest dune in pursuit of the camels. Shabanu felt her dream of educating her daughter in the city flutter and tug at her heart like a bird in a cage.

She's young, Shabanu thought. It will happen, if Allah is willing and if I am patient.

Protect her, she prayed, and she forced her feet to run back to where Rahim waited in the car.

Shabanu climbed into the back and sat between Omar and Rahim. Omar greeted her.

"I hope you've been well," he said.

She nodded. "And you?"

She felt awkward. It was the first time they'd spoken since she'd asked him to leave her alone. His jaw was so straight and broad, his eyes so dark and serious. Even through her worry and fear she felt the old longing for him sucking at her heart with a power that made her wonder how he could not feel it too. She wondered how she could have thought her feelings for him had gone away.

She was conscious of Omar's hip, thigh, and shoulder against hers, and she clenched her teeth.

"How did you find out about the accident?" she asked.

Neither Rahim nor Omar answered for a moment. The car slogged through mud and leaped from rut to rut until it reached the secondary road along the larger canal.

"Nazir's driver came with a note that there had been an accident," said Rahim. "I don't know what kind of accident, or who else was involved, or when it happened."

The car had left the dirt track for the hardtop road. It hurtled through the tunnel made of thorn trees, through the early morning mist that had grown thicker as they neared the main canal. Nazir's house was only a few miles down the main road.

"Nazir took Ahmed hunting," Shabanu said.

"What!" said Rahim. "Why didn't you tell me?"

"Zabo told me just as they left," she said, evading his question. "I didn't know where you were."

As they neared Mehrabpur they passed a broad field where dozens of workers with axes were cutting down trees that Rahim had planted only two years earlier. At the edge of the field other workers dug holes for fence posts. Large spools of wire fencing sat at intervals along the perimeter of the road.

Rahim looked back over his shoulder.

"Stop the car!" he said. His voice was dangerous and low. "That's Ahmed's land," he said.

On the other side of the road, where the fields were already strung with strands of sparkling wire, fat brown cows grazed under a low gray sky.

"That, too, is Ahmed's," Rahim said. "And those are Nazir's cattle."

Rahim climbed out of the car and walked to the edge of the road.

"Ho!" he shouted at a man who seemed to be in charge of the workers. Shabanu recognized him as Nazir's farm manager, who frequently appeared at Okurabad.

"What are you doing?" Rahim asked.

"Nazir-*sahib* has ordered us to clear and fence this land," said the man. "He's going to plant sugar."

"This is not Nazir's land!" Rahim said, his voice rising. The man stared at the ground.

"Uncle," said Omar, getting out of the car. "This fellow is just following orders." But the man wanted to speak.

"Already Nazir-*sahib* has bulldozed the village of my brother, because my brother's father-in-law said it was you who should order Master Ahmed's land cleared," he said.

Rahim got into the front seat of the car. He motioned for Ibne to drive on, and they didn't speak again until after they had passed through the village of Mehrabpur.

The village was as dusty as if there had been no rain. It was a poor village. Many mud-brick buildings stood empty and unused, their walls crumbling and roofs caving. Men stood silently in doorways and watched them pass. The shutters were drawn across the entrances of the shops in the bazaar. Even the flies were still.

Shabanu wondered whether the village was in mourning for Ahmed. For she was sure now that Ahmed was dead. She was certain Nazir had arranged a hunting accident. Perhaps he had even shot Ahmed himself—Ahmed, who would have been too excited about the hunt ever to have suspected.

She thought it likely that Zabo was all right. That would explain why Nazir had given Ahmed whiskey on the wedding night, so the marriage would not be consummated, and why he had whisked Ahmed and Zabo away the very next day. He had intended to grab Ahmed's land from the start. And Nazir wanted to be sure there was no heir to challenge his holding of the land.

The car slowed to turn into the lane that led to the broad wooden gates of the thick mud wall surrounding Nazir's house and garden.

The bodyguards stood at attention, two at either side of the gate, their red turbans starched and pleated, khaki *shal-*

war kameez pressed and creased, sandals shined, and rifles across their chests.

Ibne opened his window and spoke rapidly in Punjabi. Two of them opened the thick wooden gate, while the other two stood with their guns ready.

Ibne drove the car slowly into the courtyard. Shabanu sensed instantly that something was wrong. The courtyard was empty and quiet. Usually servants and farm workers crossed back and forth, just as they did at Okurabad. Normally goats and chickens mingled with the wild birds in the courtyard. But even the hoopoes had fled from under the saal trees in the garden. And the light was hard and sharp, despite the gray sky, outlining everything in dark edges.

Both Rahim and Omar sensed the danger. They got out of the car slowly, and Rahim walked around to where Omar stood facing the front door. Shabanu sat immobile with fear, feeling as if her spine were attached to the seat of the station wagon.

In the second before the shooting began, a glint from the balcony over the portico caught Shabanu's eye. There stood Nazir, watching, one pudgy hand with a diamond ring on the little finger rubbing the silk that stretched over his broad paunch.

The first shot came from inside the house. Rahim threw himself in front of Omar, and several bullets that would have killed his nephew ripped across his back and shoulders. Rahim fell forward, completely immobile and limp. Omar tried to drag him back into the car.

"Leave him!" shouted Ibne, who had ducked down behind the door he'd held open for Rahim. "He's dead."

"We can't leave him," said Omar, who was still clasped in his dead uncle's arms. Omar was not hurt.

"He's dead. Get in! Get in!" Ibne screamed at Omar.

Dark stains of blood appeared around the two holes at the center of Rahim's back. One of his shoulders had been partially torn away, and Shabanu stared at the fragments of bone and white ribbons of ligament that protruded from where just seconds before Rahim's skin lay whole under his shirt.

There was only a second's pause in the shooting. The guards, who seemed to have been unaware that an ambush was to take place, stood frozen beside the gate.

Still Omar dragged at Rahim's body, though bullets whistled in the air and pinged through the metal of the car. In desperation Ibne lunged through the car and over the backseat to help pull the body inside. Shabanu, who had been motionless with shock, barely managed to get out of the way.

It began to rain, and the moment seemed strangely protracted. Shabanu remembered later that she had looked up to see Nazir still standing on the balcony rubbing his belly, his ring winking in the sun.

"Get down!" Ibne shouted, and they crouched as he whirled the car and aimed it at the gate, which the lately stung-into-action guards were just pulling closed.

As the car made its turn, knocking over flowerpots and small trees in the landscaped courtyard in front of the house, a man with a bandolier across his chest darted out of the house, yanked open the rear door where Shabanu sat, and pulled her from the car.

"Stop!" Omar shouted, but Ibne paused only briefly. His eye caught Shabanu's and it said I'm so sorry, and he kept going, smashing through the closing gate and splintering it. She understood that Ibne was doing his duty to protect Omar, his new master, as Rahim would have wished.

She struggled like a newly captured bird, striking with

her fists at the man who held her by the wrist, and kicking at his legs. He hoisted her up in one arm, and she turned her face toward him, sinking her teeth into his shoulder. The man screamed with pain. He drew back his other arm, and his fist crashed into the side of her head.

When she awoke, Zabo was dabbing her face with a damp cloth. Shabanu was confused. Her body ached. Had she dreamed it all?

"Where are we?" she asked.

"Shh," said Zabo.

"No talking, please!" said a voice from behind Zabo.

Shabanu looked past her friend. A kerosene lamp was lit on the table. Beyond it she saw the dark muzzles of the bodyguards' guns.

Funny, she thought, how contemptuous of them we were in Lahore.

Zabo stayed with her. Shabanu's clothes were torn, and Zabo unfolded one of her own *shalwar kameez* for her to wear. They were silent, not wanting to agitate the guards. A servant brought dinner on trays. They ate without speaking. Shabanu barely touched the oily spiced stew.

"You must eat. Just a little," said Zabo. There was urgency in her voice.

Shabanu did manage to swallow a few bites of vegetables and bread. She thought that both she and Zabo would need their strength if they were to escape. Zabo's eyes never left her face.

The guards put aside their guns and ate noisily, crouching in the doorway.

"I thought I'd never see you again," Zabo whispered quietly enough that the guards could not hear her over their slurping and sucking at chicken bones. "I'm sorry it happened like this."

"What happened?" Shabanu asked.

"Ahmed was killed in a hunting accident," she whispered.

"And what will happen now?"

"You should get some rest," Zabo said.

Shabanu lay back against a hard pillow. She tried to focus on what Rahim's death meant: that Omar was now the leader of Rahim's people, and that he must now avenge Rahim's death. A bloodbath, she thought. Would Omar also then try to rescue her and Zabo? If he did, she would return to Okurabad, and she would be under Amina's control.

No, thought Shabanu, that is not what Rahim's death means. It means I must never return to Okurabad. If Omar does rescue us, we must somehow get away.

It means that Zabo and I must now go to Sharma. Her heart was buoyed by the thought of being with Sharma and Fatima and Zabo and Mumtaz. But she knew it would be difficult.

Nazir had what he wanted—the land. Perhaps he would let them get away. Why would he take the trouble to find two women in the desert? She felt he would leave them alone after a while, as Sharma's husband had done when she had run away.

She fell asleep, and when she awoke it was as if no time had passed. The two bodyguards remained at attention on either side of the door. Zabo sat beside her, watching her face, and the kerosene lamp glowed in the room's stillness.

Then there was a loud crash at the door that sent Shabanu's heart hurtling into her mouth. Filling the doorway was Nazir, his bulky frame swaying. The mingled odors of stale cigarettes, cologne, and alcohol floated into the room before him.

He came to the side of the bed and pushed Zabo aside. He sat down and took Shabanu's hand and belched.

"My brother is dead," he said. "It is my duty now to protect you."

Shabanu shrank back against the hard pillow and tried to pull away her hand. Nazir seemed not to notice, and went on holding it between his two fat hands. He shifted his weight, swaying the *charpoi*. The stink of him made her stomach churn.

"You murdered your brother," she said, her voice a low, dangerous growl. "I would rather die than let you protect me."

Zabo sucked in air through her teeth, and Shabanu too prepared for a blow from his huge fist.

But Nazir stood slowly and bent forward. From the floor beside the washbasin that Zabo had used to bathe Shabanu, he picked up a large, shiny brown cockroach. He held it before his face between his forefinger and thumb and studied it carefully.

"You will learn to accept me," he said. He smiled, and his teeth were brown and ragged. Perspiration stood out on his forehead and lip and chin. "It is the duty of a good man to marry his brother's widow."

"Marry you!" said Shabanu. "Ha! The thought of you makes me sick. I would die first."

Nazir smiled again and turned his head slightly away from the roach, which struggled between his fingers, its sticklike legs moving frantically.

"You will marry me," he said. "Or your sister, Phulan, and her puny husband—eh?" And with that he squashed the bug between his fingers, and the yellow liquid contents of its body splattered over Shabanu and Zabo.

Shabanu leaned her head over the side of the *charpoi* and retched into the basin on the floor. Nazir threw back his enormous head and laughed loudly.

chapter 21

S habanu and Zabo marked the passing of the next two days only by the delivery of meals. The shutters at the windows were closed.

On the second day a loud banging shook the room. Shadows of movement flickered around the lit edges of the window as someone nailed boards over the outside. The thin lines of light disappeared inch by inch until the room was dark.

A cold stillness began to grow inside Shabanu's chest until it made breathing painful.

Is this what despair feels like? she wondered. No, there is no room for that kind of thinking, she scolded herself, and she lit the lantern.

Still they were not allowed to talk. An old *ayah* brought them a bucket of water to wash with in the mornings. In the evenings she came to empty another bucket that had been brought to them to use as a toilet. The guards refused to leave the room when the two young women wanted to wash or use the toilet.

"We are under orders," they said. And Shabanu and Zabo

hung their *chadr*s from nails across one corner of the room for privacy.

At midday the room was still dark, but it had grown hot and stuffy and filled with the smell of their toilet and the greasy food that was brought to them from Nazir's kitchen. It made them ill.

A desert chill crept into the air at night, and there were no blankets. They huddled together for warmth, but neither could sleep until the room warmed in the morning.

If only I could see the stars, Shabanu thought at night. But then she disallowed those thoughts, too. "Soon enough," she whispered softly to herself. "Soon enough."

She spent some time thinking about how good Rahim had been to her. She remembered how kind he'd been when Mumtaz was born. He never said, "You must have a son," which is what many men would have said after the birth of a daughter.

When she failed to conceive again, his only concern was for her health. He was so kind she had felt a little guilty that she had chosen not to conceive. But only a little guilty.

He was a good and gentle man, she thought. If his greatest fault was in sacrificing all for his family and their land, it also was his great strength. It was difficult to realize she'd never see him again.

She thought about Mumtaz, and how happy she was among the camels and the dunes. She thought of her own childhood, and her daughter's freedom consoled her.

And she thought about Omar, about how she had tried and failed to banish him from her heart. She wondered whether he would just stay there, and if he did, would the impossibility of loving him fill her with longing the rest of her life?

These thoughts drifted through her mind in a haze, as if

they were part of a dream. Then suddenly the reality of what had happened would pounce on her.

She saw the stain from the roach on her tunic, and the picture of Rahim's blood and his shattered shoulder became fixed in her mind until she could see nothing else.

Then she caught a whiff of Nazir's lingering stench, and the thought of her waiting night after night, terrified that he'd come to her bed, drunk and smelling of the fat of meat, made her retch.

When these realities took hold of her mind, Shabanu began to fight.

There is no time to mourn Rahim now, she thought to herself. There is no time to worry about Nazir. You must think clearly, calculate accurately, plan how you and Zabo can escape! And it worked. A fine plan took shape in her mind. It calmed her.

For each step of the plan, she thought of an alternative plan. It became a fascinating game, memorizing details and then replaying them in order; it was like following a maze inside her head.

On the third day, just after their breakfast of greasy fried bread arrived with lukewarm tea, a loud explosion rocked the room that had become their world.

The guards threw open the door and looked outside. Gunfire was raining down, and explosions rocked the house every half minute. The guards stayed outside in the hallway for a few minutes, arguing about whether they should leave Shabanu and Zabo unwatched to join the fight.

In that moment Shabanu closed her eyes and whispered a small prayer: Please, Allah, guide my hands and feet that this plan might bring both of us to safety. And—please protect Omar.

"He'll have our heads if we leave them," said one guard.

"You fool," said the other. "We can lock them in. He'll have our heads if we don't fight!"

They closed the door and locked it from the outside. Shabanu waited for the clatter of their running footsteps to recede down the hallway. She went to the door and bent to look through the keyhole. No light came through. It was almost too good to believe!

Another explosion hit so close to the room that plaster dust rained down on them.

Shabanu took from the breakfast tray a stiffly starched napkin and pushed it flat under the door. Then she put her cheek against the floor, with her eye close to the crack at the bottom, and worked a teaspoon under the door to position the napkin under the keyhole on the other side.

She rose to her knees before the doorknob. She took a hairpin from the bun at the back of her neck and poked it through the keyhole. It was only a few seconds before the key dropped to the floor on the other side of the door. To her utter amazement, she pulled the napkin through the crack at the bottom of the door, and sitting atop it like a prize was the key!

"Come quickly," Shabanu said. She made a bundle of their breakfast and took two shawls from the cupboard.

But Zabo sat immobile on the cot opposite Shabanu's, her back pressed against the wall. Her eyes were huge and unblinking.

Outside, men shouted and automatic weapons fired, glass shattered, wood splintered, and more explosions made the walls shudder and the floor heave.

Shabanu took Zabo's hand, but her friend pulled back.

"We're safer out there than we are here, in the front of the house," said Shabanu. She shook Zabo's shoulders gently. "This is our best chance to get away!"

"But why? Hasn't Omar come with Uncle Rahim's men to take back Ahmed's land? Won't he rescue us?"

"If he wins, I'm sure he will," replied Shabanu. "But I cannot go back to Okurabad with Rahim gone. And you—your father will keep you a prisoner. He might even kill you. You will inherit Ahmed's land, and he wants it. We must get away before Omar comes. We must go to Cholistan." Still Zabo did not move, and Shabanu thought for a moment.

"You are not going alone. Mumtaz is already there. I am coming with you. We're going together."

Zabo stood slowly. She shook herself, as if emerging from sleep. She took the bundle of food from Shabanu's hand.

"I'm sorry," said Zabo. "I'm terribly afraid. But I'm ready. Let's go."

Outside, the hallway was dimly lit but empty. They made their way quickly to where the narrow corridor ended in a room with tattered and broken chairs against the walls, entrances to two other hallways, and two doors to the outside.

"This way!" said Zabo, and she pushed open a door that led to a back garden behind the kitchen. Most of the firing was concentrated on the courtyard and the main rooms at the front of the house.

They ran together across the garden, through just-planted corn rows, trampling newly staked tomato plants that sent their fresh, bitter smell following them to a low building at the base of the compound wall.

A heavy dew dampened the hems of their clothes. Their breath came in pale puffs of mist. The sky was a watery blue, with a soft rim of melon at the horizon.

The noise of the battle was deafening, numbing. They ducked into the shed, which was a storage place for old, disused wheelbarrows, empty cement sacks, broom handles, and other, less identifiable debris. Sunlight filtered into it through a haze of dust and spiderwebs.

"Is there another way to get outside the wall besides the main front and back gates?" Shabanu asked.

"Through the stable," Zabo said, and she led the way. The stable was the best-kept building on the property, better by far than the house. The stalls were clean and smelled only of the fresh straw spread over the floor.

The horses stamped nervously in their stalls, ignoring the basins that contained their morning meal.

Shabanu's and Zabo's eyes grew accustomed to the dimness of the stable. The horses looked out over the tops of their half doors, ears pitched forward, nickering softly, begging to be let out to escape the noise of the guns.

"I wish I knew how to ride a horse," Shabanu whispered.

Zabo shook her head. "Too dangerous," she said. "We must get out on foot."

And she led Shabanu to an ancient part of the compound wall. Outside, the earth had fallen away in a series of floods over a period of decades as the river had changed course and the water table rose and fell. The wall had been repaired from the bottom many times, leaving an old footpath gate several feet in the air on the outside. It was one of a very few gates that had been closed permanently and forgotten.

Zabo went first. Before easing through a parting of the gate's wooden planks, Shabanu stopped to look back toward the firing at the front of the house.

On a slight rise outside the front gate sat three lorries with huge guns mounted on their beds. Two were aimed at the massive steel-reinforced front gates. Behind the rise, dozens of vans and minibuses were parked, and rows of gunmen lined the rim of the hill.

The gunfire from outside the wall was overwhelming. Omar must have raised several hundred men to reclaim Ahmed's land and avenge Rahim's death.

Shabanu had wondered whether Omar's years in the West had dulled his instinct for revenge. In the Punjab, a man who murdered his brother was nearly as good as dead himself at the hands of his brother's heirs.

"Praise Allah in His mercy that all Omar's bullets fall true," she said, before letting herself fall gently to the ground beside Zabo on the other side of the wall.

Shabanu pulled her *chadr* tighter around her face, and, seeing her, Zabo did the same. Shabanu still wore her silver ankle cuffs and her country-made sandals. If anyone saw her and Zabo, Shabanu was sure they looked enough like village women to go unnoticed.

Kept company by the soft gurgle of the fetid water in the sewers on either side of the deserted lane, they made their way from the compound and the outer edge of the village until they had reached the secondary feeder canal that carried irrigation water to the farmers at the edge of the desert. Not a soul was in sight; no doubt the villagers had fled at the first sound of gunfire.

They stopped to rest at the canal, and the water lapped and sucked softly at the muddy bank. Birds sang in the trees over their heads. In the distance the battle still sounded fierce.

"Your father will suspect we've gone to the settlement where my family is, near my sister. If he survives Omar's attack, they will be at risk," said Shabanu.

"I'm sure he will carry out his threat against your sister and her husband," said Zabo. "Shouldn't we warn them?"

"I've thought of another idea. If we go to the Desert

Rangers at Derawar Fort, they will protect my family. Your father isn't likely to look for us there. But it will be a long trip on foot. Are you up to it?"

"Anything that takes me away from here," said Zabo.

They walked along the canal until they could no longer hear the gunfire at Mehrabpur. They came to an old shed at the edge of an abandoned village, and they stopped there to eat some of the food they'd brought. The sun was high in the sky. It was hot, and the air was heavy with dampness.

"We will be safer and more comfortable if we travel after dark," Shabanu said. "Let's rest for a while."

She was relieved to breathe fresh air and to be moving—doing something, not waiting for things to happen. But Zabo's face was still pale, and she looked frightened.

"Don't be afraid," Shabanu said softly to Zabo, and she brushed her friend's hair back from her perspiring face. "Soon we will be in Cholistan. We will be free, and we will be with Sharma and Mumtaz. We will be together!"

"I'm not as strong as you are, Shabanu," Zabo said. And she twisted her *chadr* around her fingers. "And I know my father too well. He is ruthless. He won't stop until both of us are dead. I know him.

"When Father brought back Ahmed's body, he was piled on top of the deer and birds they'd shot, as if he were just another head of game. He walked in with his gun over his arm, not afraid at all that anyone would guess it was not an accident.

"And when they brought Ahmed's body into the house, Father shouted at them to take him out to the stable. 'You're getting blood on the carpet,' he said.

"And, Shabanu, there is something else. I heard him tell Raoul, his farm manager. He has somewhere to hide. He thinks nobody will find him in this place. He may even have gone there before Omar and his men arrived this morning.

"He's not sane, Shabanu. Because you said you would never marry him he'll hurt us. It will be more important to him than protecting his land. You saw what they did to Uncle Rahim. It's just the way he is."

"I know you're right," said Shabanu. "But I know the Rangers will help us."

"I hope so," said Zabo.

"And, Zabo," said Shabanu, taking her friend's hands. "We must have hope."

Zabo nodded. Within minutes both of them had fallen sound asleep.

They awoke many hours later to the sound of camels coming down the canal path shortly after sunset. The large bells tied on goathair cords around their necks made a lovely gonging sound, and their large leathery feet whispered softly through the dust.

Shabanu didn't want to risk being seen, for Nazir would surely question everyone he came upon. But she wanted to see who it was, so she knelt and looked around the door frame, her heart beating rapidly.

The legs of the camels went past at eye level, looking like the trunks of young trees bent in a windstorm, moving in long, slow, deliberate strides. The camels were loaded with bags of wheat and sugar, a few cook pots and water jars, bundles that swayed and creaked against the wooden frames of their saddles as they passed.

Most likely it was a family coming back to the desert after a trip to the bazaar in Bahawalpur. But Shabanu couldn't see people. Perhaps they rode atop the camels' loads.

When the caravan had passed, Shabanu woke Zabo. The

evening was hazy along the canal, and she was sure there would be little moonlight to find their way on such a cloudy night.

"We must start moving," she said, shaking Zabo's shoulder.

They wrapped themselves in their shawls against the dampness and walked along the towpath until they reached the break in the levee that told Shabanu they should leave the canal path and strike out across the desert.

The night air was cooler and drier once they left the irrigated area. There was no moon at all, and the stars were hidden behind clouds that had been thick and gray in the sky during the late afternoon.

When they were far beyond the villages and could see no lights and hear no sounds, Shabanu switched on the small flashlight Omar had given her. In its tight little circle of light she identified the lay of the dunes and found their direction. She turned off the light and set a pace somewhere between a walk and a run, her ankle bracelets sounding the rhythm of her gait with a soft *kachin, kachin, kachin.*

Zabo had trouble keeping up at first, but they rested a few moments under a stand of thorn trees, and she seemed to do better when they started off again.

Shabanu stopped to sniff the air, but there was no musty scent yet of the *toba* near where they would turn off for Derawar.

She moved with the sureness of a desert tracker until they were about an hour from where they'd left the canal. Then Shabanu bent and felt the sand. It was coarse and pebbly. The desert nomads always dug their *toba*s in the clay depressions along the bed of the ancient Hakra River, which had disappeared many centuries ago to run underground.

The river gravel and shells still marked its course through the desert.

She found the damp spots that marked the edges of the large pond that sustained the nomads and their herds for months at a time after the monsoon rains. There she took a turn toward the east.

When they had been on the track to Derawar for less than an hour, the distant sound of the grunting and bellowing of tethered camels reached them. She put out her hand and stopped Zabo.

"Wait here," she whispered.

She sat on the ground and took off her ankle bracelets, and for the first time that evening she was glad the night was so dark.

The caravan had pulled in between two stands of trees behind a small hillock, which sheltered them on three sides. The camels were tethered on the other side of the hillock.

Three men sat around a fire, talking and taking turns sucking at a large brass *hookah* pipe. She smelled the warm, sweet aroma of fruity tobacco and brown sugar and heard the gurgle of the smoke being pulled through the water in the base of the pipe. The flames flickered a deep golden orange on their faces as they talked quietly, happy to rest after a long day's journey.

She sat for a few moments among the sticklike branches of *kharin* just behind the hillock that hid her from the men's vision. She wanted the camels to have some time to get used to her scent before she approached them.

Even so they danced back and forth in little semicircles, and their grunts became higher-pitched as she walked toward them, her palm outstretched.

One old female sat passively over a dinner of greens,

chewing calmly. As she chewed, she drew back her head to look down her long broad nose and contemplate the young woman. The female camel wore neither tether nor ankle bracelets.

"Good *daachii*," Shabanu whispered, stroking the camel's neck. "Uushshshsh." Slowly and silently the old female got to her feet.

And just as quietly Shabanu led her away, keeping the hillock between herself and the men around the fire. She walked out into the desert a half mile before ordering the camel to her knees and climbing up onto her shoulders.

"Uushshshsh!" she commanded again, and the camel lurched to her feet. Shabanu guided her back to where Zabo sat in a thicket of tamarisk.

"This old *daachii* should make our trip easier!" Shabanu said, her voice still a whisper.

The camel was docile and cooperative, and by the time the sun sent opal streaks across the sky, they could see the massive turrets of the fort at Derawar.

The weather had cleared, and it looked like a fine morning as the sun climbed higher. Zabo slept, her head against the back of Shabanu's shoulder.

chapter 22

The Desert Rangers occupied a fort made of sand and clay and cow dung that was indistinguishable from the dunes, except for the square edges of its walls in the cool, hard light of the dawn. A white four-wheel drive vehicle was parked in front.

Shabanu slowed the old camel to a walk, and the change from her gentle lope woke Zabo.

"Oh!" said Zabo. "Oh, Shabanu! That's Raoul's jeep. They've come after us! Run! Run!"

In response to Shabanu's command, the *daachii* whirled. As she did, a single shot rang out. Zabo slumped against Shabanu's shoulder.

"Hang on!" Shabanu shouted back over her shoulder as the old camel picked up her pace. Zabo's arms tightened slightly around Shabanu's waist, and she groaned softly.

Praise Allah, she prayed. In Your mercy let Zabo be all right. I would gladly give my own life to save her. Shabanu thanked Allah for having given her the wisdom to think of alternate plans.

And by the time she heard the jeep start up, they were

on the opposite side of the fort, out of sight inside the massive front gate. The camel knelt on the cobbled drive behind the wall. Shabanu pried Zabo's arms from her waist and climbed down from the hump.

Zabo had been shot through the throat, a neat hole on one side of the soft, pale flesh of her neck and a ragged tangle of flesh on the other. Blood dripped from the side of her mouth.

"Oh, Zabo," she whispered, and tears burned her eyes. Her tongue felt swollen in her aching throat. "Please, please hang on. I'm here with you. Please fight hard!"

Zabo's lovely dark eyes were open, but it was as if they were pressed behind glass. They barely moved, and she didn't blink at all. Shabanu was not sure that Zabo could see.

She lay Zabo's head against the camel's massive hump. Her breathing was ragged and bubbly.

She ran to the small door on the opposite side of the cobbled drive from the huge gate, which was pierced through with swords at its top to keep the Rajput princes' elephants from battering it down in dozens of battles over the centuries.

"Shahzada! Please help me!" she cried, hammering on the door of her father's friend, the gatekeeper of the fort of the nawab of Bahawalpur. "Please, someone, let me in!"

At that moment the engine of the jeep whined as it headed off down the track to look for her and Zabo in the desert.

Shahzada, who must have been close to his hundredth year, answered Shabanu's knock himself.

"Do you remember me? I am the daughter of Dalil Abassi. I beg you to help me!"

"Yes, child, I know who you are and why you're here," said the old man through his long and widely spaced teeth.

His bare skull was covered with the red felt fez of the nawab's army uniform. He was tall and thin and straight, with a thick stubble of white beard.

"Come quickly!" said Shabanu, dragging him by the hand to where the camel knelt. Zabo had slumped sideways, her face pressed into the camel's hump. Her blood had saturated the animal's fur and now dripped onto the cobbles.

Shahzada and Shabanu lifted Zabo from the *daachii* and propped her up against the animal's side.

"Please, Zabo, please fight for your life! I haven't betrayed you! I'm here. We'll save you," she whispered against her friend's hair. Zabo groaned faintly.

"Your sister?" Shabanu asked Shahzada. "Is she still . . ."

"Yes," he said. He tore a strip from Zabo's *chadr,* wadded it, and pressed it against the ragged hole in her throat. "Hold this. I'll fetch her." His sister was a *hakkim* of sorts—a midwife, a preparer of the dead for burial, an herbalist curer of countless ills.

"Can you hear me, Zabo?" Shabanu asked. Her hands trembled, and tears dripped from her chin and the end of her nose. When she lifted her hand to wipe them away, it was slick and red with Zabo's blood.

Zabo's eyes were closed now. Her face was so pale it looked faintly blue. Her breaths were farther apart and shallower.

"Hurry!" Shabanu shouted in the direction of Shahzada. "Hurry!"

But Zabo was gone before he returned with the withered old woman, whose only job now would be to prepare Zabo for her grave.

Shabanu was incredulous. Her one friend who just minutes ago had clung to her with strong and healthy arms—

they had been on their way to spend the rest of their lives together, free in the desert with Mumtaz and Sharma and Fatima. She couldn't be dead! Just seconds ago she was alive!

Shahzada lifted Zabo in his arms and carried her quickly to his sister's quarters, beckoning Shabanu to follow. She was barely able to stumble after him.

"Did anyone see you come here?" he asked.

Shabanu shook her head. "Whoever was in the jeep thinks we've gone into the desert."

"Praise Allah," he whispered.

His sister darted out the low doorway with a bucket of water and washed away Zabo's blood. Then she scrubbed the camel's fur and pulled the beast inside the nawab's stable.

Within a few minutes, the desert air had drunk the water and the remains of Zabo's blood, and there was nothing to show that she had died there.

Shahzada and his sister prepared Zabo's body for burial, bathing her pale skin and praying over her. Shabanu helped them, but she felt as if her hands were ineffectual, that when they meant to tuck the folds of the shroud under Zabo's shoulders, they merely fluttered. Her lips, when they meant to pray, merely uttered words of grief. Never had she felt so defeated and helpless.

When they had finished, Shahzada lay Zabo, her body wrapped head to foot in a pure white seamless shroud, on a bare wooden table in a back room in his sister's chambers. He led Shabanu to a tiny dark parlor. His sister brought a plain tray with sweetened tea in a little blue enamel teapot.

"Nazir-*sahib* came directly here to look for you," he said. "He remembered that your family went to the Desert Rangers for protection from him one other time. And, I tell you, he will not rest until he finds you. I thought you would be alone. He never mentioned his daughter."

"Where will we bury her?" Shabanu asked. "I remember you buried Grandfather's fez and sword in the lapis tomb of the army commander."

"Yes," said Shahzada. "Your grandfather was a noble soldier and a fine man."

"I know there was no room in the nawab's cemetery for a poor desert nomad. But would there be a place for the daughter of a nobleman?"

Shahzada sat back and lay a finger beside his nose.

"Perhaps for the wife of Rahim-*sahib*," he said. "With all respect to your friend, may her soul rest in peace, perhaps we should say this is your grave. Since her father does not even care to look for her . . ."

"But then there would be no grave for Zabo, and her spirit would wander about."

"You must believe me when I tell you your life is in danger," said Shahzada, his gray eyes wise with age but young as the day he was born. "Nazir will have men all over Derawar keeping watch for you. He thought you would be traveling on foot, and so he was not expecting you as early as you arrived. He had just arrived himself."

Shabanu's mind raced. Her stomach churned. What had happened to Omar? Had he too been killed? Too many killings. Oh, I beg of you, Allah, let there be no more! Her heart would hold no more grief.

"Won't the Rangers help?" she asked.

"Bah!" he said. "The new commander is a corrupt and greedy man. Nazir has befriended him so that he can hunt whenever he likes in the game preserve."

"I must get to my family and warn them. If the Rangers can't protect them . . ."

"Listen, little *Begum*," said Shahzada. "If Nazir-*sahib* thinks you're dead, he will not bother your family. If he thinks you are alive, however, he will employ the best desert trackers the Rangers have. He will never rest until you are dead or captured."

"But my family must know I'm safe. . . ."

"For their sake, I'm afraid they too must believe it was you who was killed."

"But if everyone thinks I'm dead, what is the point of living?"

"The point is that you *will* be alive. And there is hope as long as you are alive. There is always the possibility that Nazir-*sahib* will—Allah forgive me—not survive for long."

Shabanu knew that her family would grieve for her. But it was Mumtaz she worried about. It was one thing for Mumtaz to be happy and free in the desert when she also had the security of her home, including a loving mother and father. But suddenly to find herself in a wild and desolate place and to learn that she no longer had a home and that both her parents were dead . . .

Then Shabanu thought of the alternatives: She might be a prisoner at Mehrabpur, without Zabo, dreading every day that Nazir would come to her bed; or if Omar did rescue her, she and Mumtaz would be enslaved at Okurabad, forever under the power of Amina and Leyla.

And that decided for her. Never, she thought. Never, never, never.

They buried Zabo that night in a simple grave in a corner of the deserted stableyard. They marked it with a huge mound of straw so that it would be difficult to find, even for someone searching for it. They said the prayers that would speed her on her way to heaven.

And Shahzada and his sister left Shabanu to mourn her

only friend quietly until it was time to decide how she would live her life as a ghost.

Shahzada and his sister took her back to the small dark room behind their quarters. It was decided that she would be safer hiding in the fort than trying to leave just now, when Nazir and his men were looking for her. Meals were delivered to her on a covered tray. She was not to go outside the room unless Shahzada or his sister came for her, and that happened only at night.

When she was allowed outside, she searched the stars, the billions of stars that dazzled like diamonds in the sapphire desert sky. These were the same stars, she thought, beneath which Mumtaz slept. And she wondered whether Omar might be looking up at them as well.

She was grateful for the time to concentrate on the thoughts she'd begun but never finished, the hurts she'd begun to feel but never dealt with before the next catastrophe was upon her in these last weeks.

Shahzada kept watch for danger. And each morning when he visited the well, he and the herdsmen exchanged stories.

It seemed a caravan of nomads had found the body of a small woman, the little *begum* who once was a Cholistani girl. The nomads remembered her—she married a wealthy *zamindar* the year the drought had ended. She was the daughter of Dalil Abassi, the keeper of the finest camels in Cholistan.

A tall, slender girl whose father also was a landowner kept watch over the body of the little *begum,* the nomads said. Her father had beaten her and murdered her husband, and so she asked a family of gypsies to take her into the mountains with them.

That was the story that made its way around Derawar,

although nobody was able to say exactly where the story had come from. Shahzada visited the well of a neighboring village, and he heard the same story. And by the time a week had passed, the Desert Rangers had stopped looking for the two young women.

And then something strange happened. A tall, handsome young man came to Shahzada, saying he was the little *begum*'s brother.

Shahzada recalled that Dalil Abassi had not been blessed with sons. The young man blushed and looked down at the ground.

"I loved her very much, sir," he said to Shahzada. "Can you tell me, please, who would know where I can find her grave so that I might pay my respects?"

Shahzada asked him to come back.

"I will have to go to the village to ask," he said. "Please come tomorrow."

That evening he told Shabanu. She asked what the young man looked like. When Shahzada told her, she lowered her eyes. Her eyes, which already this week had shed more tears than she would ever have guessed her body could hold, spilled over yet again.

"Please," she said. "Please show him the grave. For he is one who will never believe until he sees. But, Uncle, I want to see him," she said.

And so it was arranged that Shabanu was led to a loft over the stable, where the winter fodder was stored, to wait for Omar to mourn her at her graveside.

When he came late that afternoon, Shahzada told Omar that the nomads had brought her body to him and that he had buried her in the stableyard.

"You see, *Sahib,* no one wants trouble from Nazir. So her grave site must be kept secret. It is only because I knew her—such a good and brave young woman—that I will show you."

The young man nodded slowly. His eyes held more sadness than Shahzada knew existed in the world.

"I too wish that no one else should know," Omar said.

Shahzada took him out to the stableyard and moved aside the pile of straw.

"Here?" said Omar. "But my Shabanu must have a fitting grave! A pile of straw will never do! After I have mourned a year, I shall bring a marble marker with inscriptions. Please," he said, his voice shaking. "Please leave me alone."

The sun was low in the sky. In its red-gold light, Omar's dark eyes glistened. He leaned forward and put his hand on the head of the grave. He sat for a moment, his hand over Zabo's head.

Then he turned his face to the sky. It was wet with tears.

"Shabanuuuu!" he wailed, like an animal in pain. "Shaahh-baha-nuuuuuuuuu!"

Shabanu wanted to run to him and fold him into her arms, as she had wanted to do with Mumtaz. Her heart ached, her throat ached, and once again she found herself saying silently, For the sake of Mumtaz. For the sake of Mumtaz. For the sake of Mumtaz. And she stayed hidden in the straw of the loft.

He sat beside the grave until it was almost dark. And then he reached out his hand again.

"For as many seconds as I live on this earth," he said, "you will always be in my heart."

And with that he leaned forward and kissed the ground

under which Zabo's head lay. And then he stood and gathered the straw in his arms and began to cover the grave again. Shahzada came running.

"Here, *Sahib,* allow me," said Shahzada.

But Omar held on to the straw, spreading it handful by handful until the grave was covered.

chapter 23

Shabanu arrived at the *haveli* late on a chilly night. She got out of the *tonga* at the corner of the lane and paid the *tonga-wallah*. He and his poor old horse looked as if they would fall asleep on the spot.

It had been a long and difficult journey. She had begun from Derawar before first light, wrapped in a goathair blanket and piled with dozens of other blankets onto a camel cart. The dust of the blankets had filled her nose, and several times she was barely able to breathe.

She had traveled that way for many hours, until the camels met up with a caravan. She and the blankets had been transferred to another camel cart that was to take them to market for sale. The driver of the cart did not know she was among the blankets, and he had piled on top a load of water jars. And again she was barely able to breathe.

The carts creaked along, the drivers singing and spitting into the dust at the side of the road.

She'd been bruised by the weight on top of her and was dizzy from the bad air by the time the camels reached Bahawalpur. While the drivers stopped in a stall in the bazaar to take tea, she managed to work her way out from under the pots and blankets.

From Bahawalpur she had taken the bus to Lahore. In the Mall in downtown Lahore she had flagged down an empty *tonga* and had bargained with the driver to take her to the *haveli*.

Now she drew the black *chadr* around her face as she stood in the doorway of a small shrine to look down the lane. She heard the nightstick of the old neighborhood *chowkidar* go *chunk, chunk* on the cobbled paving stones as he made his way on his rounds. She peered around the corner and saw his back retreating from the yellow circle of lamplight outside Selma's gate. He would not return for at least fifteen minutes.

She hurried to the gate and stood for a moment in the shadows inside the courtyard to listen for voices and footsteps. There were none.

Certainly Selma was asleep, the servants were asleep, the chickens in the courtyard were asleep. The *haveli* itself seemed to be asleep.

Its old doorways sagged like slack, sleeping mouths. It seemed to wheeze and creak and groan with release from weariness.

For the tenth time that day Shabanu wondered, Will it always be like this—hiding and then wondering if I've been seen when I was unaware?

Still keeping in the shadows, Shabanu made her way to the bottom of the old stairway that led up, up through the center of the house, through the open well that went from the courtyard to the top floor, which had been sealed off after the death of Selma's husband, Daoud.

She climbed in the dark, keeping to the inside of the

curving staircase, where the steps had the most support and were least likely to creak under her weight. She stopped every few steps to listen. Still there were only the groans of the sleeping house.

She was weary when she reached the roof. She unfastened her neck chain, removed the key, and unlocked the door to the pavilion. She lit one of the small brass oil lamps. It was exactly as she'd left it, with dots of cheerful light from the cut-crystal chimney dancing from the surfaces of the wood she'd polished with care.

Even the needlework she'd had in her lap when Rahim had come to Selma's parlor to summon her back to Okurabad still sat in the little basket at the foot of her Swati chair.

Her heart tumbled again when she went to the corner of the room where the small *charpoi* she'd found for Mumtaz made an L with her own.

She found the books she'd brought up, even before she could read well enough to get through them, and she felt unaccountably happy.

But then she found a picture Mumtaz had drawn for her, and she thought that now Mumtaz would never study to become an engineer. She would be a little desert girl, married to a cousin—perhaps one of Adil's sons—with a small farm like Murad's. And she fell into a mood so black and devoid of hope she feared she might never again emerge into the light.

Is this what despair feels like? she wondered. A dark and featureless landscape with only fear and pain and loss to occupy the heart? This time she permitted herself the thought.

She spent the rest of the night mourning in this way. She was unable to sleep, seeing Omar's face as he wailed her name, and wondering when she'd ever see Mumtaz again.

By now Dadi would have told Mumtaz that her mother and father were dead. She wanted to hold her, to tell her that her mother would always be alive for her. What grieved her most was the thought of her daughter's grief.

Her heart felt as if it was full to overbrimming with jagged pieces. She was desperate to hear news of her family and of Omar.

Is this how Anarkali felt, she wondered, suffocating slowly in her tomb? No, I am not like Anarkali, who died for love. I have denied love, and wonder now if life is worth living without it.

Well before dawn, she crept down the stairs to Selma's quarters on the second floor. The massive door creaked on its hinges as she let herself in, and she called to Selma.

"Who is it?" Selma asked, sounding alarmed.

"It's Shabanu." She laughed a small, mirthless laugh.

"Ay, ay, ay," said Selma, and the bedclothes rustled as she scrambled and tore at them, trying to find the light. "What happened that you are alive? And how did you get here?"

When the light came on, Shabanu went to Selma, who struggled to get into a robe. Shabanu sat beside her on the bed. Selma took her face in her hands and studied it to be sure it truly was Shabanu.

"Do I dare trust my eyes?" Selma whispered. "They've seen too much grief. . . ."

"Oh, Selma!" said Shabanu, relief washing over her. "I had no choice. I'm sorry you worried about me, after what happened to Rahim."

Selma blew her nose, wiped her eyes, and composed herself.

"Begin at the start, and don't leave out a thing," said Selma.

She interrupted Shabanu only twice—once to ask her to repeat Nazir's horrifying marriage proposal, and once to hear again how Zabo died. Selma cried again, and Shabanu wept too. The only detail Shabanu did not tell was of Omar crying beside Zabo's grave.

"So," said Shabanu. "As long as Nazir is alive, he must think I am dead. To protect my family they all must believe it was I who died, and not poor Zabo. Can I stay here, up in the pavilion, without his knowing?"

"Of course, child," said Selma. "You yourself know that nobody goes to the pavilion. They're too afraid of the ghost of my dear late Daoud. That would have given him such a laugh! Samiya can bring your meals. Nobody else need know you're here."

"Now," Shabanu said finally. "Tell me what you know about my family. And I want to know what happened at Nazir's."

Selma heaved herself up from the bed. She paced a few moments, and then let herself down into her rocking chair.

"Let me start from the beginning. Omar returned to Okurabad with Rahim's body in the car. Within a day he had gathered the clansmen and formed an army of five hundred men. That boy will be a fine leader. Rahim, may his soul rest in peace, would be proud of him.

"They had six mortar guns, and almost every man had an automatic weapon or a grenade launcher. Big guns, nasty guns—I don't know what all they had.

"Omar assembled a convoy of lorries, vans, and mini-buses. He gathered provisions for several days of fighting. And then he assembled all of the old warriors who have always followed Rahim. He was wonderful!"

"But why did he wait so long?" asked Shabanu. "It seemed forever before he came!"

"He let two days pass. There was no way Nazir could summon as many armed men on his side. So Omar expected a trap. He thought if he waited Nazir might think he'd not been able to get the support he needed.

"Omar was right. They came in the early morning and waited until dawn, when the guards were changing. And then they attacked. Nazir's men fought valiantly. Nazir ordered them not to surrender, and then he slipped away.

"Nazir lost more than a dozen men, and the house was nearly destroyed by mortar fire. It was lucky you and Zabo escaped. Two or three of Omar's men were wounded. But Omar will get Nazir, I'm certain of that."

"That means more bloodshed," said Shabanu. They sat quietly for a moment.

"Thank God you are safe," said Selma. "I am so glad you are here. And when Nazir is gone, you can bring Mumtaz back and stay if you would like."

"Insh'Allah," said Shabanu. "God willing. I should be grateful just to see Mumtaz again. Tell me what news you have of my family."

"Word reached them that you had died on the very same day. By morning they were gone, back to the desert with Mumtaz."

"And my sister?"

"Omar has posted guards at her husband's farm. For now at least they are safe. But I think Nazir believes you are dead. As long as he does, I think he will leave them alone.

"Now, child, you must get rest. You look more tired than I am, and that is considerably tired."

The weather had turned cooler, but the pavilion was pleasant. Shabanu found blankets and a small heater in the storeroom where her furniture had come from. As miraculously as the open lattice walls captured the summer breezes, they also held in the heat, as if they were made of solid stone.

In the afternoon Samiya brought Shabanu tea. Samiya was proper and formal as she entered the room, as befitted a good servant.

But Shabanu wept when she saw the small birdlike woman. She thought of the happy days she and Mumtaz had spent with her, learning to read, learning to think, as Samiya did, that all things were possible once you had access to words in books.

"Oh, Samiya," she wept, and Samiya set down the tray without a single rattle and came swiftly on her bare feet to Shabanu's side.

"Little *Begum,*" Samiya said, taking Shabanu's hands. She held Shabanu as she wept, and when she was finished crying she felt better.

"What else can I bring you?" asked Samiya then.

"Books!" said Shabanu. "I don't feel like reading yet, but I will soon. And a pan of coal for the heater. And more oil for the lamps. Can you do it without anyone's knowledge?"

"Don't worry," Samiya said. "*Begum-sahiba* has said you may have whatever you want."

Shabanu imagined her life settling into a pattern. Each morning Samiya would bring her tea and breakfast. They would sit and talk for a short time—about the weather and who had visited the *haveli,* repairs that were needed, gossip from the servants' quarters. Shabanu would ask her to bring some mending.

Afterward Shabanu would sweep out the pavilion and trim the wicks on her lamps. She would have to do her own laundry and hang it on the roof, of course, so the other servants would not guess she was there.

In the afternoon Selma came, and Samiya brought them

tea. Selma told Shabanu what news there was. A date had been set for Omar and Leyla's wedding. It was to be later in the cool season, as Amina had wished.

"Amina is furious that she won't have her parties," said Selma. Her smile was malicious. "But mourning must be observed."

Shabanu felt as if she had come home. No place would ever be home as the desert was, but she felt safe and comfortable in the *haveli*.

That evening she sat outside the pavilion looking down at the city. As the last rays of the sun touched the translucent domes of Badshahi Mosque, lights winked on below as if the rooftops had been touched by thousands of fairies.

In the small mosque at the corner, the muezzin climbed into the minaret and called out over the small parish, *"Allah-o-Akbar!"* summoning the faithful to prayer. Men hurried down the lane, removing their shoes as they entered through the mosque's one door.

Shabanu realized in that moment on a peaceful evening that the world would go on. Hope crept back into her heart, and she felt she was mending and growing accustomed to her grief. She began to understand that the grief would never go away; she would simply learn to live with it.

She missed Zabo. But gradually when she thought of Zabo she did not see the ragged hole in her friend's neck or her blood soaking into the fur of the *daachii*'s hump. She thought instead of times they'd spent together: picking flowers beside the canal, walking in the hills together at Dinga Galli, scaring themselves by telling stories about panthers. They'd climb high up on the mountains and look out on the villages that appeared so small and insignificant under that enormous sky.

She longed for Omar. She had thought that perhaps he

would come to the pavilion to mourn her, that she would see him and that they might share their love. But as she pondered this, the realization grew that it would put her family and Mumtaz in great danger. She knew now how much he'd loved her—but she could never stand against his commitment to the family. He had pledged himself to the same destiny as Rahim's, and like Rahim he would sacrifice anything to duty, as Rahim had done with his very life.

She thought of the wonderful angular planes of Omar's face, the broadness of his hands, the gentleness of his eyes. The longing still went straight to her heart, so deep it seemed to have no bottom. But it felt familiar. There are worse things than longing, she thought.

She thought of Mumtaz, and gradually the stab of loss gave way to pictures of Mumtaz beside the fire with Mama and Sharma, learning to make chapatis, kneading the dough and whirling it into flat disks and roasting it on the black pan over the open fire. In Shabanu's mind's eye, her daughter's hands were beginning to look less chubby, and more capable and slender like Mama's. She would learn to sing the desert songs in a smoky voice, and listen to the magical stories of the desert people.

She thought of Mumtaz running over the dunes with the baby camels, a child of the wind, her hair blowing free behind her.

And Shahzada had been right. She lived with hope. One day, she thought, Mumtaz would be with her at the haveli, and she would go to school and become a part of the larger world, her life far richer for having lived among her people in the desert.

But now, Shabanu thought, Omar is my heart; and Mumtaz, Mumtaz is my freedom.

Glossary

Allah-o-Akbar (*Ah*-luh *oh Ahk*-bahr)—"God is great!"
Asalaam-o-Aleikum (Uh-suh-*lahm* oh Uh-*leh*-koom)—Traditional Islamic greeting
ayah (*ii*-yuh)—A maid who tends children

baithak (*beh*-tuhk)—Gentlemen's sitting room
barsati (bahr-*sah*-tee)—A room built on the roof of a house
Basant (Buh-*sahnt*)—Festival of kites that celebrates spring
begum (*beh*-guhm)—Respectful title for a married woman, similar to "madam" in English
beldar (*behl*-dahr)—Public servant who tends a canal
bidi (*bee*-dee)—Cigarette made of tobacco and cloves
biryani (bihr-*yah*-nee)—Rice dish, either sweet or meat-flavored
bismillah (bis-muh-*luh*)—Blessing that signifies a beginning
burka (*buhr*-kha)—Sewn garment with a latticed opening for the eyes worn by Islamic women as a head and body cover

chadr (*chah*-duhr)—Plain flat cloth worn by Islamic women as a head and body cover
chapati (chuh-*pah*-tee)—Flat, round bread made of whole wheat flour and water, cooked in a flat pan over an open fire
charpoi (*chahr*-poy)—Wooden cot with a platform woven of string
chowk (chowk)—Market street, usually one known for particular goods or services, such as jewelry, pharmaceuticals, cookware
chowkidar (*chowk*-ee-dahr)—Night watchman
churidar pajama (*chuhr*-ih-dahr pah-*jah*-mah)—Pants with a drawstring waist that hug the calves
crore (krohr)—Ten million

daachii (*dah*-chee)—Female camel
darzi (*duhr*-zee)—Tailor

divali (dih-*vah*-lee)—Hindu festival of lights

dupatta (duh-*pah*-tuh)—Long scarf matching the *shalwar kameez*, worn over the head or around the neck

ghee (ghee)—Clarified butter

hakkim (huh-*keem*)—Herbal healer who uses mysticism in cures

haveli (huh-*veh*-lee)—Three-story urban house owned by a noble family

hookah (*hoohk*-uh)—Tall pipe with a brass bowl in which tobacco and raw sugar are burned

hoopoe (hoo-*poo*)—Brown, red, black, and white crested bird common in India and Pakistan

imam (ih-*mahm*)—Islamic clergyman

insh'Allah (ihn-sh-ahl-*luh*)—"God willing"

jelabee (juh-*leh*-bee)—Pretzel-shaped, deep-fried sweet

ji (jee)—Yes

kabob (kuh-*bahb*)—Cubes of meat roasted on a stick over a fire

kameez (kuh-*meez*)—Fitted tunic worn over baggy trousers by both men and women

kanal (kuh-*nahl*)—Eighth of an acre

keekar (*kee*-kuhr)—Acacia or thorn tree

khansama (khahn-*sah*-muh)—Cook

khar (khahr)—Desert shrub used as firewood; the ashes are used in soap

kharin (kuh-*reen*)—Succulent desert plant with edible blooms that are sweet and peppery

kilim (kih-*leem*)—Woven, flat carpet

kinnu (*kee*-noo)—Native orange

kohl (kohl)—Eye makeup made of charcoal

Koran (Kuh-*rahn*)—The holy book of Islam

kulfi (*khuhl*-fee)—Sweet made of boiled milk

kumbi (*kuhm*-bee)—Mushroom

kurta (*kuhr*-tah)—Straight-cut, collarless shirt with long sleeves

lakh (lahkh)—One hundred thousand

lungi (*luhn*-gee)—Cloth wrapped loosely around the lower part of the body, usually worn by men

mahendi (muh-*hehn*-dee)—Part of the marriage ceremony in which the women's hands and feet are painted with henna

mali (*mah*-lee)—Gardener

masala (muh-*sah*-luh)—Mixed curry spices

Mogul (*Moh*-guhl)—Islamic invaders of the Indian subcontinent whose dynasty lasted from the sixteenth to the eighteenth centuries

muezzin (*meh*-zihn)—Islamic cleric who calls the faithful to prayer

nawab (nuh-*wahb*)—Former prince

nukkah (*nuh*-kuh)—Formal wedding ceremony

pakora (puh-*koh*-ruh)—Fried meat or vegetable dumpling

Pathan (Puh-*tahn*)—Tribal family of Pakistan's North-West Frontier Province and Afghanistan

raga (*rah*-guh)—Instrumental song

roti (*roh*-tee)—Unleavened bread

rupee (*roo*-peeyuh)—Pakistani currency equal to roughly one-sixteenth of one U.S. dollar

saal (sahl)—Large tree of the Indian subcontinent

sahib (suh-*hihb*)—Respectful title for a man, similar to "sir" in English

sahiba (suh-*hihb*-uh)—Respectful title for a woman

salaam (suh-*lahm*)—Greeting

sari (*sah*-ree)—Garment worn by women, consisting of a long piece of cloth wrapped around the body with one end draped over the shoulder or over the head

shalwar kameez (shahl-*wahr* kuh-*meez*)—Fitted tunic and baggy drawstring trousers worn by both men and women

shamiyana (*shah*-mee-*yah*-nuh)—Tent of primary-colored fabrics pieced together in geometric designs, usually used for celebrations and political speeches

Shariat (Shuh-ree-*yaht*)—Body of Islamic law

shenai (shuh-*nii*)—Oboe-like musical instrument

sherwani (shurh-*wah*-nee)—Men's knee-length dress coat, fitted at the waist and worn over baggy *shalwar* or tight-fitting *churidar* pajama trousers.

shutr keena (*shoo*-tuhr *keen*-uh)—Camel vengeance (death for dishonor)

sitar (*sih*-tahr)—Stringed musical instrument

syed (*sii*-yuhd)—Religious figure, usually a community or tribal leader descended from the Holy Prophet Muhammad

tabla (*tah*-bluh)—Small drum with an animal-hide head

tikka (*tih*-kuh)—A patty or small roll of minced and spiced meat.

toba (*toh*-buh)—Water hole

tonga (*tahn*-guh)—Horse-drawn wooden cart

wallah (*wahl*-luh)—Owner, operator, or seller of goods or services

zamindar (*zah*-mihn-dahr)—Landlord

zenana (zuh-*nah*-nuh)—Women's quarters

$\mathcal{S}$uzanne Fisher Staples is the author of *Shabanu: Daughter of the Wind*, a Newbery Honor Book. She was a UPI correspondent in Asia for many years, with stints in Hong Kong, Pakistan, Afghanistan, and India, and later in Washington, D.C. She also worked on the foreign news desk of the *Washington Post*.

She lives in central Florida, where she is at work on a third novel.